MW00584455

"Easily the craziest, weirdest, strangest, funniest, most obscene writer in America."
—*GOTHIC MAGAZINE*

"Carlton Mellick III has the craziest book titles... and the kinkiest fans!"
—CHRISTOPHER MOORE, author of *The Stupidest Angel*

"If you haven't read Mellick you're not nearly perverse enough for the twenty first century."
—JACK KETCHUM, author of *The Girl Next Door*

"Carlton Mellick III is one of bizarro fiction's most talented practitioners, a virtuoso of the surreal, science fictional tale."
—CORY DOCTOROW, author of *Little Brother*

"Bizarre, twisted, and emotionally raw—Carlton Mellick's fiction is the literary equivalent of putting your brain in a blender."
—BRIAN KEENE, author of *The Rising*

"Carlton Mellick III exemplifies the intelligence and wit that lurks between its lurid covers. In a genre where crude titles are an art in themselves, Mellick is a true artist."
—*THE GUARDIAN*

"Just as Pop had Andy Warhol and Dada Tristan Tzara, the bizarro movement has its very own P. T. Barnum-type practitioner. He's the mutton-chopped author of such books as *Electric Jesus Corpse* and *The Menstruating Mall*, the illustrator, editor, and instructor of all things bizarro, and his name is Carlton Mellick III."
—*DETAILS MAGAZINE*

Also by **Carlton Mellick III**

Satan Burger
Electric Jesus Corpse
Sunset With a Beard (stories)
Razor Wire Pubic Hair
Teeth and Tongue Landscape
The Steel Breakfast Era
The Baby Jesus Butt Plug
Fishy-fleshed
The Menstruating Mall
Ocean of Lard (with Kevin L. Donihe)
Punk Land
Sex and Death in Television Town
Sea of the Patchwork Cats
The Haunted Vagina
Cancer-cute (Avant Punk Army Exclusive)
War Slut
Sausagey Santa
Ugly Heaven
Adolf in Wonderland
Ultra Fuckers
Cybernetrix
The Egg Man
Apeshit
The Faggiest Vampire
The Cannibals of Candyland
Warrior Wolf Women of the Wasteland
The Kobold Wizard's Dildo of Enlightenment +2
Zombies and Shit
Crab Town
The Morbidly Obese Ninja
Barbarian Beast Bitches of the Badlands
Fantastic Orgy (stories)
I Knocked Up Satan's Daughter
Armadillo Fists
The Handsome Squirm
Tumor Fruit
Kill Ball
Cuddly Holocaust
Hammer Wives (stories)
Village of the Mermaids

QUICKSAND HOUSE

CARLTON MELLICK III

ERASERHEAD PRESS
PORTLAND, OREGON

ERASERHEAD PRESS
205 NE BRYANT
PORTLAND, OR 97211

WWW.ERASERHEADPRESS.COM

ISBN: 978-1-62105-100-8

AUTHOR'S NOTE

Ever since I was a child, I've had this story in my head. There's something about this idea that always haunted me. Two children have never met their own parents, even though they live together in the same home. They know their parents are somewhere in the house with them, but they don't know where. They don't know what they look like or why they refuse to see them. Sometimes the children hear distant laughter on the other side of the house, smell cologne lingering in a room, or they find a cigarette left burning in an ashtray, but have never actually seen their mother and father in person. It's almost a ghost story, only the children are haunted by people who are still alive.

Quicksand House is one of the most personal stories I've written. Most people look back on their childhood as being safe, fun, and carefree, but I remember it as terrifying and confusing. My world always felt as if it were about to be pulled out from under my feet and I would be left with an uncertain and lonely future. This book is my attempt to incorporate those emotions into a story.

I hope you enjoy this one. It's a story that's been in my head for so many years, I'm happy to finally get it out into the world. It's one of my favorites.

- Carlton Mellick III 6/17/2013 3:05 am

CHAPTER ONE

Polly has grown too big for the nursery.

Her arms and legs spill over the sides of her little pink bed when she sleeps, resting on the cold floor like soft snakes curled against the trunk of a tree. Her blanket covers only a quarter of her massive body, her pillow only big enough for one side of her cheek.

When standing in the toy room, Polly has to slouch or else she'll hit her head on the ceiling. When sitting at the tea room table, she can barely squeeze her butt into the tiny wooden chairs without breaking them to pieces. It's all very maddening to her.

"Why is everything shrinking?" Polly asks Nanny Warburough, as she tries to fasten the back of her dress.

All of her dresses once reached down to her ankles, but now they don't even cover her knees.

"Nothing's shrinking," says the nanny, adding extra laces to the dress in order to hold it together. "You're just growing. You're becoming a woman."

Polly looks at herself in the mirror. Her entire back is exposed, showing her pale lightly-freckled skin. It's the only way she can fit into the child-sized clothes anymore.

"I don't like it," Polly says. It's what Polly always says these days. "I wish I could get new dresses…"

As Polly ties a ribbon in her hair, she stabs her wrist on one of the pointy bones growing out of her head.

"Oww!" she cries, pushing her thumb into her wrist to stop the bleeding. "Damn these stupid things."

Nanny Warburough wipes the blood from the tip of the horn.

"You have to learn to be careful with them," says the nanny. "Your antlers are only going to grow larger over time."

"I just want to rip them off," Polly says, wrapping her fingers around the pointy bones and tugging. "They make me look so stupid."

The nanny pulls the girl's hand away from her antler and straightens the ribbon in her hair. "Your antlers are a symbol of your womanhood. You should be proud of them. The larger they grow, the more likely you will attract a husband."

"I don't want a husband. I hate boys. Like Tick. He is so annoying."

"I'm not talking about boys like your little brother," says the nanny, tying Polly's bright green hair into ponytails. "I'm talking about adult men. Someday you will leave the nursery. There will be more men than you can count and you'll want to be extra pretty for them. You'll want your antlers to be tall and majestic."

Polly just sneers at herself in the mirror. Her whole life, the nanny has been telling her that one day she would be able to leave the nursery, but that day seems to never come. She is practically a grown woman now and she's still in the nursery. She thought she would have been able to leave ages ago.

"You just have to wait for your parents to come get you," says the nanny. "I'm sure it will be any day now. I'm sure they're excited to see the beautiful young woman you have become."

The nanny smiles her wrinkled lips at Polly.

Polly hates when she says stuff like that. She's been told her parents would come get her *any day now* for several years. When the nanny's back is turned, Polly draws circles all over her own face with purple candy-scented lipstick just to piss her off. With ugly bones growing from her head and ill-fitting ripped up dresses, she doesn't see a point in trying to look pretty anymore.

Tick watches his sister and Nanny Warburough through a crack in the wall. They can't see him hiding in the crawlspace. It is his territory. When Polly was younger, they both used to hide from the nanny together in those secret tunnels, but she's become far too large to use them. It all belongs to her little brother now.

"I can hear your breathing, Tick," Polly says.

Tick holds his breath.

"Stop spying on me you little pervert," she says.

"I'm not a pervert," Tick says. "I just wanted to see what you guys were doing."

"I don't *want* you to see what I'm doing," Polly says. "That's why the door's locked."

"But it's lonely all by myself out there," Tick says.

"Do you want me to kill you?" Polly says.

Nanny Warburough calmly goes to the wall and bangs her hard round knuckles three times against the plaster. "Get out of the walls this instant, child. The crawlspace is forbidden."

"But I like it in here."

"It's not protected from the creepers," says the nanny. "Do you want the creepers to get you?"

Tick looks around. The crawlspace is dark and filled with dust and cobwebs, but he's sure there's nothing in there with him.

"I've never seen any creepers in here," Tick says.

"You can't see creepers," says the nanny. "They hide in the dark and then get you when you're not looking."

"No they don't," Tick says.

"Just get out of there and get ready for school," says the nanny.

Tick crawls away from the hole in his sister's room. The passageway is dark, lit only by the dim strips of light passing through air vents and random cracks in the walls. Although there are many shadowy corners where the light never reaches,

Tick doesn't believe any creepers could be hiding in there with him. At first the crawlspace seemed dangerous and scary, but he's gone into it so many times that it now feels just as safe as the rest of the nursery. Besides, he doesn't believe the creepers actually exist anyway.

"Change your clothes," Nanny Warburough says to Tick as he crawls out of the vent into his bedroom.

"Why?" he says, his face covered in dust and soot. His black hair is scraggly and hasn't been combed in weeks.

"You're all filthy," says the nanny, wobbling her round dwarfish body toward him.

He shrugs. "So? Nobody at school's going to care."

"Well, I care," says the nanny on her way out the door. "Now hurry up or you'll be sent to school without breakfast."

Tick removes his shirt. The closet is filled with twenty-five matching school uniforms, five in each size. He is now on the largest sized suits, having outgrown the other twenty. Like Polly, he'll probably be wearing these same suits for a very long time after he outgrows them. This doesn't bother Tick, though. If he gets as big as Polly, he plans to construct his own clothes out of curtains and old pajamas.

"Breakfast is waiting," the nanny calls from the tea room.

Changing into the cleanest uniform, which still isn't all that clean, Tick crosses the hall into the tea room. The table is set for two people. In the center of the table is a display of fruits, yogurts, croissants, bacon, jelly, and soft boiled eggs. It is one of the six different breakfasts they are regularly served. There is also an arrangement of three juices: orange, grapefruit, and tomato. As well as two sodas: Dr. Pepper and Coca-Cola.

Tick grabs a piece of bacon from the serving platter and takes a bite, savoring the chewy smoked rubber flavor.

"Eat properly," says Nanny Warburough, pointing at his

seat as she leaves the tea room.

The nanny never eats with them. She uses the time to make their beds and clean up their rooms. She always calls Tick and Polly her "little piglets" because of how messy they are.

Tick fills a plate with food and sits at the table across from Polly. The teenage girl is like a giant sitting at the tea table designed for five-year-olds, her knees towering over the edge of the table. She's like the giant-sized Alice from the old Wonderland books, but with antlers growing from the top of her green head.

"You're upset," Tick says to his big sister.

"No, I'm not." Polly just stares at her plate as if she's going to slam her face into her yogurt.

"I can always tell when you're upset."

"Shut up, Tick."

Tick isn't his real name. It's actually Rick, but his sister always calls him *Tick* as an insult. She says he reminds her of a bug. Instead of being offended by the nickname, Tick decided he liked it. Now he wants everyone to always call him Tick all the time, even all the kids at school.

"Is it because Nanny told you that Mom and Dad are coming for you soon?" Tick asks.

Polly frowns, holding her miniature fork and spoon over her miniature breakfast plate and teacup.

"I'm so sick of waiting for them," she says.

"Then stop waiting for them," Tick says. He stabs his soft-boiled egg with a fork, causing an explosion of white and yellow goo across his plate. "Go to them instead. Leave the nursery and find them yourself."

Polly sighs. "Are you crazy? I'd never be able to find them out there."

"They live in this house somewhere," Tick says. "If you went searching you'd find them eventually."

"Nanny says this house is too big to ever find them no matter how much we look," Polly says. "They live on the complete opposite side of the house."

"So?" Tick says. "It's better than waiting here for the rest of your life."

"I'm not going to wait here for the rest of my life," she says. "They'll come for me eventually."

"What if they forgot about you?" Tick says.

Polly goes quiet.

"If they forget about me when I'm too big for the nursery I'm going to go find them myself," Tick says. "I don't want to be stuck here forever. I want to see the rest of the house, maybe even leave the house to see the rest of the world."

"I'm not leaving the nursery until they come," Polly says.

"Why not?"

"Because it's not allowed."

"You're just afraid of the creepers," Tick says.

Polly goes quiet again. She doesn't like to talk about the creepers.

"Have you ever even seen a creeper before?" Tick asks. "I think they're made up."

"Of course they're not made up," Polly says. "The whole house is full of them. Only the nursery is protected."

"They're not real," Tick says. "Nanny just tells us the creepers are out there so we won't leave the nursery."

"You don't know what you're talking about. Just because you haven't seen them doesn't mean they don't exist."

"Have *you* seen them?"

"Yeah…"

"Liar."

Tick dips a corner of his croissant into his runny egg and shovels it into his mouth.

When it's time for school, Tick and Polly meet up in the teleport room.

"Do you have your homework drives?" asks Nanny Warburough.

The children give their memory cards to the nanny. She inserts them into the teleport system, sending the files off to their school computers.

"I get to sit next to Darcy today," Tick says with a smile on his face.

"Who's Darcy?" asks the nanny.

"I've told you about her a million times!" Tick says.

He doesn't understand why the nanny forgets his girlfriend all the time. She's been forgetful a lot lately.

"She's the girl he has a crush on at school," Polly says, strapping a teleport helmet around her forehead. "It's so immature."

"It's not immature," Tick says. "She's my girlfriend."

"You're such an idiot."

"Come on, Polly," says the nanny. "I remember you having a crush on a school boy when you were his age."

Polly rolls her eyes and lies down in the teleport bed. "I was an idiot, too."

After the two children are in position, the nanny operates the teleport controls and their bodies go limp. Their minds go far away.

"Please, take your seats," says the teacher as Tick materializes in his classroom.

Other children materialize from opposite corners of the classroom, one at a time. They all wear black uniforms matching Tick's and all have very similar hairstyles and skin-tones. As always, everyone keeps their voices low and responds to the teacher obediently. Mr. Robertson is not very tolerant of disruptive students.

"This is no place for chit-chatting," says Mr. Robertson to no one in particular, adjusting his wire-framed spectacles. "This is a place of learning."

Tick sits down at his desk, waiting for Darcy to arrive. She'll be sitting right next to him, sharing the same table space. There are three rows of desks and each desk is big enough for two people—a boy and a girl. It has been this way ever since kindergarten. Boys and girls work together as a two-person team, to prepare them for life as a married couple when they become adults. Naturally, the boys and girls want to be partnered with those they like best. It's the first time Tick will actually be paired with Darcy—the girl he's been in love with since the third grade.

As the class fills, the seat next to him remains empty.

"Is Darcy here yet?" he asks the couple in front of him.

The boy and girl just shrug in response.

Tick waits, watching the corners of the room for her to appear.

Darcy's never been the prettiest girl in school according to anyone except for Tick, who's always had a big crush on her. She has short Pepsi-blue hair and long bangs that cover one eye. Her skin color is a slightly darker shade than everyone else's, yet smoother, shinier. She's kind of short and a little too thin, but her dark black eyes glisten when she looks at him. She hardly ever smiles, but when she does her smile is bigger than anybody's.

He always dreamed of being able to sit next to her. Yesterday she told Tick that he could hold her hand during class, maybe even the whole time as long as Mr. Robertson didn't catch them. He's now sitting at his desk, trembling with excitement. But Darcy has yet to arrive.

"I want you to change seats with me," a voice says from behind.

Tick turns around. It's Mike, the largest kid in the class. Tick's never liked him. Ever since the first grade, the guy has always been a total jerk.

"What?" Tick says.

"I want to sit next to Darcy," Mike says. "Go be partners with Tori."

"No way," Tick says. "I want to sit next to Darcy."

Mike tugs on the back of Tick's seat, pulling him away from his desk.

"Don't be so selfish," Mike says. "I deserve to sit next to her. She said she likes me."

"No, she didn't," Tick says.

Tick knows he has to be lying. He can't even believe Mike likes her, let alone her liking him. There's never been competition for Darcy's affection before. She's always been Tick's girl.

"How do you know?" Mike says. "We're perfect for each other. Everyone knows that."

"She's my girlfriend!"

Mike just ignores the statement and pushes on the back of Tick's chair, trying to tip him out of it.

"Get out," Mike says, struggling to knock Tick to the ground.

Everyone stares at them.

"Michael, get back to your seat," says Mr. Robertson.

"This is my seat," Mike says. "He stole it from me."

"No, I didn't!"

"Just sit down," says the teacher.

Mike lets go of the chair and goes to the back of the room to his seat next to the chubby girl with pigtails. When Tick looks back at him, the large boy whispers across the room, "You're dead."

Tick pokes both of his fingers up his nose and sticks out his tongue, giving him a goblin-like face.

After class begins, Darcy still hasn't shown up. Tick becomes anxious, concerned.

"Mr. Robertson?" Tick asks the teacher. "Where's Darcy?"

The teacher pauses. He's not used to being interrupted by his students.

"She's absent," says the teacher.

"But she's never absent," Tick says.

"No interruptions," says the teacher.

Tick looks at the computer screen on his desk but can't concentrate on his studies. He's worried about Darcy. Most children come to school even if they're injured or not feeling well. It would have to be serious for her to miss class. Then Tick realizes there are a few other students missing. It's strange. There have never been more than two people absent on the same day before and that only happens once a year at most. He wonders if the teleport device is malfunctioning.

By the time recess begins, Tick decides it would be best not to worry about Darcy for a while. Surely she will attend class tomorrow. He can ask her why she was absent then.

"Want to play basketball?" Justin asks Tick on the playground.

Justin is Tick's best friend at school. He's a lanky awkward kid with glasses and long hair. Everyone calls him Frog because he hops around a lot. He especially hops around a lot while playing basketball and is damned near impossible to beat one-on-one. They've been friends for a couple of years now, mostly because Tick is the only person who will ever dare play basketball with him.

"Sure," Tick says.

Darcy usually watches them play basketball from the swings. That's usually Tick's favorite part of playing basketball these days. She's always on the swings, cheering Tick on. It almost seems pointless to play without her watching.

"No three-pointers today," Justin says.

"Fine."

Justin bounces the basketball on the small concrete court and passes it to Tick. The playground isn't very large. It is the same size as the classroom, only outdoor. It is half sand and half concrete. On the sand side, there are two slides, three swings, a merry-go-round, monkey bars, and a jungle-gym, all tightly packed together. On the concrete side there are two tetherball poles, a basketball net hanging from the side of the school building, and extra room for hopscotch, jump rope, or foursquare. A fifteen foot wall circles the yard. Only the cloudless blue sky can be seen beyond the wall.

"I'm on Frog's team," Mike says, stepping toward them on the court.

Tick sees the angry look in Mike's eyes. He's still pissed about earlier.

"You can't play," Tick says. "It's one-on-one."

"No, it's two-on-one," Mike says, grabbing the ball from Tick. "I'll play if I want."

Mike bounces the ball on the court. Tick lunges to get it back, but he dribbles it away from him.

"Give it back," Tick says. "You can't play."

"What, are you going to tell the teacher like a baby?" Mike asks, focusing on the ball as he dribbles.

Justin steps in. "You can play if you find another person. I'd love to play two-on-two."

Tick glares at Justin. His friend doesn't know what he's doing. Mike doesn't want to play for fun. He just wants to play so that he can shove, elbow, and trip Tick in game, pretending it's all on accident.

"If you want to play two-on-two you better find yourself a teammate," Mike says to Tick.

Justin and Tick look around the playground. Everyone is busy jump-roping or climbing on bars.

"Nobody else plays basketball," Tick says.

"What about Simon?" Justin asks. "He used to play sometimes."

Tick freezes when he hears the name *Simon*. Nobody's spoken

17

his name in quite a while.

"Simon?" Tick asks, looking back toward the classroom door. "Are you kidding?"

"Go ask him," Mike says.

Simon hasn't gone out to recess all year. He hasn't even said anything since fourth grade. He just sits in the back of the class, staring forward, never speaking. He doesn't do any class work or ever get up from his seat. All he does is twitch and tremble in his chair, shaking uncontrollably.

"I'm not asking him," Tick says. "He's weird."

The three boys look at Simon through the window. The boy is still shaking, his teeth chattering. It's like he's gone through some horrible psychological trauma and can't snap out of it. Tick was once friends with the boy when they were younger. He has no idea what caused him to change like that.

"What's wrong with him?" Tick says.

"Are you going to ask him or not?" Mike says.

"I'm sure he'd play if you asked," Justin says.

The weirdest part about Simon is how nobody ever speaks about him. Not the teacher, not the other students. He's like a ghost that only Tick can see, haunting the back of the class. Nobody has ever mentioned why he just sits there trembling like that. Mike and Justin are the first people to even mention Simon's name in a long time, and even they don't seem to be acknowledging his creepy behavior.

"Ask him yourself," Tick says. "I'm not going near that kid."

"Then I guess it's two-on-one," Mike says, holding the ball over his head so Justin can't reach. "Me and Frog against you."

"Two-on-one isn't fair," Justin says. "It has to be two-on-two or one-on-one."

"How about none-on-none?" Mike says.

He tosses the basketball with all his strength, hurling it over the wall into the blue sky.

"Hey!" Justin cries, as his ball disappears.

"You're such a jerk, Mike," Tick says.

Mike shoves Tick as he walks away from the court.

"I'm sitting in your seat tomorrow," Mike tells Tick. "If I see you sitting there when I get to class it'll be your head I throw over the wall."

Then he pushes a kid off the swing just to watch him fall face-down in the sand.

"What are we going to do?" Justin says.

He almost has tears in his eyes. He loves basketball so much and that was the only ball they had at the school.

"We should go get it," Tick says.

"How?" Justin asks.

Tick knows there has to be a way to get the ball back. He just has to get to the other side of the wall. But he has no idea how to do that. There are no doors leading beyond the wall. The playground is completely enclosed. The only door leads into the classroom and the classroom has no exits. The school is just a room and a playground with one door connecting the two. Children teleport in and out when they come and go. The only sign of a world outside of the school is the bright blue sky.

"Let's try to climb the wall," Tick says.

"We're not allowed," Justin says.

"Help me climb up the basketball net," Tick says.

Justin sighs and goes along with him. He lets Tick use him as a stepladder to pull himself up onto the basketball hoop, one leg dangling through the net. The other kids on the playground stop what they're doing to watch.

"You shouldn't go over the wall," Justin says.

Tick slowly stands up, balancing himself with the backboard. From this height, Tick's head is level with the top of the wall. He can't see anything beyond it yet.

"I don't care if I get in trouble," Tick says.

"But it's dangerous," Justin says.

19

"Why is it dangerous?" Tick asks. "Are there creepers out there?"

"What are creepers?" Justin asks.

Tick looks down on him.

"You've never heard of creepers?" he asks.

Justin shrugs.

"You know, the things that hide in the shadows," Tick says. "You don't have creepers in the hallways outside your nursery?"

Justin doesn't know what he's talking about.

"I've never left my nursery before," Justin says. "I don't know what's outside of it."

Tick climbs down from the basketball net before the teacher sees what he's doing. He wants to talk to Justin face-to-face.

"So you've really never heard of the creepers?" Tick asks.

Justin shrugs. "Never."

Tick wonders if he was right about them. He wonders if the creepers don't actually exist at all and are just something Nanny Warburough made up so that he'd never leave the nursery.

"Are they monsters?" Justin asks.

"I don't know," Tick says. "My nanny says they're dangerous."

Justin gives him an odd face, as if he's speaking like a crazy person.

"Forget about it," Tick says. "They probably don't even exist."

CHAPTER TWO

Tick has spent years imagining what his parents actually look like. He expends countless hours drawing hundreds of pictures of them on the tea room table, concentrating as hard as he can to capture their true likeness. He believes that somewhere deep in his subconscious he knows exactly what they look like and if he just draws pictures of moms and dads enough times eventually one of his drawings will ignite that hidden knowledge.

The crude drawings are scattered all over the nursery, hung on walls and ceilings, stuffed under furniture, hidden in the crawlspace, stacked on every bookshelf in the library. Tick still isn't quite sure what they look like even after so many drawings, but he is pretty sure his father has short black hair and glasses like his teacher. He thinks his mother most likely has green hair, like his sister's.

He imagines his mother looks a lot like Polly, only taller, smarter, stronger, prettier, and her antlers probably reach all the way to the ceiling. And if he met her he knows she would always be happy and never complain about anything or hurt him just for going in her room. She would be nice to him all the time, always.

Polly often tells Tick that their mom is probably old like Nanny Warburough, but Tick can't imagine she would look anything like the old woman. The nanny is short, fat, ugly, and doesn't even have antlers at all anymore. She is the complete opposite of what their real mom would look like.

Because the nanny is too old and Polly is too young, Tick imagines his mother looks more like the women in the library. Many of the books he's read, or tried to read, are full of images of adult women. None of them have antlers or green hair—Nanny Warburough says the books in the library come from a much older time, before women had antlers—but he can imagine any of them as his mother.

He used to like to color in all the books, drawing green hair and antlers on the pictures of adult women. Nanny Warburough would be furious whenever he did that. She always told him that books are too important to color in. Tick never understood why, but he doesn't draw in the books anymore. He only uses the pictures as reference for his own drawings.

If only his parents had left pictures of themselves with Nanny Warburough Tick wouldn't be so obsessed. But it's something that's always on his mind.

"Who are these people that made me?" Tick always says. "What do they look like? Why can't they come see us?"

Nanny always tells him, "They are very important people. They are too busy to see you."

"Not even for a few minutes?"

"Not even for a few minutes."

"But what do they do on the other side of the house all the time? What is it that's so important that we aren't to be involved in their lives until we grow up?"

"It's just how parents are these days," the nanny always says, "especially your parents."

"But I want to know what they're like. I *have* to know."

"It's a big house. It would be too troublesome to come all the way over here just to satisfy a child's curiosity." Then the nanny always says, "You'll see them some day, when you grow up. They'll be ready for you by that time. And you'll become a significant part of their lives from that day forward."

Tick never argues with her beyond that, but it's still not enough to satisfy him. He still feels the need to draw their pictures on a regular basis. It's the closest he can come to being with them.

Tick pushes a button on the tea-room table. The center of the tabletop opens and platters of hot food rise to the surface. There is sliced ham, mustard, macaroni and cheese, peas and carrots, fruit cups, milk and Coca Cola Classic. It is one of the eleven dinners they are served.

"Where does all the food come from?" Tick asks, staring into the opening on the table as the food is served.

"From inside the table," Polly says. "Don't be stupid."

"But who makes it?"

"Nobody makes it."

"Well, somebody has to."

Nanny Warburough enters the tea room and wipes dirt from Tick's face with a wet napkin.

"Nanny, where does the food come from?" Tick asks her.

"The machines below make it," says the nanny. "It's all automated."

"You mean machines like the laundry machine?"

"Yeah, like the laundry machine. Only instead of cleaning clothes the machines cook food. They were programmed a very long time ago."

Tick takes a bite from a slice of ham.

"I like the cooking machines," Tick says, smiling. "They're nice."

The nanny rubs Tick's head and leaves the room.

"A cooking machine isn't *nice*," Polly says. "It's just a machine."

"I think it's nice. It makes us lots of food."

"You think all machines are nice."

"Most of them are," Tick says. "Except the baby machine. I don't like that one. The baby machine is mean."

"It's mean?" Polly snickers.

"It's a jerk."

"Why is it a jerk?"

Polly laughs at the serious look on her brother's face.

"It scares me."

"How do you know what the baby machine even looks like?" Polly asks. "You're not allowed in the baby room."

"I can see it from the crawlspace. I think the devil made that machine."

"You should stay away from the baby room," Polly says. "Creepers might get in through the baby tunnel."

"I never saw any creepers."

"But they might have seen you."

"Creepers aren't even real. At school, I mentioned the creepers to Justin but he's never heard of them before."

"You don't know what you're talking about. Of course they're real."

"I don't believe in them."

"Why don't you believe in them?"

"Do you? I've never seen them before. How can I believe in anything I've never seen?"

"You've never seen Mom and Dad either," Polly says. "You don't believe in Mom and Dad?"

"Of course I believe in Mom and Dad."

"But not the creepers?"

"No."

"If you don't believe in them then go out in the corridor and see what happens."

Tick pauses. His eyes shift downward. He's never gone into the corridor before.

"Are you scared?" Polly says. "If you don't believe in creepers then what's there to be afraid of?"

"Nothing," Tick says. "It's just dark out there."

"Then bring a light with you," Polly says. "You'll be fine if creepers don't exist."

"They *don't* exist."

"Prove it."

"I will."

"Then go out in the corridor."

"I will."
"Right now?"
"Right now."

Tick has only looked outside of the nursery twice in his life. The first time was because Polly had lit one of her dolls on fire and Nanny Warburough needed to air the smoke out of the nursery. Although there was no light in the corridor, Tick swore he saw faces out there, things moving in the dark. Nanny Warburough convinced him it was only the smoke twisting in the shadows, causing him to see horrible things that weren't really there.

"There's the door," Polly says, pointing at the nursery exit. "Go outside if you want to prove creepers don't exist."

Tick stares at the exit. The door is larger than any of the other doors in the nursery. It's made of wood but reinforced with heavy iron. Metal latches and locks line the frame from floor to ceiling.

"I'll prove it," Tick says, going slowly toward the door.

The second time Tick saw outside the nursery he was by himself. It was late and he was supposed to be asleep, but he had a dream that his parents were visiting the nursery and the idea forced him to wake. Unable to tell reality from his dream, he stumbled through the dark toward the nursery exit, excited to see his parents for the first time. But nobody was there. His parents were nowhere in sight. His sister and Nanny Warburough were asleep in their rooms. But the nursery door was wide open. He had no idea who could have opened it.

The hallway outside of the nursery looked ancient. It seemed like nobody had been out there in a hundred years. He went toward the door, about to peek around the corner, but something stopped him. A scratching sound echoed down the hallway, like rusty nails clawing against the chalkboards.

The sound grew louder, creeping down the corridor toward the nursery entrance. Tick slammed the door shut and ran back to his room.

At the time, it was proof to him that creepers did exist. But now he's not so sure. He's convinced he just dreamed the whole thing. He was most likely half-asleep and just imagined it all. There's no other explanation for the nursery door being open like that.

"Where's Nanny?" Tick asks his sister, making sure he doesn't get into trouble if he leaves the nursery.

"Doing laundry," Polly says. "Don't worry. She won't be able to hear you over the machines."

Tick nods and goes to the door. He pries the first latch open. It's stiff and rusted shut. To lift the latch, he has to pull with all his strength until his knuckles turn white and the tips of his fingernails bend backward. It seems as if nobody has opened the door in decades. After only three latches, he has to give his sore hands a rest.

"Are you going to come with me?" Tick asks, shaking his fingers in the air.

Polly snickers. "Too scared to go out there on your own?"

"No, I just thought you might want to see what's out there."

"Prove there are no creepers out there and maybe I'll follow you," she says.

It takes a while, but Tick manages to open all of the locks and latches. When he pulls on the doorknob, the door doesn't open.

"What's wrong?" Polly asks.

"It's stuck," Tick says.

He positions his foot against the wall next to the handle and pushes off, but the door won't budge.

"You're so weak," Polly says. "Let me do it."

His big sister goes to the doorknob and pulls while Tick uses two of the lower latches as handles. They shove off against the wall until they hear a loud cracking noise.

The second the door bursts open a gust of musty air fills their lungs. A cloud of dust rises. An odor like sweaty gloves hits their nostrils.

Polly and Tick poke their heads outside of the nursery like turtles from their shells. There are no lights in the corridor. It is just a long hallway going to the right and left. They only see fifteen feet in each direction before the passage disappears into the darkness.

"It smells…" Polly complains. Then she sneezes against her wrist as she breathes dust into her nose.

The stale gray carpet on the hallway floor clashes with the bright blue carpeting of the nursery. There are two paintings on the walls outside, but they are so coated in cobwebs that Tick can't make out what the paintings are supposed to be. They just look like paintings of rocks in mud.

"What do you think that door leads to?" Tick whispers, pointing down the hall.

Polly squints her eyes. Just before the hallway becomes too dark to see, there is a door. Tick could tell by her uneasy expression that this is the first time she's ever looked into the corridor before.

"It must lead to another part of the house," Polly whispers back.

"Is it somebody's room?" Tick says.

Polly shrugs.

Tick leans into the hall as far as he can without leaving the doorway. "Do you think somebody lives in there?"

"Like who?"

"Nanny said that besides Mom and Dad there are also some servants that live in this house somewhere. Maybe it's a maid's room."

There is no light coming from beneath the door. It probably

hasn't been opened in years.

"Nobody else lives on this side of the house," Polly says. "If a maid really did live in that room this hallway would surely be kept much cleaner than this."

"But what if somebody does? Maybe we even have grand-parents that live out here somewhere."

"It's probably just an empty guest room or used for storage."

"I want to go see," Tick says.

He steps out of the nursery.

"Don't go out there."

Polly tries to grab him and pull him back, but he slips out of her reach too quickly.

"I'm just going to knock," Tick says.

He moves away from the nursery entrance, squinting his eyes to see in the dark.

"Come back here," Polly whispers as loud as she can.

Tick doesn't listen.

"There's probably creepers in there," Polly says.

The further down the hallway Tick goes, the more his eyes adjust to the dark. The hallway goes another twenty feet and then ends. There are two more doors in that direction, leading to other rooms. Tick wonders what could possibly be behind all of these doors he's never seen before.

When he arrives at the closest door to the nursery, he smiles up at it like a birthday present. The wood is old and worn with several scratches across the surface like a tall cat was trying to get inside. The brass doorknob is in the shape of a sleeping swan. Tick rubs his finger along the swan's curled neck, removing a thick layer of dust.

"Get away from there," Polly says.

Tick looks back to see his sister in a panic. Even from that distance, he could see her eyes trembling, her fingers twitching against the doorframe, her weight rapidly shifting from foot to foot.

He raises his hand to knock.

"Don't do it," Polly cries.

Tick knocks three times. The sound rumbles the door and echoes through the hallway. Polly hears the echo continue on, out of the corridor, deep into the other sections of the house far away from the nursery.

Polly ducks back inside the doorway as Tick knocks three more times. These knocks are louder than the first and the echo travels so far that Polly thinks even their parents might hear it.

"Is anybody in there?" Tick says.

No one answers.

Polly closes the nursery entrance halfway. "If you don't come back I'm locking you out here."

Tick puts his ear to the door.

"I'll leave you in the dark," she cries. She doesn't bother keeping her voice down anymore.

Tick listens carefully at the door. There is a sound coming from within, but it doesn't sound like a person. It sounds more like a tree branch scratching against glass as it's blown in the wind.

"Hello?" Tick says.

He knocks twice more.

The scratching sound grows louder.

"Tick, come on," Polly yells. "I'm closing it!"

As she squeezes the door shut, leaving it open only a crack so her brother can hear her voice, the light in the hallway fades. The corridor is swallowed by shadows. Tick finds himself alone in the dark.

Putting one hand around the swan-shaped doorknob, he says "I'm coming in." Then he turns the handle.

The second he opens the door to the strange room, Polly closes the door to the nursery. He hears her closing up the latches, locking him out in the corridor. But Tick is only in total darkness for a moment. A faint brown light illuminates a section of the room.

"Hello?" he says.

It is not much larger than his bedroom in the nursery. He can make out a bed, larger than any he's ever seen before. There is also a dresser and other cabinets. There is a wide closet on the far side of the room, a door to what could be a bathroom, but no other exits.

Tick can't tell where the brown light is coming from. The source seems to be on the floor somewhere, behind the bed. The light grows brighter and darker, changing color from brown to yellow to red to blue, like holiday lights.

As Tick steps into the room, the scratching noise returns. It's like metal scraping against metal. The noise surrounds him, slicing the insides of his ears. He doesn't see anything, but he feels as if there's something in there with him, hiding in the shadows behind the furniture.

"I'm sorry to disturb you," Tick says to the shadows.

He backs into the hallway and grabs the swan-shaped door-knob. But before he closes the door, something in the room pushes on it, slamming it shut. The force throws Tick back, knocking him to the floor.

Another slamming noise shakes the ground, coming from down the hallway. Then a rattling sound as doorknobs jiggle throughout the corridor. There are things in the rooms all around him, trying to break into the hallway to get him.

Light pours in as Nanny Warburough charges out of the nursery, carrying a flashlight.

"Are you crazy?" the stumpy woman cries as she speeds down the passage toward the boy.

Tick gets to his feet, his clothes covered in a thick layer of dust from the floor.

"Get out of here quickly," says the nanny.

She drags him by the arm, pulling him back to the nursery. All the doors in the hall rattle and shake.

Tick's tears sting his eyes. "What's happening? What's making that sound?" But the nanny doesn't hear him over all the screeching and scraping noises.

After they're back inside the nursery, Nanny Warburough barricades the door, closing every latch firmly into place.

"How many times have I told you not to go out there, child?" the nanny says as she locks the door. "Now the creepers know we're in here."

Polly and Tick hide around the corner, peeking their heads into the entry room. The nanny waves Tick over to her.

"Don't just stand there, help me," she says. "This is your fault."

Tick goes to the door and helps her with the lower locks.

"What were you thinking?" she cries.

"I didn't think they were real," Tick says.

"Of course they are real," Polly shouts from the hallway.

"But they seem so made up, like a fairy tale. And my friend at school never heard of them before."

The nanny pulls Tick away the second they finish locking the door.

"They are very, very real," she says.

The scraping noises grow louder down the hallway, like hundreds of deranged creatures are trying to claw their way inside.

Nanny Warburough sits both children down in the tea room.

"You will never do this again," she tells them, leaning over the table, staring each of them in the eyes. "Neither of you. This is not a game. You must never leave the nursery until your parents come for you. It's just not safe."

Tick is too shocked that creepers actually exist to be sorry for what he's done. It's almost as exciting as it is scary. He has so many questions.

"What are they?" Tick asks.

"It doesn't matter what they are," says the nanny. "They're dangerous."

"But what do they want? Are they trying to eat us?"

"You're too young to understand," the nanny says. "When you're older your parents will explain them to you."

"Are they monsters? Like the vampires from the old horror books in the library?"

"Not exactly," says the nanny. "Just stay away from them. This is serious."

"I understand," Tick says, staring down at his filthy hands.

"No," the nanny says. "I don't think you understand quite how serious this is yet."

She holds Tick by his shoulders and looks him closely in the eyes. Her fat heavy fingers squeeze him so tightly they bruise the skin.

"I have something to tell you that I've never mentioned before," she tells him. Then she looks at his sister. "Polly was only two years old at the time. She wouldn't even remember, but she was there. She saw it happen."

An apprehensive look crosses Polly's face. It's as if her subconscious already knows what the nanny is about to say.

"You both had an older brother. His name was Roger." The nanny looks away for a moment and licks her wrinkled gray lips. "He was seven years old when the creepers took him. I never told you about him because I didn't want it to upset you. He was such a sweet, polite child."

Polly remembers having a brother. In her dreams, he was always there, playing with her and teaching her new things. She never spoke about him out loud, but in the back of her mind she always knew he was real.

"The creepers took him while he was sleeping," says the nanny. "They came into the nursery and snatched him from his bed. By the time I woke, he was gone. All that was left was a trail of blood leading from his bedroom into the corridor. I thought they took Polly as well until I found her hiding under the study table in the library."

Polly's eyes are dark red and dripping. She jumps to her

feet, throwing away the tiny tea room chair she was squeezed into, and storms out of the room. She doesn't remember any of those details exactly, but she doesn't want to hear anymore.

"I don't get it," Tick says to Nanny Warburough, when they are alone. "How did they get in? You've always said the nursery is protected from them."

"It's safer in the nursery," says the nanny. "But, really, nowhere is safe. Because the nursery has power, the creepers stay away. Creepers don't like the light. It makes them disappear. But the day Roger was taken, the power in the nursery went out. It happens from time to time. The lights go out. Then nobody is safe from the creepers."

Tick remembers the power going out a few times in the past. Whenever it happened, the nanny would take them into the playroom and lock them inside. Then she would work on the machines in the baby room until the power came back on. Now Tick understands why she acted so nervously whenever the lights were out. He always thought she was just afraid of the dark.

"Even Mom and Dad?" Tick asks.

Nanny Warburough is taken aback by his question.

"Well, no but…" she begins.

"Is that why they've never come for Polly?" Tick asks. "Did the creepers get them?"

"Of course not," the nanny says. "That's not it at all."

"But it's possible, isn't it?" Tick asks.

The nanny shakes her head. "No, it's not possible. Your parents are strong. They know how to protect themselves from creepers. It's mostly children who are vulnerable."

The nanny stands Tick up and wipes the dust from his clothes. She takes him to his bedroom, changes him into his pajamas, and tucks him into his bed.

"Now do you understand the serious situation you're in?" she asks him.

Tick nods up at her, staring into her beady black eyes behind her big rosy cheeks.

"You were lucky today," she says. "In the future, you won't be so lucky. The house we live in is a very dangerous place. You should never leave the nursery again."

Tick closes his eyes. He promises he'll never leave the nursery again. He's not even sure if he'll ever be able to sleep in the dark again.

CHAPTER THREE

Tick's mother visits him in the middle of the night. As she enters his room, she does not look like a real woman. She is made of paper and crayon, like one of his drawings brought to life. But even though she's just a crudely drawn picture Tick always believes she is the real thing. He can't tell that she's only a figment of his imagination.

"Hi, Mom," Tick says to her.

The paper mom sits down on the bed next to him. She leans in and kisses him on his cheek, her hollow paper lips pressing gently against his skin.

"Hello, my darling," she says. Her squiggly red blob lips move out of sync with her voice. "How was your day today?"

Her eyes are just two sloppily drawn sideways ovals. The pupils—two tiny asterisks—roll awkwardly within the ovals whenever she looks at him. The crooked eyelashes come together like miniature fireworks whenever she blinks.

"Not very good," Tick tells her. "Darcy, the girl I like, wasn't in class today. I think she was sick, but that doesn't make sense. She's never sick. I'm worried about her."

Then she rubs her crinkled fingers through his scraggly hair.

"Don't worry, my darling," she tells him. "I'm sure she's just fine."

As she caresses him, her paper fingers make loud scraping noises across his scalp.

"But what if she never comes back? What if she was expelled from school?"

"She'll be back," she says. "You'll see."

An edge of one of her fingernails slices against his forehead and gives him a paper cut. Tick flinches only for a second, but it doesn't bother him much. He's just happy to be with her.

"But even if she comes back I'm worried about Mike," Tick says. "He's the school bully. He says he's in love with Darcy and that Darcy loves him too."

Tick wipes away the blood dribbling down his forehead. Then his paper mom cuts him again when she kisses his cheek. It is not unusual for Tick to be cut many times when his mother visits him. She is made of paper. She can't help herself.

"He's lying," says the paper mom. "Don't worry about him. Darcy loves only you."

"But I thought I was the only one who loved Darcy."

"Darcy is a beautiful girl. I'm sure many boys will want to be Darcy's boyfriend. But she loves only you. I know she does."

"But what should I do about Mike? He says I'm dead if I sit next to her again."

"You can't let him take her away from you."

"But what if he wants to fight me?"

"Sometimes you have to fight for those you love. Don't give her up without a fight."

"Okay," he says, smiling up at her big paper face. "Thanks, Mom."

Blood trickles from the cuts on his face, but he doesn't care. He loves his paper mom so much. Whenever he's with her, all of his problems always disappear. He's not worried about Darcy or Mike anymore. He's not worried about the creepers invading the nursery. He's at peace with everything in the universe.

When he hugs her goodbye, he squeezes her so tightly that her hip crumples into a ball.

"I love you, Mommy," Tick says.

"What did you just say?"

Nanny Warburough stands over the boy, pushing him awake as he reaches out for her, trying to give her a hug. When the boy's eyes open, the crayon-drawn face of his mother transforms into the face of his nanny.

"Huh?" Tick asks, entering consciousness.

"Did you just say you love me?" the nanny asks.

She is angry. Her hand is in the air as if she's ready to slap him.

"I'm sorry," Tick says. "I didn't know it was you."

She smacks him on the forehead twice before he can cover his eyes.

"How many times have I told you not to use that word?" says the nanny, slapping his hands that attempt to shield his face. "First, you leave the nursery and now this? What's gotten into you, child?"

"I was only dreaming," Tick cries, pushing himself into the corner of his bed. "Don't hit me again."

"You know the rules," says the nanny. "You never hug me, you never call me *mommy*, and you never ever say *I love you.*"

Tick pulls the blanket over his face and cries. The nanny smacks the top of his head three more times through the blanket and then she backs away.

"Never do that ever again," she says, her voice clearly upset. "Now get ready for school. You're going to be late."

When she's gone, Tick yells, "I didn't say it to you. I was dreaming about my mom!"

But he's not sure if she even heard him.

As Tick changes from his pajamas into his school uniform, he curses Nanny Warburough for not listening to him. He doesn't curse her for hitting him, though. He knows she hates hitting him more than anything, but she has no choice. Those are the rules his parents gave to her. Any sign of affection must be answered with physical punishment.

He doesn't understand why it is such an important rule that he never tells the nanny that he loves her. He now understands why he shouldn't leave the nursery, but this rule makes no sense.

Nanny Warburough says the rule was made so that Tick and

Polly would not view her as a mother figure. She is a caretaker and nothing more. When they grow up and leave the nursery, they will never see the nanny ever again. Their love would be wasted on her. Instead, they are to focus all of their love on their real parents. Nanny always tells Tick that his parents are very jealous parents and that he is not allowed to love any other parents more than they. Even though he has never met them, he must still love them with all his heart.

Tick does love his parents with all his heart, but he also loves Nanny Warburough. Even if he never says it out loud, he will always love her. He dreads the day when she will leave his life forever.

Tick arrives in the classroom at the same time as Mike. They both look at each other, on opposite corners of the room. Then Tick runs for his seat. Mike tries to beat him there, cutting through the middle aisle, but Tick is faster.

"What are you doing in my seat?" Mike yells. "I told you I'm sitting here."

Tick looks up at the teacher.

"Mr. Robertson, tell Mike to stop trying to steal my desk," Tick asks.

"Please, take your seats," Mr. Robertson says to them.

Mike steps back, glaring at Tick.

"This is no place for chit-chatting," says Mr. Robertson. Then he adjusts his wire-framed spectacles. "This is a place of learning."

Mike shoves Tick when Mr. Robertson looks away.

"Telling the teacher on me?" Mike says. "You're so dead."

When Mike goes back to his seat, Mr. Robertson begins class. Darcy has not yet arrived. Tick looks around the room, wondering where she could be, but she's nowhere to be seen. She's absent for the second day in a row. Not only that, but almost half the class is missing. Nobody seems to notice except for Tick.

"Where is everyone?" Tick asks the teacher, raising his hand.

The teacher looks around the room.

"What do you mean?" he asks.

"The other students. What happened to them?"

"They're all absent," says the teacher.

"So many of them?" Tick asks.

"No interruptions," says the teacher.

There are only about twelve kids left in the class. Mike and Justin are among them. As Tick looks around the room, he realizes there is something wrong with many of the other kids still present. Simon, the weird kid who sits in the back of the room, is no longer the only jittery kid in the class. Rebecca, the girl who normally sits next to Simon, also trembles and shakes in her seat as she takes notes. Samantha, who sits on the opposite end of the row, jerks her head crazily from time to time, as if she is being electrocuted every three minutes. And Tori, the girl who sits next to Mike, is facing backward in her seat, taking notes and staring intently at the back wall of the class as if she's mistaken it for the white board.

Tick wonders what's wrong with them. It's like they are all mentally ill. He wonders if it's a sickness that is spreading throughout the class, causing many of his classmates to stay home from school. Looking at Samantha jerking her head, her eyes jolting in circles in their sockets, Tick becomes very afraid. He really does not want to contract such a horrible disease.

At recess, Tick goes to Justin and asks him if he knows anything about why so many students haven't been coming to school and what's going on with all the jittery weird kids.

"I don't know," Justin says, more focused on bouncing his

basketball on the playground pavement.

"Do you think they're all sick?" Tick asks. "Nanny says people hardly ever get sick anymore."

Justin shoots a basket.

"It's probably just a coincidence," Justin says.

Just like with Simon, he doesn't acknowledge the strange behavior of the other students.

"I'm worried the creepers might have gotten them," Tick says. "Nanny told me how dangerous they are. They kill kids in their sleep and take their bodies away."

Justin doesn't acknowledge the conversation when Tick mentions the creepers, focused more on retrieving his basketball and bouncing it on the pavement.

"It's true," Tick continues. "My older brother was taken away by them when Polly was little. They killed him. What if the creepers are killing all the other kids? What if they killed Darcy?"

Justin throws the ball at the basket, but misses. It bounces off the backboard. He isn't paying attention to Tick at all. It is as if he's purposely ignoring him, as if deep down he knows all about the creepers but refuses to admit they exist.

"Nanny says they can get inside of nurseries when the power goes out," Tick says. "If the power went out in a lot of nurseries a lot of kids might have died."

Justin doesn't want to hear anymore.

He says, "Are we going to play or what?"

Tick realizes he's not going to get anywhere with Justin. He wonders if it really is creepers. The weird jittery kids make him think it is probably a disease that's going around, but they might not be acting weird because they are diseased. They might be acting weird because they are traumatized by the creepers invading their nurseries.

"Wait a minute…" Tick has an odd revelation as he watches Justin bouncing the basketball. "Where did that ball come from?"

"What do you mean?" Justin asks.

"Is that a new basketball?"

"No," Justin says.

"Yesterday, Mike threw it over the wall, remember? How did we get it back?"

Justin shrugs. "I don't know. Maybe Mr. Robertson retrieved it."

"But how did he get to it? There are no doors that lead beyond the wall."

"Maybe somebody on the other side of the wall threw it back," Justin says.

Tick looks at the wall. He imagines who could have been on the other side to throw it back.

"Do people even live on the other side of the wall?" Tick asks. "I've never heard any sounds coming through the wall. No voices. How do we know anyone is there?"

Justin shoots a basket.

"Who cares?" he says. "Let's just play."

Tick agrees and Justin passes him the ball. He dribbles three times, but then he notices Mike coming toward him. The large boy has an angry look on his face, as if he plans to pound Tick to a pulp.

"Sorry, Justin," Tick says, passing the ball back to his friend. "I think I'm going to go home early."

"Really? No way," Justin doesn't seem to notice the danger Tick's in.

Tick moves in the opposite direction as Mike, toward the classroom.

"I'll see you tomorrow," Tick says to Justin.

Then he runs into the class and teleports home.

CHAPTER FOUR

Polly screams and rams her antlers into the toy box. Her face is red, her teeth grinding. She smashes a toy train against the floor and then charges forward, driving her horn-like appendages into the wall. The room is a disaster area. All the wallpaper is slashed, the doors covered in holes, broken toys scattered across the carpet. Plaster dust covers the girl's dress.

"What's wrong with her?" Tick asks Nanny Warburough.

The boy is under the study table in the library, hiding from his sister as she rips apart the nursery and attacks everything in her path. She foams at the mouth, growling, shrieking. She's gone completely insane.

"She's a woman now," says the nanny. "All adult women behave this way when they're in heat."

The Nanny ducks under the table and wraps her stubby arms around the boy. He closes his eyes and eases into her embrace. Even though he is not allowed to hug the nanny, she is allowed to hold him if she needs to calm him down, though she never refers to it as a *hug*.

Nanny says, "Don't worry. Her fit will pass soon."

Tick doesn't understand how somebody can become so enraged so quickly. Nanny never told him about any of the changes his sister would go through. He never knew she would grow to be so tall. He never knew she would grow horrible tree-like bones out of her head. He never knew she would become so violent and lust to break everything in her path.

"These fits will become increasingly more frequent," says the nanny. "But they'll never last much longer than an hour. You'll have to get used to them."

"I don't like her when she's like this," Tick says.

"She's locked in the toy room," says the nanny. "She can't hurt you."

Polly's screams and the sounds of antlers scraping against plaster echo through the library. It's as if she's in terrible pain.

The nanny continues, "Usually, women have medication they can take to calm themselves during the peak of their estrous cycle, but we have none here. The nursery was not designed for adult women."

Tick cries, "She's breaking all the toys…"

The nanny holds him to her pudgy chest and he weeps into her neck skin. "Forget about the toys. It doesn't matter. They aren't living things."

Tick covers his ears and tries not to listen. He already has to worry about the creepers and whatever is causing the other students at school to go missing, but now he has to worry about his own sister attacking him while she's in heat. He wishes his sister would go back to normal. He wishes she never grew up.

Tick doesn't recognize the dinner. He pushed the button to call the food up from the table as he does every evening, expecting to get chicken and dumplings which was next on rotation. But what has come out of the table is something completely different. It's not one of the eleven dinners that he is regularly served.

"What is it?" Tick asks.

Polly doesn't respond. She hasn't said anything since the violent episode in the toy room, too exhausted to even keep her eyes open for more than two minutes at a time. Her green hair hanging in her face. Her cheek leaning on her sweat-drenched shoulder.

"Is it even food?" Tick asks, using a fork to poke at a spiky piece of meat on the serving platter.

Polly drools onto the side of the table.

Tick yells to Nanny Warburough in the next room. "Nanny, the food's wrong!"

Nanny Warburough comes into the tea room to see what the fuss is about.

"See," Tick says. "It's all weird and messed up."

The nanny inspects the children's dinner carefully. Instead of the chicken and dumplings they were supposed to get, the food is a mash-up of several different meals, including meatloaf, crab legs, tapioca pudding, croissants and artichokes. It's like a surreal alien sculpture of food.

"Huh…" Nanny says. She pokes the sculpture with a knife and horseradish sauce oozes out like a waterfall. "The food machines must be malfunctioning. I'll have to fix them in the morning before breakfast."

"But what about dinner?" Tick asks.

The nanny scoops the strange goop onto a plate and slides it in front of Polly's face.

"You'll eat this," she says, as she prepares him a plate of the grotesque meal.

"I'm not going to eat that," Tick cries. "It's disgusting."

The nanny puts the meal in front of him.

"It is all you have to eat until breakfast tomorrow," says the nanny. "You can eat this or starve."

"But how am I supposed to eat this?" Tick points at the food. The crab claws and artichoke parts of the food look like the face of a ravenous creature staring up at him. "It looks like it wants to eat *me*."

The nanny pays no attention to the child's whining.

"It's perfectly safe to eat," she says, as she leaves the tea room. "All of the ingredients were properly cooked. Just imagine you are eating several meals at the same time."

A bubble of hot mayonnaise pops, squirting out of a meaty round growth on the top of the alien food. Tick decides it would be better to skip eating until breakfast.

Polly doesn't seem to mind the oddness of the food,

scooping it into her mouth like a machine.

"How can you eat that?" Tick asks her.

"Hungry…" she says, between bites.

"But it's so gross," Tick says.

"Don't care. Need food."

Tick can't watch her as she slurps down squirming creamy meat bubbles from her plate. But the more she eats, the less exhausted she looks. It's helping her regain her strength.

"You're scary when you're in heat," Tick says to her.

Then she glares at him as if threatening to kill him dead if he ever speaks to her about what she did in the toy room. Tick decides it would be best to forget it even happened.

Tick wakes to a scratching sound coming from the vent above his bed. He blinks twice, trying to adjust to the darkness of his room. There is another scratching sound, closer and more piercing. Something is inside of the crawlspace, lurking between the walls of the nursery.

Then he realizes the nanny was right. The creepers really can enter the crawlspace. He's not sure how they got inside, because if the crawlspaces did connect to a passage leading outside of the nursery he would have investigated it years ago. But it has to be a creeper. The sounds are identical to those he heard in the corridor.

"Don't worry, my darling," says a muffled voice from below.

Tick's paper mom crawls out from under his bed and turns on his nightlight.

"The creepers can't get you inside of here," she says. "Not with the light on."

She rolls into bed next to him, crumpling her paper limbs against the covers.

"But they're in the crawlspace…" Tick says.

"Just don't go into the crawlspace anymore. You'll be fine."

She wraps her arms around him and collapses her breasts against his face.

"You don't understand," Tick says. "There's something really important hidden inside of there."

She pets his forehead to calm him down, hushing him, "Shhhh… Just forget about it. It's surely not that important."

"It's a drawing of you," Tick says to the paper mom. "It's my *favorite* drawing of you. I can't let the creepers have it."

She hushes him again, cutting the sensitive skin behind his ear as she attempts to caress him with her sharp paper fingers.

"You don't need drawings of me," says the paper mom. "You have the real me, always contained safely in your heart."

The scraping noises come closer until they rattle against the vent above Tick's bed. The paper mom pulls the cover over his head and wraps her crumpled arms around his body, kissing his forehead, and singing him a lullaby until he falls back to sleep.

An alarm goes off and Tick throws the covers off of his face. The paper mom is no longer in the bed with him. There are no longer scratching noises coming from the crawlspace. But there is a loud siren echoing through the nursery.

"What is that?" Tick cries as he runs into the hall.

Polly rubs her eyes, leaning against the doorway to her bedroom. "It sounds like it's coming from the baby room," she says.

"The baby room?" Tick looks at the door across the hall. He's seen very little of the baby room. "Why would an alarm come from the baby room?"

Nanny Warburrough charges down the hallway toward them.

"Something's coming in from the baby tunnel," she says.

Tick remembers the nanny telling him that creepers can get into the nursery through the baby tunnel. He wonders if it's the same creeper he heard in the crawlspace.

The nanny pulls a key from her belt loop and unlocks the baby room. Flashing red lights attack them as the door opens.

"If it's a creeper it will dissipate the second it enters the light," she tells them. "You have nothing to worry about."

"What else could it be besides a creeper?" Tick asks.

Nanny doesn't answer.

The baby room is full of machines and wires. A greasy elastic tube the size of a sleeping bag hangs from the ceiling. It is what the nanny calls the *baby tunnel*. There is also a rubber sink in the middle of the room, below the tube. The nanny calls this a *crib*. She says that it is where Tick and Polly slept when they were newborns.

"Here it comes," the nanny says.

The children hide behind her as the baby tunnel quivers and pulses. Tick hopes the nanny is right about the creeper dissipating in the light. But before it vanishes, he also hopes he gets a chance to see it. He wants to know what the creepers look like.

A blob of snot explodes from the baby tunnel and the crib fills with thick gray fluid. Then a soft white ball covered in mucus oozes out of the tube, sliding into the warm rubber bowl of the crib.

Nanny Warburough puts her hand to her mouth, shocked at the sight of the glistening orb. "I can't believe it…"

"Is it a creeper?" Tick asks. "Do all creepers look like that?"

The nanny shakes her head.

"It's not a creeper," she says. "It's an egg."

She goes to the white orb and rubs her fingers down the warm surface. Something shifts and throbs inside.

The nanny looks back at Tick and Polly with a big smile on her shiny round face. "You're going to have a baby sister."

When the egg cracks open, a smell of rotten fish fills the baby room. A fat gray worm rolls out of the fleshy shell, squeaking and growling at the nanny.

"What is it?" Tick asks.

"I told you," says the nanny. "It's a baby girl."

When the nanny picks the plump squirming creature into her arms, Tick wonders if she's confused.

"That's not what a baby looks like. I've seen pictures of babies in the books in the library. They aren't like that at all."

"That's how babies used to look," says the nanny. "They don't look like that anymore."

Tick looks at his big sister, but she just nods her head in agreement.

"I thought you said our parents were done having children," Polly says.

"I was sure they were done," says the nanny. "These days, human parents give birth to children once every five years until they can no longer have children. Since the last child was born ten years ago, I thought they were done having children. Perhaps the egg has been stuck in the baby tunnel, in a frozen state for the past five years." The nanny freezes in thought for a moment. "Or maybe something happened to the last egg before it reached the nursery…"

The baby's eyes stretch out of their sockets like those of a slug.

"I guess it doesn't matter," says the nanny. "The baby is here now and that's all that matters. You both have a new addition to your family."

The nanny smiles but the children do not return the smile. Polly is angered by the presence of the infant and Tick is confused.

"I'm not taking responsibility for it," Polly says. "Last time was a nightmare."

"No, no," says the nanny. "This time your brother will be

responsible for the baby."

"What do you mean?" Tick asks.

"It will be your job to feed her," the nanny says. "Come here. I'll show you how."

Polly cringes at the sight of the infant creature and turns her head.

"I'm going back to sleep," she tells them, leaving the room.

"But Polly, don't you want to hold him first?" the nanny asks.

"No thanks," Polly says as she closes her bedroom door.

The fat worm hisses and squirts when Tick comes near.

"What's its name?" Tick asks.

"Let's see..." the nanny says. She goes to one of the computers, bouncing the slimy infant in her arms. "Your parents always send the name of the child with them when they are delivered to the nursery through the baby tunnel."

She removes a small printout from one of the computers and holds it up so she can read it. But when she opens her mouth to read the words, Tick can't understand what she's saying.

"What did you say?" Tick asks.

She reads it again but Tick still doesn't understand the word.

"This is what it says on the paper," she says, handing him the printout.

BABY #4
GENDER: female
NAME: Kjhg22yu76(y*&^m

Tick reads it out loud. "Kjhg22yu76(y*&^m? That has to be a mistake. It's not even a real word."

"Real word or not, it's the name your parents chose for this child. We must respect their wishes and use it."

"But how are we supposed to pronounce it?"

The nanny examines the nonsense-word on the paper again. "We can call her *Kajhug* for short," she says.

Then the nanny puts the baby in the crib and unbuttons Tick's pajama shirt. Tick pulls away.

"What are you doing?" Tick cries.

"I want you to hold your sister," says the nanny. "You have to hold her against your bare skin."

"I don't want to hold her," Tick says, closing his shirt.

"You have to hold her so that you can feed her," says the nanny. "She's your responsibility."

The nanny pulls Tick by the wrist to the crib and unbuttons his pajamas. The armless, legless infant squirms in the remains of its flesh-textured shell. Its large bug-like eyes blink up at Tick, opening its goopy hole of a mouth to squeak and growl.

"Make it quick," Tick says.

The nanny slides the infant into the boy's pajamas and buttons it up halfway.

"Hold it like this," she says, placing Tick's arms around the wiggling creature in his pajamas.

Tick groans as his torso is covered in mucus, holding his head away as the dead fish stink rises to his nostrils.

"It's all sticky…" he says.

The infant begins to vibrate against her big brother's belly like a purring cat.

"She likes you," the nanny says, smiling as if it's the cutest thing in the world. "I knew she would."

The purring noises make the flesh of Tick's belly go numb.

"I want to go back to sleep," Tick says.

The nanny shakes her head. "You can't go to sleep until after you feed the baby."

"How do I do that?" Tick asks.

"You don't have to do anything but hold her. She'll feed from you herself."

"Feed from me?" Tick cries. "What do you mean?"

A sharp pain hits Tick in the abdomen, like dozens of tiny

knives slicing him open at the same time.

"She bit me!" Tick yells.

"Of course she has," says the nanny. "She needs to eat."

Tick unbuttons his shirt to see the wormlike creature's mouth wrapped his belly just below his ribs, biting into him with tiny teeth similar to that of a lamprey.

"What's it doing?" Tick cries. "Get it off!"

"A long time ago, human babies were fed milk from their mothers' breasts," the nanny says. "But mothers don't produce milk anymore. These days when babies are in their larval state they drink blood from living hosts. They are parasitic. You will be her host from now on. She will feed from you five times a day until she grows out of her larval stage, which won't be for at least a year and a half."

The baby makes squirting and smacking noises as it sucks from Tick's stomach. He can feel his blood flowing out of his body and into the creature's throat.

"But why me?" Tick asks. "Why can't you or Polly do it?"

"It's your job to do it this time," the nanny says. "Polly might take over once or twice if the blood loss makes you too weak to handle it, but you're big and healthy so it probably won't be necessary. Polly was only five years old when you fed from her as a larva. She was barely able to leave her bed on some days, but she survived. You'll survive too."

Tick tries to remove the leech, but it's stuck firmly to him. Not only are its teeth like fishhooks gripping onto his belly, but its worm-like abdomen is also suctioned to his skin.

"Just make sure not to feed her too long," the nanny continues. "At this age, a baby like her is quite voracious. She will drain you dry without hesitation."

A look of horror is frozen on Tick's face as the baby purrs and squeaks against his body, growing fat and round as it fills with his blood. He now wishes it was a creeper that had come through the baby tunnel. It would have been much less frightening than a human infant.

CHAPTER FIVE

The baby squirts and hisses as it rolls across the carpet in the toy room. It just finished a big breakfast, so it is extra plump and wiggly. Tick can barely believe the monstrous insect is actually his sister.

"Why is it so ugly?" Tick asks.

The nanny sighs at his question.

"It's just the way things are," she says. "Babies never used to be ugly like this, but things change. Over the centuries, human evolution took a different path."

Tick's hands tremble as he rubs the fresh wound on his stomach. The night before, the baby drank so much blood from him that he could barely sleep during the night. He felt sick and exhausted, his bones ached. But this morning the baby seemed even hungrier. It seemed determined to suck every last drop out of Tick. He was almost too weak to pry it off.

"Babies used to be cute," the nanny continues. "Originally, humans evolved to have a cuteness factor so that human adults would become fond of them and desire to love and protect them during their helpless infant period. But that cuteness factor was lost over the centuries."

The nanny pulls Tick's worm-sister away from his leg before she can sink her lamprey teeth into him.

"Now babies are born ugly," says Nanny Warburough, picking the baby up into the air. "And while the cuteness factor used to attract adult humans to infants, these days the ugliness factor does the opposite. It causes adults to reject them. Parents don't want to have anything to do with their young until they grow up."

Tick's eyes light up.

"Wait a minute…" he says. "Is that the reason our parents refuse to come see us? Because we are ugly to them?"

The nanny doesn't answer his question right away, wrapping the baby up in a little pink blanket.

"You always said the reason was because our parents are too busy, too important," Tick says. "You lied about that, didn't you?"

"I'm sorry, I shouldn't have said that," the nanny says. "It's something your parents should have explained to you when you were older."

"So they think we're disgusting?" Tick says.

"It's not just your parents," the nanny says. "It's all human parents. That's why children are raised in nurseries. A long time ago, parents tried to raise their children themselves, but because the parents were horrified by their children they could not bring themselves to love them. In fact, they *loathed* their children. With everyone growing up unloved by their parents, it had an incredibly negative effect on human civilization. People grew cold and heartless. Now that children are raised in nurseries, detached from their parents and human civilization, they are able to be raised in a caring environment."

"What about you?" Tick asks. "Do you think we're hideous, too?"

The nanny shakes her head.

"Nannies are different," she says. "Unlike parents, nannies are driven to care for children no matter what they look like. We see nothing but beauty in you, even when you're in the blood-drinking larval stage."

Tick nearly falls over when he tries to stand up. The loss of blood has made him too light-headed to balance himself.

"It's just the way things are now," she says to him. "Don't take it personally."

Tick doesn't acknowledge her words as he leaves the toy room. He doesn't want to hear any more about mutant babies or his heartless parents. He doesn't even want to eat breakfast, knowing the nanny hasn't fixed the food machines yet. He just wants to go to school. He hopes that Darcy will be back in her seat next to him.

The teacher doesn't say anything when Tick gets to class that morning. He just sits behind his desk, staring at a stack of papers.

Darcy doesn't show up for school again, nor do any of the other kids who were absent yesterday. Three more students are absent today. Tick would be more alarmed about all of this, but he's almost too weak to care. He waits for class to begin, but after an hour the teacher hasn't said anything. Mr. Robertson just sits at his desk, staring at his papers.

Tick looks around at the other students. They remain quiet, staring up front, patiently waiting for class to begin.

"What's going on?" Tick says, breaking the silence. "Is it study period all day or something?"

The few kids in attendance look at him in shock, surprised he would speak out during class. It would normally get Tick detention, but Mr. Robertson just ignores him. For two hours, the teacher does nothing but ignore them. It is very much like Mr. Robertson to do something like this to his students. Tick always wonders if he's just trying to mess with their heads.

"If we're not going to do anything can we go out to recess?" Tick asks.

The other kids stare him down again. Another half hour passes.

The silence shatters when a basketball hits the rim of the backboard out on the playground. Through the window, he sees Justin playing out there. He's all by himself. Tick has no clue as to how or when his friend snuck outside but he does think he's got the right idea.

Tick gets out of his seat and ducks down, making sure Mr.

Robertson doesn't see him. Then he sneaks out of the classroom and onto the playground.

"I can't believe you ditched class," Tick says to Justin, walking across the court toward him. "You're even gutsier than me!"

Justin gives him a confused look.

"What do you mean?" he asks. "I didn't ditch."

Tick laughs. "Of course you did." He points through the windows at the other kids in their seats. "Everyone else is still in class. Didn't you realize you were out here by yourself?"

Justin's face is even more confused. "I'm not out here by myself…"

Tick wonders what is wrong with his friend. Obviously, Justin doesn't realize what's going on around him. He must be disoriented.

"Are you feeling okay?" Tick asks him.

Justin shrugs.

"Yeah, let's play," he says, tossing the ball.

But Justin doesn't toss the ball to Tick. He passes the ball to his left, as if somebody else were standing there. The ball bounces off into the sandbox. Justin just stares at the ball, as if waiting for an invisible person to fetch it for him.

"I'll get it," Tick says, going after the ball in the sand.

Tick knows it must be true. Justin is getting the disease, the same one that's infecting many of the other kids in the class. He's becoming weird, like Simon. He wonders how many others will be infected. Even the teacher seems to be infected. How long will it be until Tick starts acting this way himself?

"Now you're dead," Mike yells at Tick, walking across the playground toward him.

Tick isn't sure where Mike came from. He didn't come from inside the class. He came from the shadows somewhere behind the jungle gym, as if he'd been lurking out there all day, waiting for a chance to strike.

"You've had this coming ever since the day you got between me and Darcy," Mike says.

"What are you talking about?" Tick says, backing away. "Darcy's always been with me."

Justin shoots a basket and then looks at Tick. "Just let him have Darcy so we can go back to playing basketball."

"What?" Tick is shocked he'd even suggest it. "No way."

Mike stands in the center of the basketball court, cracking his knuckles.

"If you want to keep her you're going to have to fight for her," Mike says.

"I don't want to fight you," Tick says.

"You don't have a choice," Mike says.

Tick knows he's right. He has to fight. His paper mom told him that he will sometimes have to fight for those he loves. No matter what happens, he will not give up Darcy without a fight.

"You can't beat him," Justin tells Tick. "Just give him your girlfriend. You don't have a choice."

Mike charges, aiming his knuckles at Tick's face.

"I won't give her up," Tick cries, curling his fists into a ball.

When they collide, Tick ducks beneath Mike's heavy clumsy attack, then leaps fist-first, connecting with the sensitive tissue under the bully's freckled chin.

Mike falls off of his feet, into the air. Then he explodes.

Tick tumbles backward in shock as the bully's body shatters into hundreds of pixelated particles, then vanishes.

"What the hell..." Tick says, staring at the place where Mike was standing.

"What did you do?" Justin says, backing away from Tick with a terrified look on his face. "You killed him!"

"No, I didn't kill him," Tick cries. "I didn't know that would happen."

"You just killed him. You're a murderer!"

"No, my punch must have just teleported him home."

Justin runs away from Tick, fleeing through the sandbox toward the monkey bars.

"I'm telling the teacher!" Justin screams. "You killed him!"

"I couldn't have killed him," Tick cries. "Nanny says that nobody can die at school. You get teleported home if you're ever in danger."

But Justin keeps running around the playground, screaming, "You killed him! I'm going to tell the teacher!"

He runs back and forth between the swings and merry-go-round, moving frantically in a panic.

Tick realizes he's going to get into trouble if he doesn't get out of there. He goes back into class, sneaks through the aisle, and makes a run for the teleporter. Nobody, not even the teacher, seems to notice him.

At dinner, the children are served a mixture of bubblegum ice cream fish filets with sunny side up eggs for skin and cucumber toast.

"Nanny, the food machines are still broken," Tick yells to the other room.

Nanny Warburough enters the tea room with the baby squeaking in her arms.

"I thought you said you were going to fix it yesterday," Tick says.

Tick tries to act normal, as if nothing is wrong. But he can't stop thinking about what happened at school. He's not sure if he really caused Mike to teleport home or if he actually did kill the boy somehow. He can't tell the nanny about what happened. He tries not to think about it.

"Fix what?" the nanny asks.

"The food machines. They're still broken."

"They're broken?" she asks.

She acts as if she has no idea what he's talking about.

"Yes, just like yesterday."

Tick points at the food on the serving platter. The nanny leans in to examine them.

"Hmmm…" she says, poking a fish filet with a fork which causes it to erupt with a geyser of marshmallow sauce. "It looks like the food machines are malfunctioning. I'll have to fix them before breakfast tomorrow."

"That's what you said yesterday!"

It was an eventful evening last night with the baby coming and all, but Tick is still shocked that the nanny would forget something so important. He doesn't know if he can go another night without food.

"Nevermind that now," says Nanny Warburough. "Kajhug needs to be fed."

"Again?" Tick whines. "I'm still weak from this morning."

"You have to feed her five times a day," says the nanny, placing her in Tick's lap. "Make sure you eat as much as possible to keep your strength up."

"But how can I eat when the food machines are broken?"

"The food is edible no matter what it looks like," says the nanny. "Just eat it."

The baby squirms beneath Tick's shirt, slides up his torso and bites into his nipple. Tick writhes in his seat as the creature purrs and squirts against his body. It sucks blood from his nipple and Tick feels as if he's breastfeeding the hideous worm. Fishy odors rise from his clothes and attack his senses. The smell makes the food in front of him even less appetizing.

"Nanny?" Tick asks, before the old woman leaves the room.

She turns around and smiles at him. "Yes, child?"

Tick pauses for a moment, looking down at the bug in his

lap, then back up.

"Is it true that people automatically teleport home from school if they're in danger of getting hurt?" he asks.

"Of course they do," she says.

"So if somebody punched me on the playground, I would transport home the second they hit me?"

A look of concern crosses her face.

"Did something happen to you at school today?" she asks.

Tick shakes his head. "No, I was just wondering."

"It would depend on the danger level," the nanny says. "The computer doesn't pull you out of school if you get hurt, scrape your knee, or get shoved by a schoolmate. Your life has to be threatened. Like if somebody swung a baseball bat at your head."

"But what about a punch?"

"Maybe. It would have to be one heck of a punch, though."

Tick smiles.

"It was a pretty good punch," he says.

"What was that?" the nanny asks.

"Nothing," he says.

He's happy to know he most likely did not kill Mike. But then he realizes that if Mike is still alive he is going to be incredibly angry when he gets back to school and will want revenge.

Polly enters the tea room as the nanny exits.

"This looks gross," she says when she sees the food.

"You had no problem eating it yesterday," Tick says.

"I was out of it yesterday," she says.

Polly takes a few pieces of the cucumber toast but decides to skip the ice cream fish egg concoction. When she takes her seat, squeezing her fluffy butt into the tiny chair, she notices the writhing beneath Tick's clothing.

"You're feeding that thing during dinner?" Polly cries.

"That's disgusting."

"Nanny made me," Tick says, holding the creature through his clothes.

"I can't believe we have another tick in the nursery," Polly says. "Ticks are so hideous."

"Wait, you call all babies *ticks*?" Tick asks.

"Of course," she says. "Where do you think you got your nickname? When you were a baby you were just as repulsive."

"You call them ticks because they suck blood?" Tick asks, he looks down at his freakish baby sister. "I think it's more like a leech than a tick."

"It's more like a tick because they get fatter and rounder as they drink," Polly says. "Like a balloon."

"How big do they get?" Tick asks.

"They say a baby human could drink all the blood out of an elephant and grow a hundred times its size, bigger than this tea table."

"What!" Tick looks down at the ravenous creature drinking from his chest.

"I nearly died feeding you when you were in your larval stage," Polly says. "One time I fell asleep in the library and you somehow wiggled your way out of the toy room and found me sleeping on the floor. By the time I woke up, I was freezing cold from the blood loss. You were twice the size of a basketball, having sucked on me for hours. I would have died if Nanny hadn't emptied your stomach and returned most of the blood to me."

Tick lowers his eyes. He can't believe he had ever been such a horrible disgusting monster. He can't believe he almost killed his own sister.

"Is that why you've always hated me?" Tick asks, pointing at the leech under his clothes. "Because of when I was like this?"

"Probably." Polly shrugs. "Nanny says older siblings tend to resent their younger siblings for all the blood they sucked in their larval stage." Polly takes a bite of cucumber toast, chewing as she speaks. "On the other hand, due to the intimacy and nourishment provided, younger siblings tend to grow up to feel a deep connection with their older siblings."

She spits the toast out on her plate and wipes her tongue with the napkin. The hot cucumber made the toast slimy and disgusting.

As she finishes wiping the toast slime out of her mouth, she says, "That's probably why you always want to be around me so much no matter how mean I am to you."

Tick looks down at the creature. He wonders if he will grow to despise the baby the way Polly despises him. He wonders if the baby will grow to love him with all her heart.

It kind of hurts Tick to learn that he was given his nickname based on what he looked like as a baby. He always thought it was more personal than that. It was something Polly had given him. He was proud of it. The nickname always meant something to him.

He wonders if his little sister will feel the same way about her nickname when she grows up.

"I think I'll call her Leech," Tick says. "She looks more like a leech than a tick anyway."

He smiles up at Polly, but his sister just rolls her eyes at him and leaves the room.

CHAPTER SIX

After dinner, Tick searches for Nanny Warburough so he can give the baby back to her. It's his job to feed it, but he doesn't want to babysit the maggot as well. He finds her sitting in the garden, staring at the marigolds growing in the artificial sunlight.

"I was looking all over for you," Tick says.

He enters carrying the baby, holding it out to her.

The nanny has a smile on her face and a distant look in her eyes. She doesn't notice Tick standing in the room until he steps into her view.

"You look so cute holding your sister, Roger," she says to Tick. "Make sure little Polly grows up to be big and strong."

She turns her smile to the baby.

"What are you talking about, Nanny?" Tick asks. "This is Leech... I mean *Kajhug*. Polly is reading Tarzan books in the library."

"Don't be silly, Roger," Nanny says. "Polly is just a larva. She can't read."

"Why are you calling me Roger?" Tick says. "It's me. Tick... I mean *Rick*."

"Ricky?" Nanny Warburough looks away, his name rolling inside her head. "Of course it's you, Ricky. I'm sorry. My memory was mixed up there for a moment. I'm fine now."

"Why did you think I was Roger?"

The nanny shakes her head.

"You look so much like him," she says. "He grew so fast, just like you. I can't believe he's gone..."

Tick wonders why she's forgetting things so frequently these days. She forgets all his friends' names, she forgets to wake him up for school, she forgets to fix the food machines and other appliances around the house, and now she's forgotten Tick's name. It's almost as if she has the weird disease that everyone's getting at school.

"Have we given Kajhug a birthday party yet?" asks the nanny.

"I don't know," Tick says.

"We should give her a birthday party," says the nanny. She stands up, clapping her heavy hands together with excitement. "How about tomorrow? It can be an all day event."

"I have school tomorrow," Tick says.

"You do?" Nanny asks. "Well, just skip school. It's a holiday. It's been ten years since we've had an addition to the family. We need to celebrate!"

The nanny spins in a circle and runs for the door.

"I'll make the preparations," she says, exiting the garden room.

Tick is left alone, still holding the baby. He doesn't know what's going on with Nanny Warburough. She's been acting strangely. She never would have let him stay home from school before, not for any reason. He's happy he won't have to go to the school tomorrow to face Mike or Justin or Mr. Robertson's discipline, but it's still not like the old woman.

He decides it would be best to put Leech back in the baby room for the rest of the night, and then get some sleep. Lots and lots of sleep.

Tick wakes a couple hours early, just lying in bed staring at his ceiling. He wishes he could sleep more, but there's too much on his mind.

His mother sits on his pillow above his head, her paper legs crossed against his chest.

"I think Nanny has Alzheimer's disease," Tick tells his paper mom.

"What's that?" asks the paper mom.

"It's a disease that eats away your memory," Tick says. "I read about it in one of the old medical books in the library last night."

His mother giggles at him and paper-cuts his cheek. "That book is from a long time ago. People don't get many of those diseases anymore."

"But it's true," he says. "It's the one that makes the most sense."

"Maybe, but I wouldn't take anything you read in an old book too seriously," she says. "People were weird back then. They had a lot of funny ideas."

"But what if she does have it? The book said that it slowly takes away people's memories. And then they die." He lays his cheek against her crumpled leg. "I don't want Nanny to die."

"Everybody dies, Ricky," she tells Tick. "It doesn't matter what happens to your Nanny. She's only a caregiver. I'm your mother. Only I should matter to you."

"But she raised me. I love her more than I love you."

"What?" his paper mom says.

She is shocked. Tick is shocked himself.

"I can't believe you'd say that," she says. "I am your mother."

"But I've never even met you before. Not the *real* you. You're practically a stranger."

"How dare you…" Her raspy paper voice is filled with venom. "You're my flesh and blood. I'm the one who gave birth to you."

She squeezes her legs around his head, putting paper cuts all over his chin and neck.

"I love you, too," Tick says, pushing back her hands and legs. "I just don't want to lose Nanny. I don't know what I'd do without her."

Tick puts his hands in his face. His mother stops scratching him.

"I understand…" his mother says, holding him closely. "You're just frightened. It's okay. I'm sure your nanny will live

64

for several years to come."

She wipes the tears from his face. The tears turn her paper fingers to mush.

"Really?" Tick asks.

"Sure," she says. "She will live for as long as you live in this nursery."

"How do you know?"

"Because it won't be long until I come get you and take you away from the nursery forever."

"Really?" Tick asks the paper mom. "Do you mean it?"

"Of course," she says.

"When?" he asks. "When are you coming to get me?"

"Sooner than you think," she says.

"Really?"

"Really."

He wraps his arms around her and squeezes tight, crushing her hollow paper body and melting her shoulder with his tears.

"Happy birthday!" Nanny Warburough says to Leech as she brings her into the toy room. Birthdays are always celebrated in the toy room.

"This is your welcome-to-the-family party," she says to the greasy mucus-squirting creature. "It's a celebration of your birth."

There is a birthday present on the toy room table and three cupcakes. The nanny programmed Leech's birthday into the food machine the night before.

"Did you fix the machine?" Tick says, running toward the delicious-looking pink-frosted cupcakes.

"What do you mean?" asks the nanny.

Tick takes a bite of his cupcake and an explosion of nacho cheese sauce covers his face.

"Hey, we're supposed to sing happy birthday first," the nanny says. "Don't be a piglet."

Tick doesn't care that the cupcakes are filled with nacho cheese. He's so hungry that the unusual combination actually tastes good to him. He finishes the cupcake before Nanny Warburough can force him to put it back.

"Can we get this over with soon?" Polly says. "I'm feeling twitchy."

Feeling "twitchy" means that another psychotic fit might strike her soon.

"I should be fine for a while, but you might want to lock me in my bedroom tonight," she tells the nanny.

"Of course, honey," the nanny says. Her voice practically dismisses the girl, too busy putting a birthday hat on the wiggling maggot.

Tick looks over to Polly but his big sister just groans back at him. She doesn't want to be there. She'd rather not be around anyone at the moment, especially not Tick or the annoying baby bug.

"Here's your birthday present," the nanny tells Leech, pushing the present next to the blobby creature. "It's from your Mommy and Daddy."

The nanny lets the baby squirm against the present for a few minutes before opening up the package herself. It is a pink pacifier shaped like a large human toe.

"Look at that!" the nanny says to the baby. "A new suckling toy. Aren't Mommy and Daddy so nice to give you such a present?"

The baby squirts and squeals, ignoring the pacifier and trying to roll toward Tick to suck on his leg.

"Did Mom and Dad really give her that present?" Tick asks the nanny. "How did they send it here? Through the baby tunnel?"

Nanny Warburough pushes the toe-shaped pacifier into the baby's mouth. The creature just spits it out again.

"No, they didn't send it through the baby tunnel," says the nanny. "The present was already here."

"But she was just born," Tick says.

66

"All the presents you have ever received or ever will receive have been hidden in storage since long before any of you were even born," says the nanny. "Your parents bought twelve years worth of presents for up to six children, three boys and three girls."

Tick goes to the large iron toy box in the middle of the room, next to the cupcake table. It contains many toys he's received over the years, each one from a different birthday.

"Only twelve years' worth?" Tick asks. He looks back at Polly. "Is that why you don't get birthday presents anymore?"

She doesn't respond, sulking in the corner, her fluffy dress covered in baby snot and plaster dust.

"She received her last present when she turned twelve," says the nanny. "Children rarely stay in the nursery past the age of twelve. Usually they leave sometime between their ninth and twelfth birthdays, to make room for a third child."

The nursery really can only sustain two children at a time. There is a boy's room, a girl's room, and a baby room. Once a baby girl is big enough to move into the girl's room, the older sister will have already moved out of the nursery to live with her parents.

"What happens if Polly is still here by the time Leech is too big for the baby room?" Tick asks.

"I'm sure that won't happen," the nanny says. "I'm sure your parents are on their way to get her any day now."

"You always say that," Polly says.

She crosses her arms.

"It's true," the nanny says. "Have faith."

"Are we done now?" Polly asks. "Or do I have to stick around here watching the maggot leak all over the floor all day?"

"Do whatever you want," the nanny says in a disappointed tone.

"Thank you," Polly says, turning to leave the room.

But Nanny Warburough stops her before she leaves.

"Wait a minute…" the nanny says. She pauses, listening closely to the air. "Do you hear that?"

"Hear what?" Polly says.

"Bells," the nanny says.

"I don't hear anything," Tick says.

"It's the nursery doorbell," the nanny says.

She smiles up at Polly.

"They're here," she tells her. "I told you they would come. I told you."

"Who?" Polly asks.

"Your parents," says the nanny. "They're here."

Tick doesn't believe it.

"Our parents are actually visiting the nursery?" he asks the nanny. "They've finally come to get Polly?"

"Yes," the nanny says. "Isn't it exciting?"

Polly is so surprised she's about to have a panic attack. The day she's been awaiting for so long has finally come. She can finally leave the nursery and start her life as an adult.

"I'm filthy!" Polly says, looking at her dress. "I can't meet them wearing this."

The nanny goes to Polly and pushes her out of the nursery.

"You go change your clothes and fix yourself up," she tells the girl. "Your brother and I will keep your parents company until you're ready."

"Okay," Polly says. She can't stop smiling. "I can't believe it!"

After Polly leaves the room, Nanny Warburough picks up Leech and puts her in a playpen in the corner.

"How do you know our parents are here?" Tick asks the nanny.

"Because of the bell ringing," the nanny says. "Can't you hear it?"

"No," Tick says. "There's no doorbell, Nanny."

Tick begins to think that Nanny Warburough is confused about what's happening. She probably only *thinks* she hears the bell. Their parents haven't actually come.

"Come on," says the nanny. "Let's go meet your parents."

She straightens his clothes and wipes the baby-mucus from his shirt with a wet handkerchief.

"Why the long face?" the nanny asks him. "Aren't you excited to meet your mom and dad for the first time?"

Tick shakes his head. "I don't think they're really here. I think you're just hearing things."

Her wrinkled lips tremble at his words for a moment, then she giggles.

"Of course they're here," says the nanny. "They're the only ones who can possibly ring that bell."

"I think you've got a disease that affects your mind," Tick says. "Like Alzheimer's."

"Don't be silly," she tells him. "Nobody's had Alzheimer's in centuries."

She takes him by the wrist and leads him out into the hallway. The closer he gets to the nursery exit, the more he believes that she is mistaken. There is no bell. No Mom. No Dad. When Polly learns her parents haven't actually come for her, she is going to be devastated.

When they get to the entry room, Tick hears loud scratching noises coming through the door. There are creepers out there. Dozens of them. But Nanny Warburough doesn't hear them. She can only hear the bells ringing in her head.

"Don't open the door," Tick says.

The nanny flips open the first latch.

"I have to open it," the nanny says. "How else am I going to let your parents in?"

The scratching becomes wild against the outside of the door. The creepers are slamming themselves against the wood, trying to break it down.

"There are creepers out there," Tick cries. "Don't let them in!"

"Your parents surely would have cleared the corridor of creepers upon their arrival," says the nanny. "You'll be safe. Trust me."

Nanny opens a few more latches. Tick grabs her by the arm, pulling her away from the locks as the creatures outside bang against the wood.

The nanny gets angry, pushing the boy away from her.

"Stop this nonsense," she shouts at him. "What are your parents going to think when they see you acting this way? Do you want them to think you're a troublemaker?"

But Tick doesn't give up.

"Stop it, Nanny!" he cries, trying to close the latches she's opened. "You can't let them in!"

Tick knows the creepers won't enter with the lights on, but he doesn't want to risk it. They might be a different breed of creatures, ones who thrive in the light.

Finally, she stops trying to get the door open and faces the panicked boy.

"What has gotten into you, child?" she yells at him.

There are tears of distress in his eyes.

"You're going to let the creepers in," he says. His voice croaks as he cries.

A banging noise explodes from the toy room. Then Polly shrieks at the top of her lungs.

"What is that?" asks the nanny.

"The toy room," Tick says. "The creepers must be getting in through the crawlspace!"

The nanny snaps out of it. The bells disappear from her mind. She hears the scraping noises outside the door. She realizes the peril she almost put them all in.

"Danger?" the nanny says. "The children are in danger…"

She leaves the door closed and runs back to the toy room, hobbling on her stubby legs.

In the toy room, Polly is slamming her antlers into the walls. She shrieks, scratching off the wall paper, stomping on toy animals and trains.

"Polly!" Tick cries.

She's not being attacked by creepers. She's having another psychotic episode.

Nanny gets between Polly and the baby.

"Who are you?" Nanny Warburough screams at her. "How did you get in here?"

Polly shrieks and stabs her antlers into another wall, ignoring the old woman.

"It's just Polly," Tick tells the nanny. "She's in heat. Remember?"

The nanny holds out her hand so that Tick doesn't come any closer.

She says, "Don't worry, Roger. I'll make sure she doesn't hurt Polly."

Polly turns and glares at the nanny. Her eyes are deep red, wild. She doesn't look human anymore. She looks like a crazed beast.

"Just leave," Nanny tells her. "I won't let you hurt these children."

Polly charges the nanny, ramming her antlers into the old woman's chest. Nanny falls back onto the table, crushing the two remaining cupcakes.

"Stop, Polly!" Tick cries. "She doesn't recognize you. Something's wrong with her brain."

But in Polly's state, she doesn't recognize the nanny either. She doesn't even recognize Tick.

"Stay back, Roger," the nanny says, hardly able to speak. The antlers must have knocked the wind out of her.

Leech just squirts and squeaks inside of the playpen, oblivious to the situation.

"I'm not Roger," Tick says. "I'm Ricky. Remember? Ricky!"

Nanny Warburough holds her chest as she gets back to her feet. Polly charges her again, cutting open Nanny's cheek.

"You devil!" the nanny cries. "You demon! I'll kill you if I have to!"

"Nanny, don't!" Tick cries.

The nanny hits herself on the thigh in three different places. Then she tears her own leg off.

"It's my job to protect the children," she says. "And I know how to defend them."

Then she raises her severed leg over her head. Tick never knew the nanny had a fake leg. It is made of metal. The nanny stretches the leg out and twists the foot sideways like an axe-blade.

"What the heck..." Tick says.

The severed leg has been transformed into a weapon.

Polly screams as she rushes the nanny, aiming her antlers at the woman's face, as if trying to gouge out her eyes.

Nanny Warburough swings the leg, clubbing Polly in the side of the head. Blood sprays from the girl's scalp, her antlers twist to the side, and then she falls to the ground.

"Get out of the nursery!" Nanny screams, hopping on one foot toward the fallen girl.

Polly curls into a ball, shrieking like a demon, as the old woman beats her with the foot-club, hitting her in the stomach and ribs.

"Stop, Nanny!" Tick cries, running behind her and trying to get between his sister and the deranged old woman. "This is Polly! Don't you remember Polly?"

"Out of the way, Roger!" she screams.

"I'm not Roger!"

She pushes him away and swings her club again. A loud crack when the metal foot connects with the side of Polly's ribcage.

Polly snaps out of it. She stops screaming and wails in agony. Her anger turns to terror. She has no idea what is going on.

"Intruder!" Nanny cries. "I'll kill you!"

She raises the leg-club above her head, aiming to crush the young woman's skull.

Polly holds out her hands.

"Nanny…" Tears are in her eyes, melting her freshly applied makeup down her cheeks. The makeup she put on to look pretty for the parents who never actually came. "Don't…"

Tick jumps up behind her and grabs the leg-weapon by the ankle.

"I just want to meet my mommy and daddy…" Polly cries, holding the broken rib sticking out of the side of her dress. "Just let me see my mommy and daddy."

Tick loses his grip on the fake leg. He can't hold it back any longer. His fingers slide off and Nanny lowers the club into Polly's face. Like a dull axe, the metal toes of the club split open her head. She screams in one quick burst, and then her body goes limp.

When he sees his sister's face break open, the blood splashing into the air, Tick's voice becomes a high-pitched screech. "Stop it!"

He jumps at Nanny's remaining leg, knocking her off balance.

As she collapses, the old woman says, "Ricky, what is—" but her voice is cut short as she hits the side of the large iron toy box. Her neck twists back. Her face breaks off.

Then everything goes silent. The only sound left in the room is the violent thumping of Tick's heart and the hideous baby squeaking in the playpen, begging to be fed.

CHAPTER SEVEN

Tick goes to his big sister. The metal leg juts out of the side of her face, straight up in the air. She isn't moving.

"Polly?"

Tick shakes her. The metal leg wiggles in the air.

"Wake up," he says.

Tears roll down his cheek. "Wake up…"

He pushes at her with more strength, trying to shake her awake. The metal leg whips around above her.

"Wake up!" Tick yells.

Polly's arms lunge at him and grab at his clothes. Then she shrieks herself into consciousness. Tick flies back, pulling his shirt out of her clawing grasp. He thinks she might still be having her psychotic episode, but she only thrashes for a minute.

"What's happening?" she cries.

Tick can't believe she's still alive. It's a miracle.

"I can't see in one eye," she says.

The leg is still in her face. When Tick looks carefully, he notices the big metal toe has landed inside of her eye socket, crushing her right eye. The club split open the skin on her cheek and forehead, but it did not break through her skull to the brain.

"Don't move," Tick says.

"What is in my face?" she says, beginning to whip her arms into the air. "Something is stuck in my face!"

"Calm down," Tick says. "I'll get it out."

Tick stands up and examines the metal leg.

"Don't!" she cries. "Have Nanny do it. Where's Nanny?"

"She's lying on the floor over there," Tick says.

"Why is she on the floor?"

"Don't you remember?" Tick asks. "She attacked you."

"She what? Why did she attack me?"

"Just hold still," Tick says.

He grips the leg tightly and pulls. Polly screams.

"Stop!" she grabs the leg herself, holding it in place.

"I have to get it out," Tick says.

"No, just wait…" she says. "Wake up Nanny. I want Nanny to do it."

Tick looks over at Nanny Warburough. Her face has been ripped from her head, lying on the floor a few inches away from her shoulder. She isn't breathing.

"I think she's dead," Tick says.

"What!" Polly cries.

"She fell and hit her head when I pushed her away from you," Tick says.

"You killed her?"

"It wasn't my fault. She was hurting you."

Polly bawls at the top of her lungs. "You killed her!"

Tick yells, "It wasn't my fault!"

Then he rips the leg out of her eye socket. She cups the empty hole on her face and shrieks, rolling away from her brother into the corner of the room. Tick sees the remains of his sister's imploded eyeball on the end of the metal toe.

Polly doesn't look at him. She doesn't even scream anymore. Her mouth agape in silent shock.

It takes a while for Tick's sister to calm down. She refuses to remove her hand from her eye.

"Are you sure she's dead?" Polly asks.

They have been staring at Nanny's body for almost an hour. Neither of them has wanted to touch her to make sure.

"Her face is off," Tick says. "She has to be dead."

"Maybe we can put it back on," she says.

"That's stupid."

"You're stupid!"

Tick stands up and inches his way toward the old woman's body. He knows she's dead but he also knows Polly won't let it go until she's certain.

"Nanny?" he says.

The old woman doesn't move. He figured she wouldn't.

He kneels down and rolls her over. In the hole where her face should have been, there is an assortment of wires and mechanical parts.

"What the..." Tick says.

He jumps away from her.

"What's wrong?" Polly says.

"She's not human."

"What do you mean?" Polly gets to her feet and staggers closer until the nanny's body is in her view.

"She's like a machine inside," Tick says. "There's no blood or organs."

"A robot?" Polly asks. "Nanny was a robot?"

Tick picks the old woman's face from the floor. It is made of a synthetic tissue. It feels like flesh on the outside, but on the inside it's harder like a plastic.

"How is that possible?" Polly asks.

Tick rubs his finger across the wrinkled face in his hand. He now understands why it was against the rules to love the nanny. She was only a machine. It wouldn't be right to love a machine.

"I guess it makes sense," Tick says.

"What?"

"How else are Mom and Dad going to get somebody to raise us?" Tick says. "Children are disgusting to adults. A real human probably wouldn't want to dedicate their lives to raising ugly kids."

"This can't be real," Polly says. "Nanny can't be a robot. Are you sure it's really her?"

"Of course it's her."

Tick realizes that the nanny had been malfunctioning this whole time. She never had Alzheimer's disease. Her memory circuits were just corrupted. Like the food machines, she was breaking down and needing repairs.

Polly rubs her remaining eye, wiping out the tears.

"What are we going to do without her?" she asks. "We can't live without Nanny. Who's going to fix the food machines? Who's going to look after us?"

"I don't know…" Tick says.

"Can she be fixed?" Polly says. She's beginning to panic again. "If she's a machine she can be fixed. We can get Nanny back. You have to fix her."

Tick leans down and puts the face back in place. It just slides off when he lets go.

"I wouldn't know how to fix her," Tick says.

"Just fix her!" Polly screams.

"I don't know anything about robots!" Tick yells back.

She nudges him out of the way.

"Fine, I'll do it myself," she says. "You're so useless."

She leans down to examine the robot's machinery, hoping to figure out a way to fix the nanny as soon as possible. She doesn't realize that lowering her head causes a river of blood to stream out of her eye socket and run through her fingers. She doesn't seem to notice it dribbling down her cheek.

"Polly, it can wait…" Tick says.

He wipes the blood from her chin and neck, then grabs hold of an antler and pulls her head back to stop the bleeding. She shoves him away from her.

"You should go to the bathroom and take care of your wounds first."

She wipes at her cheek and sees the blood. Then she nods her head at him, realizing that she isn't thinking straight. She's still in shock.

"Okay… I'll go get a bandage." Her voice is much quieter, the tension releases from her muscles. "You stay here and fix Nanny…"

As she staggers out of the toy room, Tick looks down at the nanny. There are several tiny pieces of her machinery scattered across the floor where she landed. He picks two of them up. They were originally one piece that has broken in half. He realizes that she is well beyond repair, even if one of the children actually had the knowledge to fix robots.

"I'm sorry, Nanny," Tick says to the dead machine.

He doesn't regret what he did to save Polly from Nanny Warburough, but he's sorry she had to be broken.

"I don't care if you were just a robot," he says. "I still loved you."

He picks up the cupcake-smeared tablecloth from the floor and covers the nanny's face with it. The nursery will be lonely without her.

Tick turns off the lights and locks up the toy room. He doesn't want to go back in there anymore. He wonders if they can keep the room locked forever, so they'll never have to see her broken body again.

Leech squirms in Tick's arms, squeaking and growling at him. The little creature has no idea what's just happened. When she grows older, she'll never get to know Nanny Warburough.

"I'm not going to feed you," he says to Leech as she bites at the outside of his clothes. "I'm too weak."

He enters the baby room and gently sets the creature down inside the bowl of the crib. Then he places the large toe-shaped pacifier in the crib with her.

"Who's going to raise you now?" Tick says to the maggot. "I only have to feed you. It's supposed to be Nanny's job to take care of you."

Leech curls her chubby worm body around the pacifier toe and opens her goopy slug mouth to it.

"You're not my responsibility," he says.

She squeaks at him as she sucks on the rubber toy.

"Go to sleep."

He turns off the light and closes the door behind him. Then he goes to the entry room to close up the locks and latches the nanny had left opened.

The creepers are still out there, banging and scraping at the door. It sounds like they are even more ferocious than before, trying even harder to get inside. It's like they know that their nanny is dead and that the children are left unprotected. Tick wonders if the door is strong enough to hold them all back.

He imagines it won't be able to hold forever.

"What am I going to do?" Tick asks his paper mom.

He's in his room, pacing back and forth. He has spent the last three hours cleaning his room, organizing every inch of his closet, bookshelves, and toy box. Now he's stuck with his thoughts.

"You don't need the nanny anymore," says the paper mom. "You're a big boy now. You're practically an adult."

"But who's going to look after Leech? Polly?"

"You will," says the paper mom.

"I don't know how to take care of a baby," Tick says.

"You're a smart boy," she says. "You will figure it out."

"But aren't you going to come get me soon?" he asks. "What happens when I'm gone?"

"It'll all be fine," says the paper mom. "Don't worry about it."

"How can I not worry about it?"

She rubs his shoulder.

"Because everything's going to be fine. I'll make sure of that."

"No, you won't," Tick says. "You're not even real."

"Of course I'm real."

"You're just paper," Tick says.

"How dare you," she says. "I'm your mother."

She stomps toward him and slaps a paper cut across his face.

"You're just paper!" Tick cries.

He grabs her by the shoulders and crumples her up into a ball.

"Stop," his mother cries, as her body collapses and folds. "You're hurting me."

He scrunches her arms and legs together, crushes her abdomen inward, and wads her up into a giant wrinkled sphere.

"You're just imaginary," he says, squeezing her tightly against his stomach until she's the size of a basketball. "You're not my real mom. You're nothing."

Without Nanny, Tick knows he has to grow up. He needs to forget about his paper mom. He needs to grow out of imaginary things.

"I don't need you."

The ball of paper wiggles and shivers at Tick as he drops it onto the carpet. Then it rolls away, disappearing into the shadows under his bed.

Polly won't let Tick see her for the rest of the day. She locks herself in her room and refuses to leave. All alone, Tick lies in his bed wondering what life is going to be like in the nursery without Nanny Warburough. He has no idea if they are capable of taking care of themselves.

He can hear the baby howling and squealing through the walls, begging to be fed. Tick hasn't given her any blood all day. Without Nanny there, he doesn't have to do anything he doesn't want to do. He doesn't have to feed the baby, he doesn't have to go to school, he doesn't have to clean his room. Nobody will punish him.

The food machines can't be fixed, so Tick will have to deal with disgusting food from now on. He won't know how to fix any of the machines. If the power goes out he will be trapped in the dark with the creepers.

The only thing he can do is hold out until his parents come for him. Maybe they will know how to fix Nanny Warburough and all the machines. He hopes they haven't forgotten about him.

Tick tries to fall asleep, but the sound of the baby grows louder and more high-pitched, keeping him awake. He puts his pillow in his face, but that doesn't help. The creature is starving, wailing like a pig-banshee.

"Fine," Tick says. "I'm coming."

As he goes to the creature in the baby room, she nearly leaps out of the crib at him, biting at him through his shirt. She drinks his blood ravenously, as if trying to suck it all out in a single sip.

CHAPTER EIGHT

"Polly?" He knocks on her door, holding a plate of food. "Aren't you going to eat anything?"

He tries the doorknob but it's locked. Tick has no idea what's going on with her.

"There's pineapple chicken bagels for breakfast." He takes a bite out of one of them. "They're actually really good."

There's still no response.

"Come on, answer me," he says. "Are you alright in there?"

He puts his ear to the door. No sound comes from inside.

"There's also something I want to give you," he says. "I made it myself."

After a few minutes, he gives up. He puts the plate on the floor.

"Your food is out here if you decide to eat," he says. "I'm going to go to school."

There's still no sound coming from the room as he walks away.

In the teleport room, Tick doesn't have Nanny to help him get to school. He straps the helmet on himself and goes to the controls. He's seen Nanny do it a dozen times. He's sure he can teleport himself without problems.

"Here we go," he says, taking a deep breath.

He doesn't really want to go to school after what he did to Mike, but he has to get out of the nursery. He needs to see people again. He needs to talk to Justin or Darcy. He'd even settle for talking to Mike, if the bully would actually forgive him for what happened the other day.

Tick pushes the button and his vision explodes into a bright light. He is sent far away, through a glowing teleportation tunnel, toward school.

When Tick arrives in the classroom, the place is empty. Nobody else is there. This doesn't make any sense to him. He's late, so he should be the last kid in class, not the first.

He walks down the aisle toward his desk and looks around.

"Is anybody here?" he asks.

His voice echoes in the abandoned classroom.

The sky is dark outside the window.

"What time is it?" he asks, wondering if he's come to school at the wrong time of day. It seems like it's night outside.

When he turns around, there are three students sitting in the back of the room.

"Where did you come from?" he asks them. "I didn't see you teleport in."

The kids don't respond. They just sit in their seats, staring at the front of the room. One of them is Simon. Tick goes to him.

"What's wrong with you, Simon?" he asks. "Why don't you ever speak anymore?"

Tick leans in closer. The boy is just vibrating, quivering in his seat.

"Are you sick?" he asks.

Something's wrong with the kid, that's for sure, but Tick has no idea what. He puts his hand on Simon's shoulder. The vibrations crawl up Tick's arm.

When Tick pulls his arm away, the vibrations don't stop. His arm quivers, shaking so fast that his fingers look almost like a blur.

"Oh…" Tick says. "Now I'm infected…"

He shakes his arm. It's all numb.

"What's going on?" he says.

A loud thumping sound makes Tick jump. Something slammed against the window outside.

"What was that?"

He goes outside onto the playground. It's dark out there. He's never seen the playground at night. When he looks at the sky, he expects to see stars and a moon, but there's nothing there. It's not really night time. The sky has just lost all of its color. It's all gray. No clouds. Just a flat gray color.

A basketball rolls across the court. Tick goes to it and picks it up. He decides the basketball must have been the thing that hit the window. But looking around, he has no idea who could have thrown it. The playground is empty. Nobody is there.

As Tick goes back toward the classroom, he tosses the ball over his shoulder. His arm vibrates crazily as he tries to get the door open.

"You killed him!" screams a voice from behind.

Tick turns around. It was Justin's voice, but he doesn't see him anywhere.

"Justin?" Tick calls out.

He goes to the darker section of the playground, behind the jungle gym. Justin isn't there.

"You killed him!" the voice screams again.

Tick looks around. He can't tell where the voice is originating. It sounds as if it's coming from everywhere at once.

"Where are you?" Tick asks.

There is no response. He searches every inch of the playground, but there's nobody in sight.

"I'm telling the teacher!" cries Justin's voice.

It's the same words Justin was saying the last time Tick saw him.

He explores the playground, following the sound of Justin's voice until he realizes where it's coming from. It sounds as if it's coming from the other side of the wall.

Tick puts his ear on the brick surface.

"Are you there?" Tick asks.

"I'm telling the teacher!" cries Justin's voice.

"What are you doing on the other side of the wall?"

Tick goes into the classroom and grabs a desk. His vibrating arm infects one leg of the desk, causing it to quiver and rattle. He brings the desk outside and pushes it against the wall. Then he goes back and gets another.

The other kids ignore him as he steals desks and chairs from the classroom. When he's finished, there is a tall ladder of desks leaning against the outer wall of the playground, all of them rattling wildly due to the shaking disease. Tick has no idea why the disease in his arm was transferred to inanimate objects, but he doesn't want to worry about that now. He's more interested to see what's on the other side of the wall.

"You're a murderer!" Justin cries.

Tick climbs to the top, infecting more sections of the desks he touches. The entire mountain of furniture rattles and quakes by the time he reaches the top.

He peers out over the wall for the first time.

"Where is everything?" Tick says.

There is nothing on the other side. No city. No streets. Just the color gray.

"This isn't real," he says.

There isn't even a ground. At the bottom of the wall, there is just gray. The same color as the sky. It's like the school is just floating in empty space.

"You killed him!" Justin screams.

Tick didn't notice him at first, but Justin is there. He's not on the other side of the wall. He is *inside* the wall. He's stuck in there, only half of his body sticking out into the gray emptiness.

"You killed him!" Justin screams.

He's running in place. His body moves back and forth, twisting in a circle, trying to escape but he can't get anywhere. He's stuck inside the wall.

"Justin…" Tick says. "What's going on…"

His friend doesn't notice him, just jittering and running in place.

Tick climbs down from the ladder of desks and runs back

to the classroom. When he enters, the class is upside-down. The chairs and desks are on the ceiling. The lights are on the floor.

Tick looks up as he crosses the room. The few children remaining just stay in their seats, staring straight ahead, waiting for class to begin. When he gets to the corner, Tick teleports out and finds himself lying on the floor of the teleport room, curled in a weird angle with his head twisted toward his armpit.

He never really left the teleport room. Only his mind was teleported to class, leaving his body behind to crumple to the floor. He stands up, rubbing his shoulder. His arm is back to normal, no longer vibrating.

He tries to come up with a rational reason for everything that happened at the school, but he can't accept the only one that makes sense. None of it was real.

Tick sees that the breakfast he left for Polly is still on the floor. She never took it.

"Polly?" he asks through the door. "Are you awake?"

He knocks a few times.

"Are you going to stay in there all day again?"

After a few more minutes, Tick begins to panic. He wonders if Polly's wounds were more severe than he thought. He wonders if she's dying in there, bleeding internally. Maybe she's already dead.

"Let me in," Tick yells.

He tries to force the door open.

"Polly, you're scaring me. Just say something. Anything."

The door won't budge.

He doesn't know what to do. He puts the plate of food down and goes to his room, looking for something that might pick the lock. Then he catches sight of the vent above his bed. Whenever Polly used to lock him out he always went into the crawlspace to see what she was up to through the crack in the wall.

"But I can't go in there…" he says to the vent.

There are creepers inside. He's heard them. It would be too much of a risk. But what if his sister is in trouble? He can't lose her.

He gets a light from Nanny's room and shines it up at the vent. There is nothing inside when he opens it. He puts the light inside the crawlspace and then climbs up, squeezing through the open vent.

The crawlspace hasn't looked this frightening to him since he was a little kid and Polly forced him to go inside to hide from Nanny Warburough. She wanted Tick to pretend as if he were taken by creepers. It was supposed to be her revenge on Nanny for making her go to school on a day she wanted to stay home. Tick had to remain hidden up there all day, listening to the nanny call out to him. He didn't respond to her calls, afraid of what his sister might do to him if he gave himself away. Tick eventually grew fond of the crawlspace. It was a nice private area he could escape into.

But now the crawlspace looks like a death trap as he slithers on his belly through the shaft, shining the flashlight in front of him. Every three feet he pauses and listens. The first sign of scratchy noises and he plans to get out of there as quick as he can.

His flashlight goes out.

"No," Tick cries.

It is the worst thing he feared would happen. He bangs the light twice and it comes back on.

"How?" he whispers to himself.

He just put fresh batteries inside the light, worried about the batteries dying while inside the crawlspace. But the light went out anyway. The batteries are fine. It must be something wrong with the bulb.

Looking back and then looking forward. He isn't sure if he should keep going with the faulty flashlight. The next time it goes out it might not come back on. He decides to keep going.

He has to make sure Polly is all right.

"Please stay on…" he begs the light.

When he gets to Polly's room, he doesn't have to look through the crack in the wall. There is a larger opening. The vent has been broken off and the bookcase that used to block it has collapsed to the floor. Polly put the bookcase there a long time ago so that Tick wouldn't stare at her through the vent when she was changing.

"Polly?" Tick whispers into the room.

It's dark in there. He's not sure why the lights are off.

"Polly?" he says again, a little louder.

He shines the light into all of the corners, but there's nothing in there. Polly is missing. When the thought of creepers breaking into her room and getting her in her sleep comes to his mind, he shivers in a panic. There is no nightlight in the room, no light of any kind. Maybe the creepers smelled the blood from her wounds and came after her. What if she's dead?

A scraping noise echoes through the vents behind him, then he hears shuffling, the sound of knees and elbows bumping into the crawlspace walls.

Tick turns his flashlight to the sound but the battery goes out, leaving him in darkness. He hears shuffling noises ahead of him. He doesn't move. He tries not to breathe. Then he attempts to bang the flashlight back on without making any noise.

A scraping noise squeals across the metal walls, coming slowly toward him. He decides there's no point in being quiet. He has to get the light back on. He slams the shaft of the flashlight against his hands with all of his strength, but the light stays off.

His eyes begin to adjust to the darkness. There are strips of dim light entering the crawlspace from other parts of the nursery and some light comes in behind Tick from his bedroom. It's enough to almost make out what's in the vent with him.

In the darkness, he sees the silhouette of a woman's body.

The scraping sound comes from the woman's antlers, scratching against the ceiling as she crawls through the vent toward him.

"Polly?" Tick asks the figure crawling through the dark. "Is that you?"

He can't see the girl clearly, but it looks like Polly. She has long hair and antlers, the same size as hers. But she's not wearing any clothes, crawling naked in the dark.

"What are you doing in here?" he asks her. "Why aren't you wearing clothes?"

She doesn't respond, just scraping at the ceiling as she crawls toward him.

"I thought you couldn't fit in the crawlspace anymore..." Tick says.

As she nears him, entering the light emanating from Tick's room, he notices she's much thinner and bonier than his sister, almost like a skeleton. And her hair is black and scraggly. This woman isn't Polly at all.

He bangs his flashlight three more times. The light comes back on for just a second and then turns off again. In that brief flash, he sees the woman's face. Her skin is black and charred, as if made of soot. Her eyes are black balls of coal. Her lips like wrinkled licorice whips. She's not like Polly. She's not even human.

The second she sees Tick in her cold dead eyes, the creature shrieks. She raises her claws and thrashes toward him. Tick throws his flashlight at her, but it misses and lands on the other end of the crawlspace.

"Get away!" Tick screams.

Just before she can grab him, Tick dives through the vent into Polly's room. He lands on the collapsed bookcase on the floor. He looks back and sees claws reaching out for him through the vent, but she can't get to him. The size of her antlers prevents her from getting through.

He flips the light switch on and the woman disappears. There's nothing there but an empty hole where the vent used to be.

"Where'd she go?" Tick says.

He takes a few steps closer, peers into the crawlspace. There's nothing there. The woman just vanished.

"What were you doing in my room?" Polly yells at Tick when she sees him in the hallway.

She has a large bandage over her eye wound, strapped to her face.

"Polly?" Tick cries. His face lights up when he sees her, relieved to see her still alive. "Where were you? I thought you were dead."

He wants to hug her with all his strength, but is afraid he'll hurt her wounded body.

"I was in the library," she says. "I spent the night in there. I kept hearing noises in the crawlspace, so I decided to switch rooms."

When she enters her room, seeing the disastrous state it's in, she glares to Tick as if she's ready to kill him.

"What did you do to my shelves?" she shouts at him.

"It wasn't me," Tick says. "A creeper was in the vent. The bookcase was already knocked down."

"You saw a creeper do this?"

He points up at the vent.

"It disappeared when I turned the light on. Just like Nanny said would happen."

"You better not be lying," she says.

"I'm not. I swear."

Polly stares up at the opening, as if afraid to look away from it.

"We need to barricade the vents somehow," Polly says. "I'm not sleeping in here again until I feel safe."

Tick tells Polly about what happened at school that day. He explains how the sky had no color, the class was upside down, and how Justin was trapped in the wall, speaking in a loop.

"It must be a computer glitch," Polly tells him, her remaining eye puffy from lack of sleep and crying too much.

"A glitch?"

"Yeah, they happen sometimes. Nanny usually fixed them before they got too bad."

Tick suddenly feels the urge to run away from this conversation. He doesn't know why. He just wants to get out of there and hide under the table in the library.

"The school is a computer program?" Tick asks.

"Of course." She laughs. "You didn't think any of it was real did you?"

"Just the classroom, right? The people are still real, aren't they? Justin and Darcy live in other nurseries in other houses far away."

"They're fake, too," Polly says. "All of it was just a simulation."

"But it was real... I could feel the desks and touch the people. Darcy kissed me behind the jungle gym."

"It was designed to give the illusion of a classroom experience," Polly says. "You had a teacher, a bully, a best friend, and a love interest. So did I. All of those are important to childhood development."

Tick sits down. Although it seems obvious now, he can hardly believe any of it. He doesn't *want* to believe any of it.

"So Darcy isn't really out there somewhere? She never really existed?"

Polly becomes frustrated with her little brother.

"It was all fiction. None of the people were real. Your friends weren't real, your teacher wasn't real, even Nanny wasn't real. The only real human being you have ever known in your life is me."

Tick is shocked by her words. He can't speak.

"I can't believe you didn't know," she says, shifting her eye bandage. "I was younger than you when I figured it out."

Tick suddenly feels incredibly lonely. His universe has become small. The only real person he's ever known has been his big sister, and she's always despised him and pushed him away.

"We've always been alone," she says. "Just us."

There's also Leech, but she's just a weird bug thing. He hardly believes she'll grow up into a real human being.

"There's not just us," Tick says. "There's also Mom and Dad. They live in the house somewhere."

"But you've never seen them before."

"They're still with us in spirit," he says. "They'll always be with us in spirit."

CHAPTER NINE

Tick barricades the vents, using hammers and nails from the storeroom. But there aren't enough supplies to seal up all of them, so he breaks apart the tables in the library and nightstands from bedrooms to get more wood.

Polly doesn't help him. It was her idea but now she says she's too injured to do it. Lifting her arm to hammer nails sends shooting pains through her ribs, so Tick has to do it all by himself. Just like he has to take care of Leech all by himself and clean the nursery all by himself.

When he's finished, all the vents are sealed up airtight. Nothing will be able to get through. Nothing will even be able to see through.

Tick realizes that he might have made a mistake. The light shining through the cracks in the vents might have been what was keeping the creepers away. Now that not even small strips of light can enter the crawlspace, the creepers might come in larger numbers. Not only that, but Tick realizes he might also have just cut off the air supply to the nursery. If the vents are sealed airtight, they might suffocate.

He wonders if he should take down the boards and start over. Metal bars over the vents might be more effective. But he's been working all day and he's too exhausted. He can barely stand anymore and it's already time to feed Leech again. Until they prove to be a problem, the boards are going to stay where they are.

The bathroom door is open a crack and Tick can see Polly's

naked body reflected in the mirror, examining her wounds and whimpering at the sight of herself. Tick cringes at the dark footprint-shaped bruises covering her body. The entire left side of her torso is black and purple, stretching all the way down to her hip. There's a visible dent in her body below her left breast, the center of the massive bruise. Three of her ribs are poking out of the flesh like skeletal fingers.

Now Tick understands why she's not able to do any work around the nursery. She can hardly move one side of her body. She probably can't even breathe through one lung anymore. He has no idea how that's going to heal without Nanny to fix her up.

Polly coughs up dark blood into the sink. She tries applying ointment to the wound, but even the slightest touch sends a shooting pain through her chest. Tick can hardly watch. She shivers and whines in agony, staring at her horrible wounds with a terrified expression. She's confused and frustrated by her injuries, because she has no idea what to do about them.

The gaping hole where her eye used to be looks worse than before. The swelling has gone down a little, but the entire area of her face has become a large black scab. It looks as if half her face burned off.

She cries at her reflection in the mirror. At first, Tick thinks she's crying about the pain, but that's not it.

"I'm so ugly," she says to herself.

She punches at her wound, cracking the scab open, as if she can rip the wound away to find beautiful skin beneath. Then she screams at her reflection, grabbing one of her antlers and trying to rip it off. When she raises her arm too high a stabbing pain shoots up her chest. She calms down and droops against the sink, tears rolling down her face.

"I'm a hideous monster," she says in a soft voice, inches away from the mirror. "Mom and Dad are going to hate me…"

Tick comes closer and catches her eye through the crack in the door.

94

"Can you still cry with your eyeball missing?" Tick asks.

She slams the door when she sees him, covering her hideous body.

"Go away," she cries.

Tick doesn't leave.

"I brought you something," he says. "I meant to give it to you earlier. I made it for you."

"What is it?" she asks.

"It's for your eye," he says.

She opens the door a crack, and peeks out at him. He holds up the gift so she can see.

"A doll?" she asks.

"It's just the face of a doll," he says. "I turned it into an eye patch for you."

"I'm supposed to wear that on my eye?" she asks.

"It'll cover up your wound," he says.

She pulls the eye patch into the bathroom with her and closes the door. When she comes out, she's wearing a clean dress, a ribbon in her hair, bright red makeup, and the porcelain doll face over her wounded eye.

"Do you think Mom and Dad will think I'm pretty when they meet me?" she asks.

Tick smiles at her.

"They'll think you're the prettiest girl ever," he says.

She smiles back, touching the porcelain face on her eye as if it does somehow make her prettier. As long as she can cover up her ugliness, she won't feel so bad.

When dinner is served, a terrible stench comes out of the tea table. Tick can't tell what kind of food mash-up would cause such an odor. It looks like tuna casserole, bacon and pork chops but it smells worse than anything Tick has ever smelled.

"Why does it stink so bad?" Tick asks.

Polly nearly collapses when she enters the tea room. She cups her mouth, trying not to throw up.

"The meat is rancid," she says, waving the air away from her face.

"It's rotten?" Tick holds his nose. "This is what rotten smells like?"

"Get rid of it," she cries.

Tick pushes the button and the table disposes of the food.

"What are we going to eat?" Tick asks.

"You can't eat food that's rotten like that," she says. "It will make you sick or kill you."

"But why was it rotten?"

"The food machines are getting worse," she says.

In the morning, they try the machines again. A breakfast of moldy bread and rancid egg soup stinks up the tea room. Not a single bite of the food is edible.

"We can't eat any of this…" Tick says. "What are we going to do?"

"I don't know…" Polly says.

"We can't stay in the nursery anymore," Tick says. "We have to go find Mom and Dad."

Polly's eyes widen when he says this. Her antlers tremble.

"But what about the creepers?" she asks.

"They're only dangerous in the dark," Tick says. "We just have to take lights with us."

Polly shakes her head violently.

"No," she says. "We have to fix Nanny. If we get her back she'll make the machines work again."

"You don't know how to fix her," Tick says.

"I'll figure it out."

"You've been saying that for days but you haven't even tried to fix her yet."

"I'm sure I can fix her if I try."

"Even if you got her to work, she might try to kill you again."

"No, she won't," Polly says. "She'll remember me."

"There's no time. If we don't leave we're going to starve to death."

"Then *you* leave," Polly says. "I'm staying here and fixing Nanny."

"You'll die," Tick says.

She marches out of the room and says, "No, *you'll* die."

The water is the next to go. While taking a shower, Tick feels the water pressure drop until only a small trickle of fluid comes out. He quickly plugs up the drain, then fills up as many buckets of water as he can. By the next morning, the water doesn't come out of any of the faucets anymore.

When he tells Polly she doesn't reply, busy sitting in the toy room, putting pieces of machinery back into Nanny's face. She has to guess where they're all meant to go.

"We have enough for only a week at most," Tick says. "If you don't fix Nanny by then, I'm leaving the nursery with or without you."

Polly just stares into the robot's face, ignoring him.

"Did you hear me?" he asks.

She turns and glares at him. "Will you leave me alone? I was almost onto something when you interrupted me."

Tick frowns and says, "Just don't drink it all."

As he is about to leave the toy room, the lights flicker on and off. Then the power goes down for a moment, the lights dim. Tick and Polly lock eyes for a moment, then the power returns to normal.

"We can't stay here," Tick says. "Once the lights go out..."

Polly shakes her head. "We'd be safer out there? Even if the lights go out, I'd rather be barricaded in the nursery."

Tick wishes she was on his side. He turns around and mumbles, "I'd rather be with Mom and Dad..."

Tick feels like he's suffocating as he sleeps. He's not sure if it's because of the boarded air vents or if it's just his paranoia playing tricks on him.

Just to be safe, he removes the middle board from the vent above his bed. It doesn't help. He's still having problems breathing. Perhaps it has something to do with the loss of blood. He feeds Leech regularly, but he might be giving her too much. Without Nanny around he's not sure what the proper amount should be.

"You can't stay here," says his mother's voice.

The crumpled ball of paper rolls out from under his bed. It turns to him, the drawn-on face of his paper mom flattened onto the outside of the ball.

"You have to leave the nursery and come find me," she says.

Tick turns away from her. "I thought I got rid of you. You're not real."

"But I *am* real," she tells him. "You just have to leave the nursery and come find me."

"I thought *you* were supposed to come get *me*."

"I can't come right now," she says. "You have to come to me."

"How do I even find you? Nanny said this house is too big to find you without a map."

"Then you should find a map."

"Where do I find one?"

"You can find one in the house. In a map room."

"That's what Nanny said, but what is a map room?"

"You'll find it if you look."

"Whatever."

Tick rolls over and tries to go to sleep. The paper mom isn't helping. She never tells him anything he doesn't already know.

After a few days with no food, Tick can't bring himself to feed Leech anymore. He's already too weak. The little worm looks fat and healthy enough to go without being fed for awhile.

"I'm sorry," he says to the squeaking blob as he hammers a metal chair leg into a point. "If I have to starve then you have to starve too."

Leech wiggles across the library floor toward him.

"No you don't," Tick says, as she's about to chomp down on his ankle.

Tick moves to the other side of the room, taking the hammer and chair leg with him. He continues pounding the piece of metal until it forms a sharp point.

Leech huffs and puffs, growl-snorting, desperately looking around the room with her big bug eyes to find where Tick went. When she finally sees his new position, she squeaks and squeals and inches her way across the carpet toward him.

"Stop coming after me," Tick says, when she gets within range of his ankle. "You're not a carpet shark."

He picks her up and faces her mouth away from him, then brings her back to her crib in the baby room. She squeals and growls as he walks away and shuts the door. He can hear her squirting and pouting as he goes back to the library.

The metal chair leg is sharp. He tests it by stabbing it into the reading couch. It cuts right through. The metal does not bend. He straps the blade of metal onto a broom handle, creating a spear. He drives it into the couch, impaling a couch cushion.

He makes armor out of wood scraps left behind when he barricaded the air vents. There's a round board strapped to his chest, other thin boards protect his forearms and legs. For a helmet, he uses a metal waste bucket with eyeholes broken out of it with the sharp side of the hammer.

Now he's ready for a fight.

"What are you doing?" Polly cries when she sees her brother opening the locks on the front door of the nursery. "Have you gone crazy?"

The creepers bang and scratch on the other side of the door.

"I'm not leaving," Tick says. "I just want to test out a theory."

"You're going to let them in!"

Tick opens the door and the scratching noises stop. They both look out into the corridor. Nothing is there.

"Where are they?" Polly says.

"Nanny said they dissipate in the light, right?" Tick says. "We should use the light to dissipate as many of them as we can."

Tick closes the door again. The second the door is shut, the scratching and banging noises return.

"What..." Tick steps away from it.

"They're back," Polly says.

"But I made them disappear..." Tick says. "They should be dead now."

Tick opens the door again. He slowly steps out into the corridor, pointing the spear in front of him.

"Whatever you do, don't close the door..." he says.

He looks down the corridor. There is nothing out there. For as far as the light reaches, there is nothing. But in the shadows beyond the light, there is movement. He hears footsteps and gentle scratching noises. The creepers are still there.

Back inside the nursery, he closes the door and the banging immediately returns.

"What's going on?" Polly says.

Tick looks around the room. He takes three deep breaths, then goes toward the light switch on the wall.

"Get behind me," he says.

Polly does what he says, but asks, "What are you going to do?"

"Don't be scared," Tick says.

He turns off the light in the entryway. In the shadows, there are several black creatures with jagged antlers and gnarled teeth, clawing at the walls.

Polly screams when she sees them and grabs Tick by the shoulders. The creatures turn to her. They raise their claws, filling the room with high-pitched shrieks. Then they attack.

Tick flips the light back on and the creatures vanish.

"Where'd they go?" Polly cries.

"They're still here," Tick says. He's trembling but tries to appear calm and unafraid. "We just can't see them."

Tick is ashamed he had been so stupid.

"I'm sorry, Polly," he says. "The nursery isn't safe anymore." He looks up at her. "I let the creepers in."

A look of panic crosses her face once she understands the danger. Although they can't see, hear, or touch them with the lights on, the creatures are still inside the nursery with them. They'll never be able to turn out the lights in the nursery again.

CHAPTER TEN

"This is just perfect," Polly says. "You did this on purpose, didn't you? Now we have no choice but to leave."

She follows Tick as he runs through the nursery, turning on all the lights.

"Stay out of every shadow in the house," Tick says, ignoring her complaints.

He grabs lighters and candles, setting them down on the tea room table.

"We need everything that we can find that will generate light," he says.

Polly gathers many battery-operated toys from the toy room, the ones that create light. Tick grabs flammable liquids, cloth, and pieces of wood, hoping he can make torches with them. He also has a pack of self-charging batteries.

"Where's the flashlight?" Polly asks. "Nanny has a flashlight somewhere."

Tick shakes his head. "It's in the crawlspace."

"What?"

He grabs a big toy spaceship, one that shines a beam of light out the front. It's the closest thing they have to a flashlight.

"Put the rest of these in a bag," Tick says. "I have something I want to check out."

"What's that?" she asks. "You're not going into the corridor again are you?"

"Yeah," he says. "I want to see where the other doors lead."

"You're going to let more of them inside," Polly cries.

"I know," Tick says. "But we have to find a way out."

Polly grabs him by the wrist.

"Don't be an idiot," she says, trying to keep him from leaving.

"Put whatever water we have left into a bottle," Tick says, pulling himself out of her grip. "We'll need it if we're going to cross the house."

Before he leaves the room, Polly says, "Are we really going to leave the nursery?"

She tears up as she thinks of the possibility.

"We don't have a choice," he says.

Then he heads back to the nursery exit.

Tick takes the big wall mirrors from the two bedrooms and sets them up in the corridor. They reflect the light of the nursery all the way down the passage, lighting his path. He also turns on the toy spaceship's beam, creating extra light in front of him.

He can still hear creepers in the shadows at the end of the hall, their antlers clacking together, soft growls under their breaths. But Tick is invisible to them. They can't hear or see him when he's in the light.

With his homemade spear in one hand, the spaceship in the other, he goes to the closest room. It is the same room he investigated the first time he left the nursery.

He pushes open the door, then shines the spaceship light into the room. It is just an ordinary bedroom. It still confuses him that there's a bedroom here. Who is supposed to use it? It looks like it hasn't been slept in for decades. The bed is large enough for a Polly-sized adult. There is a dresser and a closet. A mirror reflects the beam of light back at him.

There is still a light source in the room, coming from the floor behind the bed. The light shifts from red to blue to yellow to brown. He decides not to enter the room to see what it is that generates the light. He doesn't want to leave the safety of the brightened hallway.

"One of these has to be a map room," Tick says, moving on to the next door.

The next room is less confusing. It is an ordinary storeroom. He shines his light on the shelves and is surprised to see it is filled with birthday presents.

"Happy birthday…" he says to himself.

He's never seen so many presents in all his life. Every shelf is full of them. Nanny said she had presents stored away somewhere for all the birthdays the children will ever have. He wonders if this is the storage she was talking about. But that doesn't make sense to Tick, because Nanny never left the nursery. This must be storage for backup presents in case something happened to the original ones stored in the nursery closet. It would be devastating to children if the closet were to catch on fire and burn all the presents. Then they'd never get any presents for the rest of their lives.

Tick moves on from the present closet and continues to the door at the end of the hallway. This door has been broken open, the wood splintered across the floor. It must be where all the creepers came from.

He shines his light through the doorway. He can't see much, but the walls are taller out there, the ceilings higher. It opens up into a massive room. It is the entryway to the rest of the house.

"Big," Tick says. He doesn't know what else to say as he moves closer to the exit. "Really big."

In the doorway, he raises his toy light to the walls; they are so tall his light can't reach the ceiling. Rows of white pillars line the center of the hall and the room seems to go on forever. He's never seen so much open space in his life. The closest thing he can think of is looking at the sky while on the playground at school, and that wasn't even real.

The sound of antlers scraping the walls echoes through the vast chamber. There are also loud clacking sounds of antlers colliding, as though a group of creepers are attacking each other.

He steps through the doorway into the massive room. The light from the corridor only reaches the first pillar. If he can get inside far enough, he might be able to see how many exits lead out of the room. He hopes one of the exits leads to a map room.

"There's got to be one here..." he says. "I'm sure of it."

He moves slowly, shining his light in every direction to make sure nothing sneaks up behind him. Halfway to the pillar, he sees them surrounding him. He can only see them in the corners of his eyes, but they are there. Just as he can just barely perceive their presence, the creepers can just barely perceive his. He doesn't dare step an inch outside the path of light coming from the corridor.

He sees no exits leading out of the massive room. There are pillars, tall walls, dusty tile floors, but no doors. They must be on the other side of the room, beyond where his light can reach.

As he reaches the pillar, he turns around. In the corners of his eyes, he can see hundreds of the black creatures. An entire crowd of them, filling the great hall. An army. The spaceship shakes in Tick's hand. The things lean in toward him, as if they see parts of him in the shadows but can't make a whole boy.

One creeper leans toward him even further, his gritty coal eyes rolling up and down his body. Tick turns the light on it, causing the thing to vanish. But then another creeper leans in on his other side and he has to swing the light in its direction to get rid of it. There are too many of them. The spear in his hand feels useless now. He wants to just drop it, but he's worried it will attract attention if it lands in the shadow.

He takes one step toward the nursery. Then the path of light goes black. Polly's scream echoes in the distance. It doesn't take Tick long to grasp what has happened. The power in the nursery finally went out.

Tick puts his back against the pillar so that none of the creatures can get him from behind. Then he holds the light of the toy spaceship over his head, shining down on him so that he'll be invisible.

But the creatures don't seem interested in Tick. They turn their charred black faces toward the corridor, attracted by Polly's screams. At once, the mass of gnarled figures charge forward, piling into the corridor, heading toward the sound of Tick's panicking older sister.

"Polly, they're coming!" he screams. "They're coming!"

He's not sure she heard him, but his voice carried far within the massive chamber. It is enough to attract some of the creepers back to him.

Tick runs for the corridor. Holding the light in front of him, vanquishing the army of creepers in his way, he charges back toward the nursery.

"Polly!" he yells. "There's too many of them. Use the light."

As he gets halfway down the hallway, the beam light from his spaceship bounces off the mirrors he's set up outside the nursery. There is gnashing and screeching sounds against his ears. In the reflection, he can see an army of creepers running behind him, closing in.

He turns around to shine his light at the invaders, but they collide with him before the light can reach. Tick falls to the ground and the spaceship clatters from his hand. One of the creatures tramples the boy, stomping on his chest and belly. Another creeper kicks the spear out of his hands when trying to jump over him. None of them seem to notice him yet, they seem more interested in trying to get into the nursery.

Tick can't reach his light in time. The demons crush it under their pointed heels, leaving him in darkness.

To escape the frantic beasts, he rolls into the room to his left and closes the door behind him. Lying there, catching his breath, he hears the sound of antlers scraping across the door outside as creepers run past.

He blinks twice. Then he realizes something odd about the room.

"What...." he says, when he realizes he's no longer in the dark.

Even though the power in the nursery went out, killing all lights inside, this room is still lit. The strange light comes from behind the bed. It shifts from yellow to brown to red to blue.

Tick gets to his feet. There do not appear to be any creepers in the room with him. They are all too interested in the nursery. Tick steps around the bed until he sees the thing sitting in the corner of the room.

It is a birdcage, but instead of birds inside there are six miniature planets, spinning around a sun. He reaches out to grab it. The second his fingers touch the handle at the top of the cage, the sun in the center brightens the entire room.

"What are you?" he asks the planets in the cage.

Holding it up, he doesn't understand where its power source comes from. The sun seems to power itself.

"You're beautiful," he says, as he looks at the planets rotating around the sun. It's almost as if they are real planets, as if he's holding a real miniaturized solar system in his hand.

Tick leaves the bedroom and the light from the miniature sun fills the corridor. The entire horde of creepers in the hallway is vanquished, disappearing as if they were never even there.

He heads quickly for the nursery. Before he gets there, he smells the smoke.

"Polly?" Tick yells.

The nursery is on fire.

"Polly!"

Smoke fills the entryway. Flames crawl through the halls. There is usually a sprinkler system to put out fires, but it doesn't seem to be operational.

"Tick," he hears his sister crying. "Where were you?"

She runs into the entry room, holding a cloth in her face,

coughing on the smoke. Tick can see cuts and tears on her arms and dress. She did not escape the creepers unscathed.

He ignores her question. "What happened?"

She leaves the nursery and collapses into the corridor, coughing up smoke. A water bottle falls to the floor. There's a large puncture mark in it, the shape of an antler tip. Most of the water has leaked out.

"I started the fire," she says, when she catches her breath. "It was the only light I could create bright enough to keep them back."

"What were you thinking?" Tick asks. "You'll set the whole house on fire. Mom and Dad will kill us."

She points at the cage in Tick's hand. "Where did you get that?"

"In one of the rooms," he says. "It will protect us from the creepers."

Polly gets to her feet and takes the cage out of his hand. She staggers down the corridor with it, away from the flaming nursery.

"Where are you going?" he asks.

"Let's get out of here," she says, continuing down the hall.

"We can't leave yet," Tick says. "Where's Leech?"

"Who cares?" she says. "Forget about that repulsive maggot."

"She's your sister," Tick cries.

"It's probably dead already," she says. "Let's go."

Tick gives her a look of disgust.

"I can't believe you," he says.

Then he runs back into the nursery.

"Come back," she yells at him, but Tick won't leave his baby sister, even if she is just a blood-sucking blob.

Without the cage of light, Tick has to rely on the fire to protect him from the creepers. But the flames are erratic. He can see the creatures disappearing and reappearing all around him as the fire flickers across the walls. Their shrieks flash in and out, as if vibrating. Black antlers flash in and out of his path.

He runs for the baby room, covering his mouth. He can barely see through the smoke. He doesn't dare breathe.

When he busts open the door, he sees Leech hopping and wiggling in a panic within her crib. The creepers never broke into the baby room and very little smoke has gotten in, but the heat of the fire permeating the walls has turned the baby room into an oven.

Tick grabs Leech from the crib and the worm slimes up his torso into his arms, chirping and gurgling in a panic.

Without having a free hand to cover his mouth, he just makes a run for it. The fire is massive once he exits the baby room. The flames quickly swallow the nursery, eating away the only world he's ever known. The thought of Nanny Warburough's body crosses his mind, lying on the toy room floor being burned away to nothing but charred metal. He's thankful he doesn't have to witness that.

Leech wiggles in his arms, squeaking up at him.

"Stop your squeaking," Tick says, hugging the creature close.

When he gets out of the nursery, Polly is already at the end of the corridor, poking her head through the doorway into the great chamber to breathe clean air.

"Come on," Tick says as he reaches his big sister.

They enter the great chamber, holding the cage of light above their heads. It brightens the room enough to see all the way to the end. There are three exits.

"We need to find a map room," Tick says. "There's got to be one somewhere."

But Polly doesn't care about which exit they take. She just runs. Holding the cage for dear life, she charges through the massive room, far away from the smoke and flames, and enters the closest door she can find. Then she takes that corridor until she comes to another door. As long as there are passages to enter, she keeps running.

Tick knows that if he doesn't keep up with her frantic pace she will surely leave him behind without a second thought.

CHAPTER ELEVEN

"Do you think they're still following us?" Polly asks.

"We're invisible to them in this light," Tick says. "They won't follow us. But that doesn't mean there aren't other creepers here, hidden in the dark."

Leech squeaks and gurgles, strapped to her big brother's back.

"So this is the rest of the house…" Polly says. "It's not what I was expecting. It's so big…"

Tick nods. "Our whole nursery could fit twice in this one room."

They stare at paintings of old men that line the walls in some kind of gallery section of the house. The lack of food has caught up to them, their adrenaline worn off, but they keep moving at a staggering pace. Polly holds her side as she lurches through the gallery. Escaping the creepers made her injuries worse. Tick can't tell with her black dress on, but he thinks she might be bleeding again.

"I wonder when the last time our parents were in this section of the house," Tick says. "There are so many rooms that seem like they are never used. I don't understand their point."

"I'm sure there's a point," Polly says. "Mom and Dad wouldn't have these rooms unless there was a good reason."

Polly stops walking for a moment, holding her side. The agony is visible on her face.

"I need a rest," she says.

She sets down the cage of planets and uses both hands to hold up her hips. Tick is worried if she sits down she'll never be able to get up again.

"We should keep moving," Tick says. "It's going to take all day to get to the other side of the house."

"Do we even know where we're going?" Polly says.

"We will if we find a map room," he says.

Polly nods. She picks up the cage of light and they continue moving.

Pointing at the paintings, Polly says, "I bet Mom and Dad would have taken us through here if they had come to get us. They would have explained the significance of each of the people in these paintings. Perhaps they are our ancestors."

"Maybe," Tick says. "Or maybe they just hung up a bunch of random pictures because they have more space than they know what to do with."

"Nanny said they *are* really rich," Polly says, smiling. "They probably can afford to have all the pointless rooms they want."

"So you think all these rooms are pointless, too?"

"No, I think they have a point. They just don't *need* to have a point."

Her eye sparkles as she watches the paintings, pretending to walk hand in hand with her mom and dad through the gallery, imagining what their voices would be like when explaining the history of all the people in the paintings.

"Tick?" Polly asks.

"Yeah?"

"We're really going to see them, aren't we?" she says. "We're really going to meet our parents?"

Tick nods and smiles back.

"We might even get to see them as soon as today."

They go from room to room, hallway after hallway, but can't find any map room.

"We've been searching for hours," Polly says. "I can't go any further."

Tick points to a door up ahead, near an intersection of hallways.

"Let's just try one more room," he says.

111

"You said that three rooms ago."

"I don't think we should stop until we find a map room," he says.

"This better be a map room..." she mumbles.

It isn't a map room. It's a bedroom. The biggest bedroom they have ever seen. Just the bed is the size of Tick's whole room. There are velvet curtains lining the walls, a lace canopy over the bed, a bathroom, a vanity, tables and chairs. All the furniture is ornate, made of emerald, carved to look like the faces of lions and the tentacles of octopi.

"It's so fancy..." Polly says. "Like the pictures of luxurious penthouse hotel suites from books in the library..."

Tick crosses the room, takes Leech out of his back harness and lays her on the bed. She squirts and growls, sore at him for keeping her on his back so long.

"It's so clean," Polly says. "Much cleaner than the other rooms we've been in."

"Maybe a maid lives somewhere in this region of the house," Tick says. "This could be a guest room that needs to be kept clean in case visitors stay over."

"I don't think this is a guest room," Polly says, placing the cage of light on an end table. "I think it's a backup room for our parents." She looks into the vanity mirror, straightening her doll face eye patch. "Think about it. With such a big house they probably wouldn't have just one bedroom, they would have tons of them. They could move to any area of the house whenever they want."

She touches the bed, bouncing the mattress next to Leech.

"They could have slept in this very bed," she says.

Then she picks up a pillow and smells it. There's a lingering perfume scent.

"It's Mom," she says, inhaling the perfume deeply. "I know it is."

Tick goes to the bathroom. There's no doorway leading inside, so it's not private, but it is a separate room. The cage of planets doesn't brighten much of the bathroom from around the corner, so Tick goes for the light switch. It doesn't work.

His worn out face stares back at him in the dimly lit mirror. He's covered in dried sweat and soot from the fire. He desperately needs a bath. Without thinking, he goes for the faucet and nearly falls over with shock when water gushes out.

"It works..." Tick cries.

He puts his face into the sink and drinks.

"Water!"

Then he splashes a handful into his face. When he looks into the mirror, rubbing water out of his eyes, he sees a black figure in the shower behind him where the light doesn't reach.

Tick jumps out of the bathroom.

"There's creepers in here," he says.

Polly limps to the bathroom doorway.

"Are we safe?" she asks, looking at the twisting figure in the corner.

"As long as the light is on and we stay out of the shadows," he says.

The second Tick says this, the sun in the cage dims down to a brown light. Dozens of black creatures are revealed in all the corners of the room.

"What happened?" Polly cries.

The creatures turn to her.

Tick runs to the cage and touches the handle. The sun brightens and floods the room with light until the creepers disappear.

"It powers down if you let go of the handle for too long," Tick says.

"So we have to keep holding that thing all night?" Polly asks.

"What do you mean *all night*?"

"Aren't we going to spend the night here?"

Tick shakes his head. "No, we have to find a map room first. What if we're only minutes away from Mom and Dad and don't even know it?"

"Or it could take another whole day just to find a map room,"

Polly says. "We have water and a bed. We should rest here."

"But it's not exactly the safest place…"

"I'll keep my hand on the cage the whole time I sleep if I have to."

Tick thinks about it for a moment. Then he nods. He knows that there's really no place safe in the house anymore. And he feels bad about dragging Polly around with such serious injuries.

"I hope this is a good idea," Tick says.

He goes back to the entrance of the room and closes the door. The instant the door is shut, scraping and clawing sounds erupt against the walls outside. The creepers know they're in there. It's going to be difficult to sleep knowing they're surrounded inside and out.

"Are you going to sleep with that stupid armor?" Polly says to Tick.

He's lying on the giant bed, still wearing his homemade wooden shields. His helmet is long gone. He doesn't even remember where he lost that, probably back in the nursery.

"I'm not taking this off," he says. "I'm surrounded by monsters."

Polly takes her dress off and looks at herself in the mirror. She doesn't care if Tick sees her anymore. The wound on her ribs is looking worse. It's turning green and covered in pus.

"It's so itchy…" she says.

Polly tries washing it, but that only breaks the wound open more. The room fills with a horrible stench.

"What is that smell?" Tick says, covering his nose.

She frowns at him. She doesn't mind the smell, as if she's already gotten used to it.

"It's infected," she says.

"It smells like the rotten food in the tea room," Tick says.

"I need antibiotics. There was probably some in the nursery. I'm sure Mom and Dad will have some."

Tick begins to worry. He suddenly thinks staying the night is a bad idea. They shouldn't just lie around while her infection spreads.

"We should only rest for an hour," Tick says. "Then we need to find you medicine."

"I need a full night of sleep," Polly says. "The medicine can wait."

Tick gets up from the bed and goes toward her. The closer he gets, the more intense the pungent odor of her rotten wound becomes.

"It's so gross," Tick says.

Her face turns red with anger. "Shut up, *Tick*."

"If it spreads higher will your boob rot off?" he says.

"Shut up!" she shrieks.

He's trying to work her up about it. She's acting like it's nothing, but the infection is obviously serious. If they had two light sources he would let her sleep and go look for antibiotics on his own, but they have to stick together. She has to come with him to search for the medicine. He can't let her ignore it.

"I don't even know if I can sleep in the same room with you," Tick says. "It's like rotten eggs. If you don't get it cured soon you'll probably smell like that forever. Nobody will ever want to go near you."

Polly doesn't respond. She just glares at him, fuming. Her eye turns red. She growls.

"So do you still want to sleep here all night and let the infection spread? Or search for Mom and Dad so we can get you help?"

Her eye is locked on his. Foams leaks from the corner of her mouth. She steps forward, not caring that she's only in her underwear.

"Polly?" he asks.

She hisses and aims her antlers at him.

"Not now..." he says. "You can't do this now."

He thought he'd seen the last of her episodes, but his older sister is still in heat. She is still prone to fits of psychotic sexual rage.

"Calm down…" he says.

She screams like a bloodthirsty animal and charges at him. Her antlers connect with the wooden plate on his chest and he flies backward, landing skull-first into the floor.

Dazed, he finds himself unable to dodge when Polly jumps on top of him, clawing at the wood on his arms.

"Stop it…" Tick cries.

She slams her head into his face. The tip of one antler opens up a large gash down the center of his forehead, an inch away from gouging out his eyes. He pushes her back. She writhes on top of him, biting at the air above his nose, digging her claws into his forearms.

"Watch out," he says. "Your wound…"

Blood leaks across the tile floor as she rips open the wound on her side. She doesn't seem to be able to notice pain anymore, moving her body with such intensity, as if she has no idea she's injured at all.

The putrid egg stench fills Tick's nostrils. He turns his face, gagging on the odor, dry-heaving, coughing drool down his cheek. If he had any food in him he would have thrown up.

"Get off!" Tick cries.

He wiggles out of her grasp, but there's nowhere to run. If he escapes into the hallway without the cage of light, he will be killed by the creepers out there. If he takes the cage with him, Polly will be killed by the creepers in here. But if he stays in here with her, she'll probably tear him apart.

She grabs him again and bites down on the board of wood on his arm. The loud cracking sound makes Tick think she's breaking out all of her teeth, but it's only the wood splintering.

The sun in the cage dims down and the room fills with shadows. Creepers peer at them, eyes filled with venom, their gnarled figures twisting through the dark.

Polly is thrown off by the dimming of the light. She loosens her grip on Tick. The boy uses the opportunity to run for Leech. He sweeps the baby up. Polly charges after him. He drops to the floor and crawls under the bed. The wiggly grub in his arms squeaks and bubbles in his ear as Polly tries to follow him under the bed.

Her antlers are too big for her to get through. They stab and scrape at the bed frame. She reaches her hands inside, swiping at him. He crawls away from the edge toward the center.

In the shadows, he becomes visible to the creepers in the room. Those who spot his position shriek and come at him, disappearing from the shadows in the corners. He can't see them while they're in the light. But once they get to the bed, he sees their claws reaching in, swiping at him. Their antlers are also too big to get through.

When Polly gets bored with Tick, she turns to the half-visible creepers in the corners of the room. She charges at a group of them, antlers-first.

"Polly!" Tick cries. "Stay away from them!"

Her antlers collide with the antlers of one of the creatures. The two of them fall away from each other. She attacks again, hooking their antlers together, but when she pulls back, into the light, the creeper disappears.

Tick crawls back to the edge of the bed.

"Over here!" Tick yells.

Polly turns her crazed eye toward him. Several creepers close in on her from the shadows.

"Come to me," he says, waving his hand out from under the bed at her. "Attack me, not them."

Polly charges at him and stabs her antlers into the mattress, ripping open the comforter. Tick just barely rolls back to safety.

"Come on," he says. "Come get me."

He teases her, holding out his hands inches away from hers so she feels as though she's just about got him. He can't let her attention go back to the creepers.

For the next hour, Tick has to keep this up. Polly shrieks,

thrashing her hands at him, grinding her crotch against the corner of the bed. The blood leaking onto the floor sends Leech into a squirming frenzy, trying to break out of Tick's grasp to drink up all the fresh food that's getting wasted.

Tick wakes to a squeaking sound. He doesn't know how long he's been out. Exhaustion must have gotten the best of him.

He looks around for Leech, but the little bug is no longer in his arms. He crawls out from under the bed and lifts the cage of light, bringing the room to its full brightness. The creepers in the corners fade away.

Polly is unconscious, lying on the bed, exhausted. Sweat pours down her cheeks. Her face flushed. She looks as if she has a fever from the infection.

Leech is on top of her, drinking from her open wound. The little insect must have followed the trail of blood to her.

"No!" he yells at the grub baby. "Get off of her!"

Leech squirts and growls at him.

He runs at the bed. The baby looks fat, having swallowed a large amount of her blood. If he slept any longer she might have sucked his big sister dry.

"She's too sick," he says. "You can't drink from her."

The maggot squeals like a cranky piglet when Tick pulls her off of Polly.

"Bad bug," Tick says to her.

Leech snaps at his nose.

When Tick examines Polly's wound, he notices that it doesn't stink anymore. It's not rotten.

Leech squirts and sniffs in his hands.

"Did you do this?" he asks the baby.

Polly's wound has been sterilized. All of the dead infected flesh has been eaten away. The bad blood has been sucked out. Leech was just being her usual greedy gluttonous self, but inadvertently stopped Polly's infection from spreading.

He puts his hand on Polly's forehead. If she had a fever before, she doesn't now. She's going to be okay.

"You ugly little worm," Tick hollers at the baby, lifting her up over his head. "I could kiss you!"

The maggot squeaks and gurgles at him.

It growls when he kisses the top of its head.

Tick allows Leech to drink from Polly a little longer, just to make sure her wounds are clean. He only lets her drink from the eye wound for a few minutes, worried about what Polly would do if she woke up to a bug sucking on her eye socket. But his big sister is in a deep sleep. He covers her with a blanket. Then he lies down next to her, holding the cage of light between them. Leech, on the other hand, is harnessed to the side of the bed. She might have saved Polly's life, but she could easily kill either of them if left to feed unsupervised.

Falling into sleep, Tick has dreams of exploring the massive house. At first, it's a wondrous dream filled with many beautiful, strange rooms and fascinating sights that he encounters on his journey. But then his dream goes bad. He dreams that he is an old man, still exploring the house, spending his entire life looking for his parents that are never to be found.

CHAPTER TWELVE

Polly is disgusted when she learns Tick let the baby drink from her. She wants to bite into the creature's bubbly flesh and drink out its blood to see how it likes being fed upon.

"But she cured your infection," Tick says.

"It's still gross!" she cries. "Never let that thing touch me again. No matter what."

"She might have saved your life," Tick says.

"Whatever," she says. "Let's get out of here."

They drink as much water as they can fit in their bellies and fill the only water bottle they have with them. Because of the large hole in its center the water bottle can hold very little, but there's nothing else in the room that they can use.

When they continue their journey through the maze of corridors, Polly has a smile on her face.

"What?" Tick asks, wondering why she looks so happy all of a sudden.

"Nothing," she says, shaking her head. But then she says, "What do you think Mom and Dad are like?"

"Mom and Dad?"

"I bet Dad is smart, handsome, and popular," she says. "Mom is probably caring, pretty, full of wisdom…"

Her eyes go distant, fantasizing about them.

Tick nods. "I can't wait to meet them."

"Do you think they'll like me?" she asks. "I hope they like me."

Tick nods.

He's all of a sudden not so enthusiastic about imagining what they're like.

"What's wrong?" Polly asks. "You don't want to talk about them?"

Tick shakes his head.

"I was just thinking," he says. "You always worry about whether they'll like you or not. But what if we don't like them?"

"What do you mean?"

"What if they aren't friendly? Mom could be stupid and selfish. Dad could be scary. I'm worried that they won't turn out to be good people."

"Don't be silly," she says. "They're our parents. Of course they're good people."

They check every room they come to, but none of them are map rooms. They find a couple more bedrooms, smaller than the previous one. These rooms are just as clean, but do not have water in their sinks. Some rooms are filled with machines. A couple of rooms are filled with boxes of flooring tiles and other carpentry supplies. There is a laundry room, a billiard room, and an entire gymnasium filled with strange exercise equipment. All of these rooms are set up as if waiting for people to use them, but everything is dead. No sign of their parents. No sign of any people at all.

"What's that?" Polly asks, pointing toward a lit doorway halfway down the corridor.

"A light?" Tick asks.

Light pours from a doorway up ahead. When they get closer, they see a shadow in the light stretching across the hall. It is in the shape of a person.

"Somebody's in there," Polly says.

They rush toward the doorway.

"Hello?" Tick says. "Is somebody there?"

The closer they get to the doorway, the more human-shaped the shadow looks. But it doesn't move.

They turn the corner and see a woman standing in the hall, her back to them. She is in a small lobby, lined with elevators. The light panels on the ceiling are turned on, but only immediately above where the woman stands.

"Hello?" Polly says to the woman.

She doesn't turn around. She doesn't move.

"Is she alive?" Tick asks.

"Maybe it's just a statue…"

When they go to the front of the woman, they realize she is not a statue. She has short purple hair that matches her wide motionless purple eyes, and a small heart-shaped mouth that looks like it is giving the air a kiss. She wears the uniform of a maid.

"She's frozen in place," Tick says.

He touches her. The skin is flexible.

"She's like Nanny," Polly says. "A robot."

"Are you sure?" Tick says.

He touches her eyeball. It is wet with a synthetic liquid.

"She must have broken down while cleaning," Polly says.

"Do you think all the servants in this house are robots?"

"Maybe," Polly says. "It's a big house. It would make sense to have robots clean it."

"But we didn't see any maids until now. Where are all the others?"

"Maybe they've also broken down," Polly says.

"Why doesn't anyone repair them?"

"Maybe the robot that repairs the robots is broken down, too."

Tick shakes the robot woman. She's like a dummy. When he pushes her over, her posture doesn't change. She stays in a standing position, staring straight ahead at nothing, even though she's lying horizontally on the floor.

"What did you do that for?" Polly asks. "That wasn't nice."

"I wanted to see if she'd turn back on," Tick says.

"She's not turning back on," Polly says. "She's broken."

They step away from the robot on the ground and search the lobby.

"Hey," Polly says, pointing at a sign on the wall.

"What?" Tick says.

"The map."

A sign that reads *MAP* is hanging on the wall with an arrow pointing to the left.

"That's it," Tick says. "The map room!"

They run down the lobby, searching for the map. The arrows point them down another corridor until they get to a small gray door with the words "Map Room" positioned above the doorframe.

When they enter the room, small lights flicker on one at a time, illuminating the maps on display. The room is filled with dozens of maps. There are so many that it seems like a map museum.

"Which map is for this house?" Tick asks.

There are too many of them. Polly steps closer, examining each of them carefully.

"There must be a map here for every house in the neighborhood," Tick says.

"So many rooms…" Polly says.

Each map has hundreds of rooms, so many that it's difficult to read the tiny labels explaining what each room is supposed to be. She touches one map and it zooms in, showing her the details of the area she touched. The maps aren't made of paper. They are plasma screens.

"This one," Tick says.

He is standing in front of the only map with a blinking red dot on it.

"It says *you are here*." He points at the dot. "This must be the map for the house we're in now."

Polly leans over his shoulder, and pushes the red dot. The screen zooms in to the map room, their current location. Leech chews on her locks of green hair as they hang in her chubby face.

"So where would our parents' chambers be on this map?" she asks.

"I don't understand the names of half these rooms," Tick says. "Nylurg Room? Ongoing Prayer Room? Video Arena?"

"It probably wouldn't be called *parent's quarters*," Polly says. "Maybe something like *main quarters*? Master bedroom?"

Tick shakes his head. "I don't see anything like this on the map."

"There are so many rooms. We can't just explore them one at a time. It would take days."

"We'll just have to study each room on these maps until we find the place they'd most likely be."

Polly nods and continues examining the giant map on the wall.

"Wait a minute..." Polly says, zooming out on the map. "We passed a row of elevators on the way here."

"So?" Tick says.

"If there are elevators that means this house has multiple floors, but there's only one level shown on the map."

"So where are the other levels?" he asks.

Polly turns around and looks at the dozens of maps on the walls.

"There..." she says.

"All of them?"

"These aren't maps of multiple houses," she says. "Each map is for a different floor. It's all just one house."

"But that means this building is almost a hundred stories tall..."

"And a hundred miles wide..."

"It wouldn't just take days to explore the whole house," Tick says. "It would take years."

Polly pushes away from the map, ripping her hair out of Leech's mouth. She clenches her fists, wishing she could just ram her antlers into every map screen so that she wouldn't have to face reality.

"It's impossible," Polly says. "Even if we searched this house for the rest of our lives, we would never find them. It's the size of a whole city."

Tick shakes his head. "It's the size of a whole country."

Tick tries not to allow the immense size of the building to discourage him. After grumbling for most of an hour, Polly finally comes around as well. The house is huge, but if they can figure out exactly where they need to go it won't be such a long voyage.

"We're on the sixty-third floor," Tick says. "Each floor seems to be divided into eight sections, with elevators in the center of each section. There is also a map room near the middle of each section. If we can just figure out which floor Mom and Dad are on it shouldn't be too difficult to get to them."

Polly stares at the map.

"How much distance have we traveled so far?" she asks, trying to get a grip on how large the map really is.

"Pretty far, but we've barely covered even a tenth of just this one floor."

She points at a cluster of rooms near the vicinity of the blinking red dot.

"This is the nursery?" she asks. "It's just around the corner from where we are now." Her voice becomes angry. "Have we just walked in a circle and are back where we started?"

"No," Tick says. "That's not the nursery." He points at a cluster of rooms further away, to the northwest of the blinking red dot. "We came from the other direction, way over here."

"But it says *nursery* here," Polly says.

It says nursery in both locations. Tick zooms in on the map.

"It has a number next to it," Tick says. "Nursery #505."

"What does our nursery say?"

Tick zooms in on the section of the map they came from.

"Nursery #507," he says.

"There is another nursery in this house?" Polly asks.

"If these numbers mean anything then there could be over 500 other nurseries in this house," Tick says.

Polly's jaw goes slack. For a moment she can't even speak.

"How is that possible?" Polly says. "Nanny never said anything about this. Are there kids in every one of them?"

"I don't know…"

"We have to go to one," Polly says. She turns toward the door. "Right now."

"But what about the maps?" Tick says.

"The maps can wait," she says. "We'll come back. It's just around the corner."

"It's not just around the corner," Tick says. "It's at least a mile away."

Polly won't listen. She grabs the cage of light and leaves the room. Tick has no choice but to follow her.

"Slow down," Tick says, trying to catch up to his sister. "What's the rush?"

She doesn't slow down.

"I have to see if there's really another nursery."

"Why?"

"I have to see if there are other kids in it."

"But why does it matter?"

She stops and turns around.

"This is our parents' house," she says. "If there are other nurseries in this house then that means they have other kids besides us."

"So?" Tick says. "That should make you happy. It means we have other brothers and sisters we don't know about."

"That's the problem," she yells, her eye becomes moist as if she's about to tear up. "Don't you get it? If they have tons of other kids then what does that make me to them? I wouldn't be special. I'd just be one of their hundreds of children raised in one of their hundreds of nurseries. They won't want to have anything to do with me."

She turns and continues on.

"You don't know that for sure," Tick says, following after her. "We don't know anything about this place. For all we know, Mom and Dad *don't* own this house. There could be tons of people who live here. If there are kids in the other nursery maybe they belong to another set of parents who live in another part of the house."

Polly doesn't respond. She picks up her pace. She has to see for herself.

CHAPTER THIRTEEN

When they get to Nursery #505, it looks exactly like the one they grew up in. Only this one appears long abandoned. The door has been broken open, antler and claw marks cover the surface. The power is out. The air is stale and musty, as if it hasn't been breathed in years.

"Do you think children ever lived here?" Tick asks.

"I don't know," Polly says. "Maybe it's just a backup nursery in case something happened to ours..."

They search through the rooms. All of the rooms are dusty, but fully furnished. Other than the dust and the antler marks on many of the walls, the nursery is in pristine condition. The rooms seem unlived in. The beds are tightly made, as if they've never been used.

"Maybe you're right," Tick says. "Maybe this nursery was only meant as a backup."

But when they enter the baby room, they realize that's not the case.

"Gross..." Polly says, looking down at the dead bodies.

The remains of four dead human larvae are in the room. In the bowl of the crib and scattered on the floor are the remnants of eggshells and worm-shaped skeletons. They are covered in cobwebs.

"What happened to them?" Tick asks.

Polly looks them over. She holds her face to her nose as if the bodies smell, even though all the flesh rotted away so long ago that the only smell left in the room is dust.

"The eggs were delivered through the baby tunnel," she says. "But there must have been nobody in the nursery to take care of them. They died one by one, alone in the dark."

"Shouldn't this nursery have a nanny to take care of them?"

"Maybe there was one that broke down before these children were born," Polly says. "Like the maid by the elevators."

Tick looks at Leech, imagining she could have been one of these larvae skeletons on the floor if she was born in this nursery.

"It's so sad…" he says, petting Leech's head.

Leech just squeaks and poofs, oblivious to the bodies around her.

They explore the rest of the nursery and sure enough they find a broken down robot in one of the rooms. It lies on the floor, its chest torn open by antlers. It is obviously the work of creepers.

"She looks exactly like Nanny Warburough," Tick says.

"They probably all look like Nanny Warburough," Polly says.

"Do you think she was exactly like our nanny?"

"Maybe."

"I like the thought of there being other versions of Nanny out there in other nurseries. It's like she's still alive out there somewhere."

"She was never alive," Polly says. "She was just a robot."

They go through the store rooms, looking for supplies. Polly takes some antibiotics and pain relievers from the medicine dispenser. Tick grabs some bottles that can be used to carry water next time they come across some.

As he passes the boy's room, Tick suddenly feels as if he's back at home, back in the nursery he was raised. It makes him wish they could stay there for a few nights. He rushed out of the burning nursery so quickly he didn't have a chance to give it a proper goodbye.

"You have to keep going," says a voice from the boy's room.

It is the voice of Tick's paper mom. He hears her unfolding

herself out of the closet, smoothing out the wrinkles on her stomach, but she doesn't show herself. The room is covered in shadows, so Tick doesn't enter.

"You still have to find me," she says.

"I'm trying," Tick says. "Nobody ever told me the house was so big."

"It's big, but you will find me if you don't give up," she says.

"Of course I won't give up," Tick says.

"I love you, my darling," says the paper mom.

"I love you, too, Mom," he says.

Polly comes up behind Tick, holding a pile of supplies in her hands, including a brand new dress.

"Who are you talking to?" Polly asks.

Tick looks back at her and shakes his head. "No one. Just myself." He points at her dress. "What are you going to do with that?"

"I need new clothes," she says. "I'll have to modify this dress so it fits, but the one I'm wearing is nearly ruined. You should get some new clothes as well."

Tick nods.

"The food machines don't work," she continues. "The water doesn't either. There's nothing here. We should go back to the map room."

Tick nods again.

"If there're any other nurseries in the area we should check them out," she says. "Maybe one of them will even have a food machine that works."

When they leave the nursery Tick checks out the other rooms in the outer corridor, hoping to find a second birdcage full of planets. It would have been good to have a second light source. But there's nothing like it that he can find.

"We should focus on finding food," Polly says on the way

back to the map room. "There's got to be a nursery we can get food from somewhere."

"I think we should just focus on finding Mom and Dad," Tick says. "They can give us food when we get there."

"But who knows how long it will take to find them," she says. "If the nurseries are marked on the map, they'll be easier to get to."

"Let's study the map before we decide," Tick says. "If we find an area of the house that seems a likely place for Mom and Dad to be, I say we head in that direction and stop off at any nurseries that might be along the way. There might also be other places on the map where we can get food besides the nurseries."

Polly agrees. "Sounds like a plan."

Tick is surprised by her response. She hardly ever agrees with anyone.

For a few minutes, they walk in silence. In their path far ahead, prowling creepers appear and disappear in the shadows. The monsters don't alarm them as much as they used to. As long as they have the light, they feel completely safe.

Polly watches him as they walk. Just watches.

When he notices her watching him, she says, "Back in the nursery, I heard you talking to somebody."

"I said I was talking to myself," he says.

"But I heard you say, *I love you, too, Mom.* Why would you say that if you're talking to yourself?"

"It's nothing," he says. "I sometimes imagine Mom is with me. I talk to her. She comforts me when I'm sad. She's not real, though. It just makes me feel good to pretend I'm with her."

Polly's eye widens when she hears him talk about it.

"You, too?" she asks.

"What do you mean?"

"Ever since I was little I had an imaginary Mom that only I could see," she says. "She talked to me all the time. She still does. I thought I was going crazy whenever she was around."

"Me, too," Tick says. "I talk to her almost every day. She used to sing me lullabies and help me go to sleep."

"What does she look like when you imagine her?" Polly asks.

"She looks like one of my drawings of her," Tick says. "She's not a real person, though. She is like a paper drawing come to life."

Polly seems unfazed by the idea of Tick's paper mom.

"My imaginary Mom is big," she says. "*Really* big. She barely fits in my room. Even though I'm practically an adult now, she can still pick me up and put me in her arms as if I'm the size of a baby. It's weird, isn't it?"

"How does she pick you up if she's imaginary?" Tick asks.

"I don't know," she says. "I think she mostly comes to me in my dreams. She can pick me up when I'm dreaming."

"Why do you think we both have imaginary moms?" Tick asks.

"Maybe it's normal," Polly says. "Maybe we want to have moms so badly that our brains invented them for us."

Tick nods his head. He's not sure if her explanation is correct, but he's glad he's not the only one who has an imaginary mom. It makes him feel much less insane.

Back in the map room, they spend hours studying the locations. There are eight nurseries on every floor except the lower levels which don't seem to have any nurseries at all. The nurseries on their current floor are labeled #504-512. There really are hundreds of nurseries in the house. Nursery #640 is the last one on the highest floor.

"That many…" Polly says. "It seems like too many to fathom."

She pauses to slip on a new dress she has just finished modifying.

"I think I'm beginning to believe what you said before," she says. "There *has* to be more parents living in this house besides Mom and Dad. How could they have enough children to fill

640 nurseries? That would be crazy."

"What if there is one set of parents per floor?" Tick asks.

"Maybe," Polly says. "If that's true then they might not be too far away. We should focus on studying the map of this floor."

"You do that," Tick says. "I'm going to study the lower floors."

"Why?"

"There are no nurseries on the bottom five floors. Nanny said the reason human children are raised in nurseries is because they don't like to be around kids while they're growing up. They think we're disgusting. It makes the most sense to me that they'd live on the floors where there aren't any kids."

She nods. "You search those. I'll search these."

Tick gets straight to work, but he doesn't make much sense of the maps on the lower floors. The rooms are bigger. The names of the rooms are words he's never heard before.

Polly makes a discovery before he does.

"Here it is!" she cries.

Tick goes to her. "What?"

"I found it." She points at a room on the other end of their floor. "It's where Mom and Dad are. I know it is."

"Why? What is it?"

He looks at the room. It reads Master Hall.

"So?" Tick says. "It just says *Master Hall*. That could be anything."

"No, look at all the rooms around it," she says.

He looks more carefully and realizes that it's actually a whole cluster of rooms with the word *Master* in the title: Master Hall, Master Bath, Master Gym, Master Store, Master Aquarium, Master Dining. They are all on one section of the house on the same floor. They are also very far away.

"It has to be it, right?" she says. She looks at the other maps. "There are rooms named this on every floor. It has to be true— one set of parents per floor."

Tick nods. "Yeah, it's far away. But it might be exactly what we're looking for."

"There are at least three nurseries along the way," Polly says. "I'm sure we'll find food in one of them. Let's go."

She picks up the light and heads to the map room exit, smiling impatiently. Tick frowns, puts Leech back in her harness, and follows after. Polly is confused by his expression.

"What's with the face?" she asks. "Aren't you excited?"

Tick nods slowly. "I'm fine. I'm just tired. Let's go."

He doesn't want to explain the real reason he's acting the way he is. Before he stepped away from the map he saw a room in the same area called *Master Nursery*. He wonders if that means there is a prime nursery, one that raises kids that are more important than other kids in the other nurseries. He wonders if their Mom and Dad only care about the Master Nursery kids. He decides not to tell Polly about it. He doesn't want her to have to worry about that.

On the way to the master rooms, they take a detour to one of the nurseries. It is Nursery #508. The door is locked, barricaded on the inside. They knock and yell out, wondering if there are kids or a nanny in there somewhere. Nobody answers. There is a doorbell, which parents probably use when picking up their children, but they're not sure if it works. They don't hear any noise coming from within. When Tick puts his ear to the door, all he hears is the light scratching of antlers against the inner walls of the nursery.

"Let's go," he tells Polly, shaking his head.

They go to Nursery #511 next, but also can't get inside. Not because the door is locked, but because a pile of rubble blocks their way into the entry room.

"What happened in there?" Tick asks, as Polly shines the cage of light into the ruins.

"The ceiling caved in," Polly says. "If any kids were living in there they'd have been buried alive."

They try to find Nursery #504, but all the rooms on its section of the house are charred black. A fire must have swept through a long time ago, burning everything down.

"Every nursery we come to is dead," Tick says. "What if there aren't any left?"

"There are 640 of them. We've only been to a few. There's got to be some that still have power."

"I haven't been hungry all day," Tick says. "I haven't eaten in forever. Why am I not hungry?"

"Your body is eating itself," she says. "You're not hungry because you're living off of your fat."

"I don't have that much fat," he says.

"Don't worry," Polly says. "We didn't get food in the nurseries, but we'll get food once we get to the master rooms. Even if Mom and Dad aren't in them, I'm sure there's a Master Tea Room or someplace similar where we can eat."

"But it's really far," Tick says. "My feet are all blistered. I've never walked for this long in my whole life."

"What about me?" she whines. "I'm in far worse shape than you and you don't see me complaining."

"I'm not complaining," Tick says.

"Then come on."

When they finally arrive at the master rooms on the other side of floor 63, Tick is ready to collapse. Polly is in even worse shape than Tick, but she's so excited that she puts up with the pain.

"Through there?" Tick asks, pointing at the double doors at the end of the hallway.

Polly nods.

"Right through those doors our parents are awaiting our arrival," she says.

"No, they're not," Tick says.

She smiles, "Let me pretend. This is what I've been waiting

for my whole life." She straightens her doll face eye patch and wipes dust from her new dress. "How do I look?"

"Fine," Tick says. "Let's just go. We need food and sleep. You still need medical attention."

Polly giggles. "I don't care about any of that. I just want to meet them. It's all I've ever wanted."

They can see light coming through the crack between the double doors.

"People are in there," she says. "I know they are."

The closer they get, the louder they hear a commotion.

"It sounds like voices," Tick says. "A lot of voices."

"Maybe Mom and Dad are throwing a party," she says. "It sounds like a crowd of people talking. Maybe they're even ballroom dancing."

The smile on her face is so wide that it nearly causes the scab under her eye patch to break apart.

When they get to the doors, they don't open them right away. They turn to each other. There is clearly a crowd of people on the other side. One of them is bound to be a parent of theirs. They're sure of it.

"This is it," Polly says.

Tick nods.

"Are you ready to meet Mom and Dad?" Polly says.

"Let's do it," Tick says.

On the count of three, they plan to open the doors.

"One," Polly says.

"Two," Tick says.

"Three," they both say.

When they open the doors, bright light pours into the hallway and wind blows so hard against their faces that they can hardly see.

There aren't any people. The sound they mistook for a crowded party was the white noise caused by a wind tunnel blowing through the room.

Tick holds onto the side of the doorway, protecting Leech

from the strong winds. Polly steps forward into the room.

"No…" she says. Tick can barely hear her voice over the wind. "It can't be…"

Tick has to raise his hand to block the light of the dark orange sun to understand what he's looking at. There aren't any master rooms beyond the double doors. At least, not anymore.

Ten feet past the doorway, the room becomes a sixty-three story drop off. The rest of the house, beyond this point, has long since collapsed.

CHAPTER FOURTEEN

Polly stands on what is now a balcony, looking out at the vast world beyond their parents' home. She is on her knees, tears flowing down her face, wind rippling her green locks of hair. A third of the giant house has broken away like a landslide and become a mountain of rubble below. It seems to have happened a long time ago.

Tick steps out, slowly, careful not to get too close to the edge. The black and white tile floor is still crumbling away one section at a time, tiles blowing away into the breeze like lost birds. He looks up at the remains of the building above him. The destruction extends for two dozen levels, all ending in jagged balconies ready to collapse at any minute. Then he looks down. The pile of debris stretches for miles. All the master rooms would be in the wreckage below. If their parents did live in this section of the house they would likely be long dead.

"What do you think caused this?" Tick asks.

Polly doesn't speak. The sight of such massive devastation overwhelms her. She just sits there, looking over the edge.

"The whole side of the building tumbled down," he says. "Do you think it was an accident? Maybe a big earthquake hit. I read about this kind of thing happening to houses."

He squints his eyes and looks out past the rubble of the house. There are rolling orange mountains and rivers of red water. In the far distance, he can see other houses, dozens of them. All seem like they could be the same size as their parents' house. These homes also appear to be in a state of ruin.

There are no signs of life outside the dead houses. No planes in the air. No vehicles on the streets. Just strong winds beating at their skin.

"It's like everyone's dead," Tick says. "Could there have been a war? Nanny never said anything about a war."

The sky is reddish in color, but Tick thought the sky was supposed to be blue. There are peach-colored clouds and three large spheres in the air. The spheres take up much of the sky.

"Planets..." Tick says.

The planets are so close they seem like they can touch the ground. A blue water planet hangs beyond the clouds like a moon. The top half of a brown gas giant grows out of the horizon. A yellow planet with rings like Saturn is the farthest away, but still close enough to be visible with the naked eye. The sun itself is blood red. It is massive, but it isn't very bright. It appears to be dying.

"Where are we?" Tick asks. "This can't be Earth..."

He looks down at the cage of light in his hand. The planets within are identical to the ones in the sky.

Polly looks up from the rubble at the planets in the red sky. She doesn't recognize anything about this landscape. None of the pictures from any of the books in the nursery library looked like this. The world was supposed to be a place of blue skies and green valleys.

"Aren't we supposed to be on Earth?" Tick asks.

Leech growls and squirts at the wind as it strikes her wet bug eyes. When Tick sees the ugly grub is suffering, he goes back inside the hallway, turning his back on the red atmosphere. He always used to dream about what it would be like to see the world beyond his parents' house, but this is not the world he was expecting. It scares him. It is big, and crushing, and dead. And haunted.

"Mom and Dad are dead, aren't they?" Polly says.

Tick turns back.

"Everybody's dead," Tick says. "The whole world."

Tick and Polly have never felt more exhausted and drained as they retrace their steps, back the way they came, to find the nearest elevator. They feel like the living dead stepping through these hallways, dragging their blistered feet.

"One of the nurseries somewhere in this building still has power," Tick says. "We'll find it."

When they get to the elevators, the button doesn't work. The elevators in this section don't seem to have power.

"Let's take the stairs," Polly says, pointing toward a doorway at the end of the row of elevators.

They trudge down one floor and head toward Nursery #495. Along the way, Tick feels himself falling in and out of consciousness. His paper mom comes up behind him, wraps her crumpled arm around his waist and helps him stay upright. He lets his weight rest against her hip.

"I'm not really dead," says the paper mom.

He rests his cheek against her hollow body.

"I did not live on that section of the house," she says. "I'm still alive."

"No, you're not," Tick says. "You're dead. Everything is dead."

The paper mom giggles at him.

"No, my darling," she says. "If I am dead then where did your little sister come from? She was born only recently."

Tick thinks about it for a moment. His paper mother is right. She has to be alive somewhere if she just recently gave birth to Leech.

"But the house is in ruins…" Tick says.

"Most of the house still stands," she says. "I live in a more secure area of the building, lower down."

"Really?"

"Yes, darling. You know this to be true."

"Where?"

"You'll know when you find me," she says.

140

Tick snaps out of it when he nearly falls over. He has been sleepwalking for a few minutes. Leech squirms and growls on his back.

When he tells Polly about his dream, she says that she also just had a similar talk with her imaginary mother. The world outside the nursery is not at all what they were expecting, but they believe there could possibly still be a chance that their parents are alive in the house somewhere.

There is a dim light shining through the corridor outside of Nursery #495. At first, Tick thinks it's their planet cage reflecting the light back at them, but it is coming from within the nursery.

"Is the power on?" Polly can barely believe her eyes.

The front door to the nursery has been smashed open. Claw marks cover the walls. The lights are on inside, but it is silent.

"Hello?" Polly asks. "Is anyone there?"

There is no answer. They step inside.

"Hello?" she asks again, walking across the entrance room.

The walls and floor have all been sloppily painted white. Toys and trash litter the entryway. The place looks recently deserted.

"I don't think anyone's here," Tick says.

They step further into Nursery #495, going down the hallway toward the tea room. They pass the girl's room. The lights are on. The room is a mess, filled with toys and clothes scattered across the floor.

"Hello?" Polly says, sticking her head inside the room.

There's no one inside, but somebody has obviously lived here in the not too distant past.

"It's weird," Polly says.

"What?"

She looks at the stuff on the floor. "Seeing this room. It

looks exactly like *my* room. It has the same clothes in the closet, the same toys on the floor…" She steps inside and walks in a circle. "But some other girl has been living in it."

"Do you think she's still here?" Tick asks.

Polly shakes her head. All the claw marks covering the walls and furniture tell her everything she needs to know.

They go to the boy's room. The room is clean, but has also been lived in. The nanny's room is empty. The toy room and library are disaster areas. Furniture has been ripped apart. Holes and claw marks cover the walls. Blood stains on the carpet.

They don't find anyone anywhere.

"Their bodies must have been dragged off," Polly says. "I'd say it happened less than a year ago."

"But all the lights are still on," Tick says.

Polly shrugs. "There was nobody left alive to turn them back off."

The food machines seem like they could be operational, but they still have a few hours before breakfast will be served. They decide to get some rest until then.

Tick removes the homemade wooden armor from his body. He doesn't think he'll put it back on. Though it saved his life on two occasions, the straps have been chaffing his skin and have made travel unbearable.

He moves the bed from the girl's room into the boy's room, so they can sleep in the same room together with the cage of light, just in case the power goes out. However, they put Leech in the baby room. The maggot is so hungry that she'll probably try to drain them of blood in their sleep given the opportunity.

"There's no water," Polly says from the bathroom.

"That's not a good sign," Tick says. He doesn't know what he's going to do if the food machines don't work.

When he goes to Polly in the bathroom, he sees her peeling

off her fingernails.

"What are you doing?" he cries.

He cringes at the sound when she tears off another. Beneath her nails there are hard black lumps, shiny like marble.

"What's wrong with your fingers?" Tick asks, his voice getting soft as he steps toward her.

"Nanny said this would happen," Polly says. "I'm just going through puberty. Just as I've been growing antlers, I'm also beginning to grow claws."

Tick examines the lumps on his sister's fingers. "Claws?"

"Soon they will become long black razor-sharp talons," she says. "A woman's beauty is measured by the length of her talons."

"I thought it was the height of your antlers?" Tick asks.

"That, too."

Lying in bed, Tick can't sleep. The thought of Polly growing talons frightens him. She already has antlers. Why does she need talons as well? He worries about what she'll be like when she's in heat with such fearsome claws. She's already deadly enough with her antlers.

"Polly?" Tick asks, wondering if she's still awake.

"Huh…" Her eyes are closed but she's not asleep.

"I was just thinking…"

"About what?"

"Your claws," he says.

"What about them?"

He pauses for a moment, wondering if he should actually talk to her about what's on his mind. But he has to get it off of his chest.

"You've already got antlers. You go into fits of violent rage. Now you are growing claws… It sounds to me like you're turning into one of the creepers."

Polly turns to him and laughs.

Lying on her pillow, facing him, she says, "That's ridiculous."

"Think about it… You are beginning to look and behave more and more like them every day. What if humans turn into creepers once they grow up? What if the creepers in the hallways were originally kids born in nurseries?"

Polly shakes her head.

"Just because they have the antlers and claws of humans doesn't mean they are humans. How come they disappear in the light? No matter how many changes my body goes through it'll never be able to do that."

"Well, what do you think the creepers are then?"

"Seagulls," Polly says.

"Seagulls?" Tick asks.

"I read about seagulls and sea turtles in a book once," she explains. "I believe we're like the turtles. Sea turtles don't raise their young. They lay dozens of eggs in a nest on the beach and then they abandon them. Kind of like how our parents abandoned us in our nursery." She rolls over on her back, staring up at the ceiling as she speaks. "When the turtles hatch, they have to fend for themselves. They leave the safety of the nest and try to cross the beach to get to the sea, to the place where their mother lives. But it is dangerous. There are seagulls on the beach that hunt the baby turtles. A lot of them are killed and eaten."

"So that's why you think creepers wait outside our nurseries? So they can catch us and eat us like seagulls?"

Polly nods. "But sea turtles as a species survive because they lay so many eggs. The seagulls can't possibly eat them all, so some are able to cross the beach and escape into the sea. I believe that's why there are so many nurseries in this house. If hundreds of children are born in this place then odds are some will survive, even with so many creepers waiting in the shadows."

Tick takes a deep breath and shakes his head.

"The sea turtles have it easier than us," Tick says.

"Why's that?"

"The beach we need to cross is falling apart around us. Everything is dying and crumbling. Nothing works. Our parents didn't lay their eggs on a beach. They laid them in quicksand." Tick closes his eyes. He's so exhausted he can't hold them open anymore. "I don't think even a single sea turtle would survive if they had to cross quicksand."

"Yeah," Polly says. "Especially if there was no sea for them to escape into."

CHAPTER FIFTEEN

"Are you my mommy?" says a little boy hovering over Polly's forehead.

When Polly wakes to see the boy smiling at her, his pudgy grubby face beaming with excitement, she shrieks and flails her arms until she falls out of the bed.

Tick sits up and sees the kid standing over his sister.

"Where did you come from?" he asks.

The boy opens his mouth in a wide goopy smile, holding a mucus-stained teddy bear in his stubby grub-like arms. He is probably two or three years old, so he's in the awkward stage between maggot and human. Not quite out of his larval stage, yet has a recognizable humanoid shape.

He wobbles toward Polly and tries to give her a hug.

"Eww, get him away from me," Polly screams, rushing away from the boy to stand behind Tick.

Tick steps toward him and leans down.

"Have you been here the whole time?" Tick asks. "Are you all by yourself?"

His lips stretch out like a balloon and then he puts the teddy bear's head in his mouth.

"What's your name?" Tick asks.

He doesn't reply, just sucking on the plushy fur.

"Where's your Nanny?" Tick asks.

The boy spits the slimy teddy bear out of his mouth.

"She stopped talking so we buried her in the toy box," says the kid.

The kid smiles at Polly again and tries to get past Tick's legs.

"Who's *we?*" Tick asks, holding him in place.

"Mommy," the kid says, pointing at Polly's face. "Why is

your eye a baby head?"

"Stop calling me that…" Polly hides her face in her hand. "I'm not your mommy."

The boy looks at Tick. "Are you my daddy?"

"No," Tick says. "We're just kids like you. We come from another nursery."

"Oh," he says. "Which nursery?"

"You know there are other nurseries?"

"Two," says the kid. "No… Three."

Then he asks, "Are you from the wet one?"

"The wet one?"

"I didn't see you there," he says.

"What?"

"We just came back," he says.

"Who else is with you?"

The sound of footsteps comes down the hallway toward them.

"Drool, where'd you go?" It's a girl's voice. "I told you never to run off. It's dangerous."

The girl pushes the bedroom door open. She's about ten or eleven years old, sickly thin, deep circles under her eyes. When she sees Tick and Polly she freezes, shocked to find them there. Then she pulls out a knife.

"Who are you?" she shouts, her voice trembling. "What are you doing here?"

Tick raises his arms when she points the knife in his direction.

"It's Mommy and Daddy," the maggot boy cries, but the crazed girl ignores his words.

"Get away from him!" the girl shrieks, pulling the little boy away from Tick and Polly. "You can't take him. Don't you dare take him!"

"We're not trying to take him," Polly says. "We're just looking for food."

The girl is frantic. Her eyes wild like an animal.

"Are you my mom?" she asks Polly, pointing the knife.

"No," she says.

"Then why do you have antlers?" she asks. "Why are you here? Why did you leave me with that crazy woman?"

"I'm too young to be your mother," Polly says. "I'm only fifteen."

"I'm not going with you," the girl yells. "Neither of us are *ever* going with you. Not after what you did. I'll kill you if you try to take us."

"Calm down," Tick says.

"You calm down," she cries, stepping forward, touching the knife to Tick's throat.

Then Tick sees something in her eyes. He thought her voice sounded familiar, but he couldn't place it before. Now, at this distance, he's sure it is her.

"I can't believe it," Tick cries. "It's really you."

The girl steps back, inching toward the doorway. Tick steps forward with a smile. He disregards the knife pointed at him.

"You know her?" Polly asks.

The girl twitches. Her eyes dart between Tick and Polly.

Her blue hair is much longer and rattier. Her creamy gray skin is covered in bruises and sores. She's malnourished and bony, with the expression of a rabid animal. But it's her. It's Darcy.

"Of course I do," Tick says. "She's my girlfriend."

The crazed girl takes the boy and runs from the room. She jumps into the baby room, then closes and locks the door, screaming about how she'll never let them take her away.

"Your girlfriend?" Polly asks.

"The one I always tell you about," Tick says. "From school."

"It can't be," Polly asks. "None of that was real. It was just a computer program."

"I know," he says. "It doesn't make sense, but she looks exactly like her. She even has the same heart-shaped birthmark on her forehead."

"It's got to just be a coincidence," Polly says. "All of that was fake."

"But what if it wasn't?" Tick says. "What if some of the other kids *were* real?"

"Everyone has their own school program," Polly says. "Two people can't go into the same one."

"But it looks exactly like her…"

After a few moments of mulling it over, they realize they've forgotten about something very important.

"Wait a minute…" Polly says.

"What?"

"She locked herself in the baby room…"

Tick's eyes pop out. "Leech!"

They run to the baby room and bang on the door, kicking and yelling for the girl to let them in. She doesn't respond.

"Don't hurt her," Tick says. "She's just a baby."

Tick slams himself against the door until finally the little bug boy opens the lock for him.

"It's getting big!" says the little boy.

They enter the room and see the crazy girl lying on the floor with her shirt unbuttoned. Leech is attached to her belly, feeding on her with ravenous speed. The baby has drunk so much that she has grown twice her size.

"So hungry…" the crazed girl says in a weak voice, trying to push away the swollen baby. "She was so hungry."

Instead of causing Leech harm, the girl attempted to feed her. But she wasn't aware of how starving the baby had been for going so long without eating.

Leech squeaks and purrs as she drinks, then growls and squirts when Tick pulls her off and puts her back in the crib. The girl he thinks is Darcy closes her eyes and falls unconscious, weak from the blood loss.

"Let's put her to bed," Polly says, lifting the girl by the

shoulders. "Maybe she'll calm down after she's had some sleep."

"Oatmeal…" Tick says, staring down into his bowl of mush.

The food machines in this nursery are operational, but just barely. The only food they serve for each and every meal is a slimy gruel that smells like walnuts and ham. The center of the table is just one giant vat of the stuff. No fruit. No sausage. No toast or jam. Just a foul-smelling mush.

Tick has always hated oatmeal and this is the worst oatmeal he's ever had.

"At least it's food…" he says to his bowl.

The bug boy is at the table with him, eating the mush with his hands. The goop is all over his fingers and smeared across his face.

"Don't you use a spoon?" Tick asks.

The kid seems like he's never used a spoon in his life.

"Chewy…" the kid says.

His nickname is *Drool*. He doesn't know his real name.

Polly enters the room and squeezes into a tiny chair. She takes three helpings of the mush. Oatmeal has always been her favorite.

"How is she?" Tick asks.

Polly shakes her head. "She must have been through a lot."

"Did you talk to her?"

"Yeah, for awhile," she says. "After I finally convinced her that I wasn't her mom, I was able to get her to answer some questions. Her name actually *is* Darcy, just like you said."

Tick's eyes light up. "It's really her? Does she remember me?"

"That's the weird part," Polly says. "She hasn't been to school since first grade, so she can't be the girl you knew."

When she says this, Tick doesn't respond. The excitement fades from his face, but he just listens on as he attempts to get down small spoonfuls of mush.

"She originally comes from Nursery #488," Polly continues. "Her nanny went insane one day and drove her out. I don't think she understands that her nanny was just a robot that malfunctioned. It really messed her up. She was only six years old at the time."

"She's been out of her nursery for five years?" Tick asks.

"She found what she calls a *glow suit* on the bones of some long-dead kid in the halls. It's what kept her alive all these years. It turns her entire body into a giant light bulb when she wears it, but it needs to be recharged every thirty minutes. So she hasn't been able to explore much of the house, just small sections at a time."

"What about Drool?" Tick asks, pointing at the worm boy. "Isn't he her brother?"

"He's originally from this nursery," Polly says. "Out of all the nurseries Darcy explored, this was the first to have kids still alive in it. The nanny here let her move in, but she broke down soon after. This place has been slowly falling apart ever since. They don't have water here, so they have to get it from another nursery within the vicinity that's been flooded."

"The wet one," Drool says, holding up a hand of oat mush.

"There's plenty of water there but not much else," Polly says. "They go there every couple of days. That's where the two of them were when we found this place."

"What else does she know about the house?" Tick asks. "Does she know how to find Mom and Dad?"

Polly shakes her head. "I don't think so. She seems to know less than we do about the house. She has no interest in finding her Mom and Dad. She blames them for everything that's happened to her."

Polly takes a fourth serving of oatmeal.

"But it seems she knows a lot about surviving around the creepers..." she continues. "Though she doesn't call them *creepers*, she calls them *lurkers*. She painted all the walls in here white so that the light reflects better, making the rooms brighter and the shadows smaller. She also says they hunt by sound, so if you ever find yourself in the dark you just have to be really quiet and they won't attack you. You can't kill them, but you can trap them if you lead them into rooms and lock them in. They aren't very smart."

"Does she know what the creepers are?" Tick asks.

"She thinks they are ghosts of dead adults who once lived in the house," Polly says. "She tries to sleep with her eyes open, because she thinks they can see her when she closes them. She swears they watch her from behind her eyelids."

Tick is done with his food. He pushes it away.

"Are we going to end up like her someday?" Tick asks.

Polly shakes her head. "Not if we find Mom and Dad."

Later in the day, Polly locks herself in the toy room. She's still in heat and feeling another psychotic episode coming on.

"Don't let them know about this," she tells Tick. She doesn't make eye contact. "I don't want them to be scared of me."

Tick does as she says, but neither Darcy nor Drool seems to notice when Polly tears apart the room, screaming at the top of her lungs. He guesses they think she's just another creeper in the shadows.

Darcy doesn't say more than two words to Tick until late in the evening, after Polly becomes quiet. They're in the garden. Though all the plants and flowers are long dead, it's still a nice place to relax. The concrete benches are warm and soothing. They remind Tick of Nanny Warburough.

"It's the most peaceful room in the nursery," Darcy says. She sits down next to him on the bench. "No matter what nursery I visit, the garden room is always my favorite."

She rocks her knees back and forth as she sits on the bench, rubbing her elbows. She seems to have problems sitting still.

"Yeah, I like the garden room," Tick says. His *favorite* room, however, is the toy room. He has no idea why anyone would like the garden room more than the toy room, especially when all the plants are dead.

There is a long moment of silence. The girl stares forward, swaying her head and jerking her fingers. She seems like an adult woman in an eleven-year-old's body, hardly like a kid at all. Tick imagines it's because she left the nursery so young. She had to grow up fast. Her face looks withered from malnourishment and never getting enough sleep. So many wrinkles around her eyes...

Though she is so different than the Darcy that he knew, he still feels a connection to her. She still feels like his girlfriend.

"I think I know you," she says. She makes eye contact with him for only a second before looking away.

"What do you mean?"

"In school," she says. "I remember a boy that kind of looks like you. I don't remember his name. I remember he was nice to me. Not many kids at school were nice to me."

Tick is happy to hear that she knows him, but he isn't incredibly surprised. He already guessed that her school would have a version of him just as his school had a version of her.

"I think it *was* me," Tick says. "Well, not the real me. A copy of me. I believe that the school program bases its characters after kids from other nurseries. The boy that looked like me was a computer clone of me. The girl that I knew named Darcy was a computer clone of you."

He's not sure why they would do this, but it's the only explanation he can come up with other than it all being a big coincidence.

The girl has a hard time keeping eye contact with Tick. She looks him in the eyes for a second, then lowers them to his neck, then looks at her twitching hands, then at the empty pots that used to contain flowers, and then at him again.

"So I was really your girlfriend at your school?" she asks.

"Yeah," Tick says. "Since fourth grade. I had a crush on you for longer than that though."

Darcy smiles and looks away. She likes the idea of there being another version of her out there in the universe, living a happier, less frightening life.

"This other version of me…" She tries to stop smiling, as if smiling is making her appear weak, but she can't help it. "What was she like?"

Tick smiles back at her. He also can't help himself. Darcy's smiles were always so infectious.

"She was quiet," Tick says, feeling a little awkward telling her about herself. "Everyone thought she was shy but she was actually the most talkative kid in school. She just didn't like to speak with words. She always spoke with her eyes and body movements. Sometimes we'd have whole conversations with each other without saying anything out loud."

"Hmmm…" Darcy snickers for a second. She kind of remembers being like that when she was really young. "What else?"

"She wasn't athletic but she could go higher than anyone on the swings. Everyone else was too scared to swing as high as she would. And when she jumped off she would always land on her feet, every time, no matter how high she jumped."

Darcy likes hearing about the version of her that Tick knew. It makes her think of what she would have been like if things had gone differently in her life. It seems like a fantasy world to her.

Tick tells her story after story, all the experiences he had with her, all the things she said and did on the playground or during class. He feels kind of awkward telling her about the times they kissed behind the monkey bars, but she still wants to hear about it. She wants to know everything.

"She was my favorite person I knew," Tick says. "I felt empty once I learned she didn't really exist."

She smiles gently at him and then looks down at his hand. The Darcy he knew would have taken his hand at a moment like this. She always liked to hold his hand in her lap. But this Darcy is not her. She just looks at his hand for a second and then shifts her eyes away. Then she wants to hear more about the happier version of herself.

As Tick makes himself a bed on the reading couch in the library, he has a permanent smile on his face. For a while there he felt like he was with Darcy again, *his* Darcy. She's a completely different person, but he wonders if it's possible for him to develop a relationship with this new version of her. He wonders if she can be his girlfriend again.

Polly enters the library with a distressed look on her face. She's exhausted from her violent episode, but something else is bothering her as well.

"I think we should get out of here," Polly says.

Tick turns away from the couch bed. "What do you mean? Why?"

"The kid said they buried their nanny in the toy box," Polly said. "While I was in there, I broke into it. I saw the body. The nanny didn't break down. She was killed. There were stab wounds in her back."

"Are you saying Darcy did it?"

"Yeah, that's what I'm saying. She's a psycho."

"Are you sure they weren't from creepers?"

"They were knife wounds. The same size as the knife she held to your throat. I don't trust her. She's dangerous."

"Maybe the nanny went crazy and she *had* to kill her. Like what we had to do."

"But she told me the nanny just didn't wake up one day. They found her lying in her bed, no longer moving. Why else would she lie about that? She was scared the nanny would go crazy and kick her out just like the nanny did to her when she was a kid. So she killed her."

Tick doesn't want to listen to this. He just got his Darcy back. He doesn't want to leave her.

"So what?" he says. "The nanny is just a robot. Who cares if she killed a machine?"

"She could do the same to either one of us," Polly says. "She's a psycho. I'm not going to be able to sleep in the same place with her."

Tick shakes his head.

"I don't care," he says. "I'm not leaving. We have food and other people. We can't leave. I don't think she's crazy. She's just scared."

"That's what I'm afraid of," Polly says. "Scared people do scary things."

Tick doesn't respond. He crawls into his couch bed and pulls the covers up to his face, refusing to believe that Darcy would ever do anything to harm anybody.

CHAPTER SIXTEEN

Over the next few days, Polly doesn't let Darcy out of her sight. She definitely doesn't turn her back on her. Though Darcy is only eleven and her antlers are only barely starting to peek out from her frazzled blue hair, Polly is scared to death of her. It's hard to rest easy with somebody whose behavior is so unpredictable. Not to mention the crazy girl carries a knife around with her everywhere she goes.

"I want you to pretend I'm the other one," Darcy says to Tick.

They're sitting in the library reading old books. Many of the books are the same ones from Tick's nursery library, but there are some that are new. Tick is excited to read new books for a change. He'd already read most of the ones in his nursery three times over.

"What do you mean?"

Tick puts his book down. *James and the Giant Peach*. It's one of the best he's read.

"I just want to see what it's like to be her," Darcy says. "Just for a while. You don't have to if you don't want to."

Darcy's book lies on her lap. She doesn't know how to read very well, so she mostly just looks at the pictures.

"No, it's okay." Tick can't believe she'd ask him such a thing. It's exactly what he's wanted to do for days. "I'd love to."

He smiles at her, but she doesn't smile back. Her face is distant, as if she's putting all of her focus into trying hard to bury a particular darkness in the back of her mind.

"So how do we start?" Tick says.

Darcy looks at him, her glistening black eyes reflecting his face. "However you want. Just pretend I'm her."

Tick gets up and moves closer to her, sitting next to her on the reading couch. She inches away and faces him.

"It's hard," Tick says. "We were never in the nursery together. We were always in school."

"Just try," Darcy says.

"Okay."

Tick decides what he wants to do most is hug her. It's what he's wanted to do since the second he laid eyes on this Darcy. He moves forward and opens his arms, trying to wrap them around her, but she jerks out of his embrace and jumps back.

"What are you doing?" she cries.

"I'm hugging you. I always hugged you."

"Don't touch me," she says, moving as far away from him as possible without leaving the couch. "You can't touch me."

"But Darcy liked to hug me," Tick says. "We didn't talk much. She liked to hug and hold hands instead of talk. Sometimes she'd kiss me."

"I don't care," Darcy says. "I don't want you touching me."

She shivers on the couch, holding her arms like she's just gotten out of a shower and is trying to keep warm.

"Then what am I supposed to do?" Tick says. "We can't go on the swings or climb the monkey bars."

Darcy is nervous, yet frustrated. She wants to instantaneously become this other version of herself and doesn't like that Tick is unable to make this happen.

"Just make me feel like her," Darcy says. "I don't care how you do it, just make me feel what she felt. And don't touch me."

Tick realizes what she's asking now. She doesn't want to pretend that she's his girlfriend. What she really wants is for Tick to make her feel happy.

"I can think of only one thing that will make you feel that way," Tick says. "But it means I have to touch you."

Darcy shakes her head frantically.

"I just have to hold your hand," he says. "That's all."

Darcy's eyes dart away and then down and then to Tick.

"No," she says. "I don't think…"

"It won't—"

She interrupts him to say, "Okay."

Tick nods.

"We sit facing each other," Tick says. He moves so he can cross his legs on the couch in her direction. "I'm going to put my hand out. You can take it when you're ready."

He puts the palm of his hand out to her. She looks down at it and chews a hangnail on her middle finger.

"Then we look into each other's eyes," Tick says. "You always liked doing this. You said it was how to have a conversation without words."

Darcy looks into his eyes. She tries to hold eye contact, but looks away every few seconds. She moves closer to him and drops her hand into his like it's a dead rat.

Tick smiles. He takes her hand and weaves his fingers into it.

"Just relax," Tick says.

He takes a deep breath. Darcy takes a deep breath to mimic him, but it's mechanical. It doesn't relax her.

There's not a lot of warmth in her hand. It doesn't feel like Darcy's. It's rough and gritty. The fingers are bony and twisted. And at this proximity, Tick can smell that she hasn't bathed in weeks.

"Is this all?" Darcy says.

Tick shakes his head. "You have to get into it. When you look at me, focus on going through my eyes, into my mind. Enter my thoughts. When you hold my hand, feel like we are connected, like our blood is pumping into each other's bodies."

She tries to do as he says, but it doesn't seem to work with her. She's too stiff and closed off. The Darcy he knew was so open. But there is one thing that makes this Darcy feel like the one he knew. There is one thing she is doing right, and she's probably unaware that she's doing it. He can feel her energy flowing into him through his hand. It's like a current of electricity.

Tick smiles at her when he feels her current entering his hand. Then she looks away from him and the current disappears. She grips his hand tighter.

"What are you doing here?" she says.

She isn't looking at Tick, she's looking past him. He turns to see if Polly entered the room but nobody is there.

"Get out of here," she yells.

She squeezes his hand, digging her nails into his skin. Tick recoils at the pain.

"Darcy?" Tick tries to loosen her grip on his hand.

She squeezes tighter, crushing his fingers. Blood trickles down from where her nails break the skin.

"I told you never to come here!" she cries.

Then she pulls out her knife.

Tick holds out his other hand, getting ready to block in case she tries to stab him. But she lets go of his hand and jumps off of the couch. She runs to the corner of the room and waves the knife at something she sees standing there.

"I'm not going to look for you," she says. "I don't care about you. I'd rather die than be with you."

Then she stabs at the wall where the unseen invader would have been standing.

When Polly enters the room holding a hammer from the storage, Darcy rushes past her, still screaming at the top of her lungs as if something is following after.

Tick and Polly stare at each other once they're alone.

"I told you," Polly says. "She's a psycho. We can't stay here with her."

"She didn't try to stab me," Tick says. "It was something she saw. She wouldn't hurt me."

"Well, you're bleeding," Polly says, pointing at the blood on the outside of his hand.

"This was an accident," he says, wiping the droplets of blood away. "You don't understand what happened."

"Then what did happen?"

Tick stands up and goes to the door. He makes sure Darcy isn't listening. She's still making noise, somewhere in the tea room, but seems to have calmed down a little.

"She was talking to her mom," Tick says, gently closing the door.

"What do you mean? Her *imaginary* mom?"

"Yeah, like ours. Only she hates her imaginary mom. And she might not realize that she's only an illusion."

Polly looks at the holes in the wall that Darcy made when she stabbed at her invisible mom. Then she looks at all of the holes and cuts all over the walls of the library.

"These marks," Polly says, rubbing her hand along one of the cracks in the wall. "And the ones that are on the walls all over this nursery. They weren't created by creepers."

Now that he looks at them Tick realizes it, too. He assumed all the scratches covering the walls were from the claws and antlers of creepers, but they're not.

"They're knife marks," Polly says.

Hundreds of scratches and holes cover the walls, furniture, books, and toys. Darcy created them all.

For the next two days, Tick tries to pretend that he never saw what happened. Darcy and Tick have *conversations without speaking* a few times per day. She wants to keep doing it until she feels like how the other Darcy felt, but Tick thinks it's impossible. Although Darcy has been able to maintain eye contact with him, she's still awkward and unable to relax. Her fingers twitch when she holds his hands, as if they really don't want to be there.

There's still a lack of happiness in Darcy's eyes, but she's beginning to enjoy having these moments with Tick. She swears that she can now enter his mind and talk to him inside of there. Sometimes she'll refer to a conversation they had, but Tick will have no idea what she's talking about. He likes spending time with her, though. Even though she's crazy, she's still nicer than Polly sometimes.

Learning that Darcy has an imaginary mom starts giving Tick ideas. He learns that Drool also has an imaginary mom, though he won't tell Darcy about her out of fear that she might try to kill her.

"What if the imaginary moms are real?" Tick asks Polly, while eating oatmeal in the tea room.

"How can they be real?"

"Well, it's something Darcy told me," Tick says. "She had an older brother in her nursery. When he was eleven, he said that his mother was calling to him, telling him to come find her. He didn't think she was imaginary. He thought she was more like a projection of his real mom, giving him instructions on what to do. So he left his nursery to go look for her."

"Where did she tell him to go?"

"That's the thing," Tick says. "She told him that she is in the lower levels. That's what my imaginary mom told me. If they are just figments of our imaginations then why would they tell both of us to go to the same place?"

"So you think Mom is trying to talk to us through these visions?" Polly asks. "She's trying to tell us to go down to the ground floor?"

Tick nods.

"That's what I think," he says.

"We should go there and check it out. Just to see."

"I agree," Tick says. "We should pack up food and water and go as soon as we can."

"But we're leaving Darcy here," she says.

"What? No, we can't leave her here."

"She won't want to go find her mom anyway," Polly says.

"We'll come back for her if we find something."

"But she's survived in the hallways for way longer than we have," Tick says. "We need her."

"You'll see," Polly says. "There's no way she'll want to go with us."

Darcy says she wants to go with them.

"But why?" Polly says.

"I want to explore more of the house," Darcy says. "I need to find a safer nursery for Drool, but I've only been able to go short distances using the glow suit."

Darcy sharpens her knife with the edge of a brick. Nobody knows where she got the knife. It didn't come with the nursery. There aren't many sharp objects allowed in the nurseries.

"But we're not exploring the house," Polly says. "We're going to find our mom and dad."

"I'm not going anywhere near my mom and dad," Darcy says. "But I can go with you most of the way. If we find a good nursery I'll stay there and you can go on without me."

Darcy goes to her room to pack before Polly can say another word.

"This is a mistake," Polly says. "We should have left her."

"I don't want to leave her."

"Are you in love with her?"

Tick is quiet for a moment. "I love the part of her that reminds me of the old Darcy."

"You know she might be your sister, don't you?" Polly says. "If all the kids in this house have the same parents you could be related. She can't be your girlfriend if she's your sister."

Tick has known about the possibility but hasn't wanted to admit it.

"She's not my sister," Tick says.

"How do you know?"

"She doesn't feel like a sister. We don't look alike."

"We'll see," Polly says. "If we find Mom and Dad we'll know for sure. When that time comes, don't be surprised if it happens to be the case."

Tick knows she has to be wrong. Darcy looks nothing like him. They have to have come from different parents. They just happened to have been born in the same house.

CHAPTER SEVENTEEN

The children wander through dead corridors, searching for a working elevator. They want to take it down to the ground floor and start the search for their parents from there, but just finding an elevator that functions has been difficult enough. If it's avoidable, they'd prefer not to take the stairs.

"She's much gentler than Drool was," Darcy says, holding Leech under her shirt.

She has been feeding Leech regularly, giving Tick a break from losing so much blood all the time. He actually feels like he has strength and energy again.

"I kind of like the feeling," Darcy says. "When she drinks my blood, it's peaceful. It calms me down."

"It makes me feel like I'm going to die," Tick says.

Darcy looks down at the wiggling maggot in her arms and pets her on the plump part of her forehead.

"She purrs when she's feeding," Darcy says. "I feel like she's a part of me. I wish I had enough blood to feed her all day."

Once Drool can no longer move anymore, they find a bedroom to camp out in for the night. Polly, Drool and Leech go straight to sleep, but Tick and Darcy stay awake. For hours, they hold hands and stare into each other's eyes. Tick doesn't care about rest; he would do this all night if Darcy wanted him to. By the end, Darcy smiles and tears roll down her cheeks. He wonders if she's actually done it. He wonders if she actually felt like the happy version of Darcy for a moment.

They find a working elevator a few hours away, in a section of the house where vines have started growing through the floor. It's as if plants from one of the nursery gardens have spread out into the halls and overtaken a wing of the building.

"Ground floor," Tick says, as they crowd into the small box and push the button.

The elevator rattles and squeals as it descends, moving slower than they would have if they took the stairs. Something seems to be holding it back, as if the vines from the hallway above have also grown into the elevator shaft and wrapped themselves around the cables.

Somewhere between the third and fourth floor, just before they make it to the bottom, the elevator breaks down. It just stops its descent, making a loud wailing sound, rumbling in place as if still attempting to move.

"Let's get out," Polly says.

They pry open the elevator doors and crawl out, squeezing through the crack at the bottom and dropping down to the third floor. They didn't want to climb up onto the fourth floor, just in case the elevator started moving again.

"That was fun," Drool says, dragging his teddy bear along with him.

Tick and Polly scan the area. The building is different on this floor. The lobby is bigger, brighter. The light overhead actually works.

"Maybe this floor still has electricity," Polly says.

They take the stairs down the rest of the way. The ground floor does not have electricity. It's pitch dark. They wish they could have stayed on the third floor.

The creepers seem to be following them from the outskirts of the shadows, beyond where the light can reach. Tick can hear them back there, sharpening their antlers and grinding their teeth.

Everything is larger on the ground floor. The halls are wider and taller. There are auditoriums, movie theaters, ballrooms, basketball courts, and indoor swimming pools. Although all of them are in various states of disrepair, Tick wishes they had the time to enjoy these new parts of the house. He's never been in a swimming pool before, nor has he ever seen basketball courts the size of the ones on the ground floor.

"Should we take a rest somewhere soon?" Tick asks, knowing that Drool is looking a little worn out. "We've been walking all day."

"We still have miles of house to cover," Polly says. Her voice is a moaning tone when she speaks. She is sweating profusely. "I think we should keep going."

"What's wrong?" Tick asks her.

She holds out her hand and empties a small bottle into her palm. Two pills fall out. They are the last pills in the bottle.

"I'm out of pain medicine," she says, then pops the last pills in her mouth. "It's the only thing that's been keeping me going for days."

"You mean since the injury? Since Nanny attacked you?"

"I started taking a triple dosage," she says. "But lately that hasn't been enough, so I started taking twice that amount."

"You went through all the pain medicine in the nursery storage?" Darcy cries. "That wasn't yours to take."

"I can't even move without it," she says. "That's why I don't want to stop. I want to find Mom and Dad before the medicine wears off. After that, I'm not going to get very far."

Tick thought she was able to move around with such severe wounds because she was healing. He didn't know that they were just getting worse, and that she was masking the pain with medicine.

"You've been walking on your injuries all this time?" Tick

says. "You could kill yourself."

"I'll be fine if we find Mom and Dad," she says. "Let's just keep going."

After a couple of hours, Polly can't keep going anymore. She tumbles to her knees, knocking over the lantern of light, whining in agony.

"We're taking a rest," Tick says, helping Polly to her feet.

He finds the nearest bedroom. It's larger than any of the bedrooms he's seen before and contains two king-sized beds. Darcy and Tick bring Polly to the closest one. She rolls onto it, holding her side, taking very shallow breaths.

"Let me see the wound," Darcy says.

Polly's eyes roll back and sideways while Darcy removes her dress. When she sees the wound, Darcy jumps back in horror.

"She was walking around like *this* the whole time?" Darcy cries.

"It was even worse before," Tick says.

"She has bones sticking out of her," Darcy says. "They need to be put back in."

"But we don't know how," Tick says.

"You just shove them back in place," Darcy says. "I had to do it to myself once."

She pulls down her sleeve and shows Tick her left arm. He didn't notice it before, but her forearm is slightly crooked in the middle with a large scar down the front.

"I fell down the stairs when I was little," she says. "The bone broke in half and popped right out of the skin. I had to force it back in myself."

"And it worked?" Tick asks.

"It healed eventually," she says. "It's not pretty but I can move it again."

Tick looks down at Polly's ribs poking out of her chest.

"Do you think you can do the same to Polly?" he asks.

"Rib bones are different from arm bones, but I'll try," she says.

Tick nods and agrees to help. He hopes it will make Polly feel better to have her bones put back into place.

Polly screams so loud that she coughs up blood.

"Stop yelling," Darcy says. "I can't do it if you keep yelling."

Tick holds down his thrashing, screaming sister while Darcy jams the ribs back inside her chest. There is working water in a bathroom across the hall, but they don't think just water is enough to keep the wound clean as Darcy puts Polly's bone back in using her bare hands.

"They're not going in properly," she says. "I think they're broken in too many places."

Polly shrieks, pushing the girl away.

"I also think her lung is broken," she says.

"Can you break a lung?" Tick says.

"Well, it looks smashed in," Darcy says.

Darcy does the best she can, bending the bones back into place. When they're done they allow Leech to drink from the wound, thinking maybe she'll sterilize it like she did before. Then they cut up a clean bed sheet to make the bandage, wrapping Polly's chest up tight.

Polly is out cold. The pain was too much for her. Tick hopes it will help her heal better. If they find their parents soon he's sure they will be able to do a better job with it.

"Thanks for helping my sister," Tick says to Darcy, after they leave Polly alone to sleep, sitting on the other side of the room by the door. "It means a lot."

"Now's our chance," Darcy whispers.

She grabs all of her things and hands Tick his bag.

"For what?" he says.

"Let's go while she's still asleep. I'll get Drool, you get the baby."

"Go where?"

"Just like we planned," Darcy says. "We're going to leave her here so we don't have to go look for her mom and dad anymore. Instead, we can look for a new nursery for us to live in. Just the two of us, and the little ones."

She goes to her little brother and shakes him to wake him up, but he doesn't want to leave the bed.

"What are you talking about?" Tick says.

"Our plan," she says, keeping her voice down so Polly doesn't hear. "You said you didn't care about finding your mom and were only doing it because your sister made you."

Tick watches in shock at what she's saying. He has no idea what she's talking about.

"It was your idea to abandon her. You said you wanted to just live with me and not have to deal with her anymore."

Tick just looks at her with his mouth agape, more confused than he's ever been in his life.

"Don't you remember?" she asks, frustrated with him.

"No," Tick says, shaking his head slowly. "I don't remember at all. When did I say all this?"

"Just last night," Darcy says.

"When did I say this last night?"

"We were talking all night," Darcy says. "Don't you remember? We were *having a conversation without words*. I entered your eyes and went into your mind where we talked about this for hours. I can't believe you don't remember."

Tick steps back. He had no idea she would take that so literally.

"I didn't have that conversation with you," Tick says. "That was all in your mind."

"No, it was all in *your* mind," she says. "We didn't go inside of my mind until after that conversation."

Tick shakes his head. "No, that's not what I mean."

He pauses for a moment, sits her down. He's not quite sure how to explain this to her.

"Look," he says. "When I said the old Darcy and I used to *have conversations without words*, I didn't mean we would speak telepathically with each other through our eyes. It was a non-verbal way of communicating. We spoke to each other with our feelings. They weren't actually conversations."

Darcy doesn't stay seated. She gets to her feet and paces in front of him. She doesn't try to keep her voice down anymore.

"What are you saying?" Darcy says, her eyes getting wet. "That you never said any of those things to me?"

"We never had any of those conversations," Tick says. "None of it was real. You just made it up."

"I did *not* make it up," she says. "You're just lying because you're chickening out."

"No, I'm serious," he says. "We never spoke telepathically."

Darcy doesn't seem to know what that word means.

"Let's just go," Darcy says. "I don't care if the conversation wasn't real. We should still leave her."

"I can't leave her. She's my sister."

"But she looks too much like my mother," Darcy says. "I hate my mother."

"But I *want* to see my mother," Tick says. "I've been waiting my whole life to see her."

"You told me you hated your mother," Darcy screams.

"That wasn't me saying that," Tick says. "That was some other version of me you made up in your head."

Darcy sits down and looks away from him. She rubs her eyes with her gnarled fists.

"Just do it for me," she says.

Tick grabs the glow suit so he can go across the hall to the bathroom. He has nothing else to say to Darcy. There's no way he would ever leave his sister like that.

"The other version of you would do it for me," Darcy says, as he steps out of the room with glowing white skin.

It's the first time Tick has worn the glow suit. The fabric is very thin and covers his entire body, even his head and feet. The glow is as bright as a high-watt light bulb and it emanates from his whole body.

In the bathroom mirror, he watches himself illuminate the room. He feels like an angel descending from heaven, shining magnificence across a world of shadow.

The strange sight helps him forget about the conversation with Darcy for a moment, but it doesn't take long for the thoughts to come flooding back. He wishes his Darcy was more like the old Darcy. This new one is too selfish, too crazy.

"How could she ever think I would leave Polly?" Tick says to the mirror. "Would we have just left her to die in a room somewhere? Who could do such a thing?"

He also doesn't understand why she'd go through all the trouble of fixing Polly's broken bones only to abandon her a moment later. Did she realize they would have left her with no light or food or water? Did she know that Polly would have died? Tick wonders if she's not able to grasp the consequences of her actions.

After he uses the bathroom and washes Polly's blood from his face and hands, he returns to the room to find that it's completely dark inside.

"What's going on?" he says.

He looks through the room, wondering if the cage of light has run out of power. But it doesn't make sense. He thought it generated its own power.

"Darcy, where's the light?" he asks.

But when he looks up, he realizes that Darcy is gone. Drool

is gone. Even Leech is gone. They took the cage of light and left.

"Darcy?"

He goes out into the hallway and looks in both directions. There is no light coming from either path.

"Darcy!" Tick yells out.

His voice echoes down the hallway. There is no reply. Darcy is long gone. He has been left all alone with his severely injured sister and a glow suit that has only twenty minutes of power remaining.

CHAPTER EIGHTEEN

"Polly, wake up." Tick frantically pushes at his sister in the bed. "We have to get moving. Quick."

The shadows in the corner of the room shift and growl. Black antlers scrape against the walls.

"Come on," he says, shaking her violently. "We don't have much time."

It takes her a while before she even opens her eyes.

Her voice is sluggish. "What's going on? Why are you glowing?"

"Darcy left and took our light," he says. "We only have this glow suit now."

"Our light's gone?" She tries to sit up but can hardly move the middle section of her body. "I told you not to trust her."

"We only have twenty minutes to find another light," he says.

"It's impossible," Polly says. "We'll never be able to find one in time."

Tick tries to help her up from the bed.

"We have to try," he says.

When he gets her into an upright position, she shrieks and holds her side. Then she falls back to the bed.

"I can't," she cries. "I can't move."

"You *have* to move."

"Leave me here," she says. "I might be safe if I lock the door and keep quiet."

"There are creepers inside the room," Tick says, trying to pick her back up. "They already know you're here."

"You'll move faster without me," she says.

"You'll die if I leave you."

Tick doesn't have time to argue with her anymore. He drags

her to her feet no matter how much she screams out or tells him to stop. She leans all of her weight onto him, unable to move most of her body except the lower part of her legs.

"Come on," he says. "Try to walk."

Because she's so much bigger than Tick, he can barely hold up her weight. They move one step at a time until they reach the door. By the time they get out into the hallway, Tick and Polly are already both exhausted. There's no time for rest.

"Ignore the pain," Tick says.

Polly tries her best to walk on her own, but it's impossible. The best she can do is to try not to put so much weight onto Tick.

"Where's the next nursery?" she asks. "If I could get some more painkillers…"

Tick shakes his head.

"The closest one is at least an hour away," he says. "We'll never make it."

"Then what do we do?" she asks.

"Let's just go room to room," he says. "One of these rooms might have power or a light."

They check every door they come to, but there's nothing in the rooms. Most of them are large and empty, as if they haven't been moved into yet. One of them is filled with boxes which might contain lights they could use, but they decide it would take too long to search through them and move on.

Polly gets heavier the further they go.

"We're not going to make it, are we?" she says.

"Just keep going," Tick says, dragging her along.

"Leave me here," she says. "It's useless."

"No," he says. "I made a decision when we left the room. We're either both going to make it or neither of us are."

"You're an idiot, Tick," she says. "I would have left you."

Tick laughs. He knows she wouldn't have really left him if things were reversed. She's too big of a coward to go on all by herself.

CARLTON MELLICK III

When the twenty minutes are up, they are still in the hallways without another light source. The glow suit flickers and fades, getting ready to go out at any second.

"This is it," Tick says. "A few more minutes and then we'll be in the dark."

"You never should have trusted that girl," Polly says.

"I don't regret trusting her," he says. "I just wish things would have turned out differently. I should have spoken to her more."

Tick looks like a dim brown light bulb walking through the halls. The suit lasts a little longer than expected. They make it to the end of the hallway, turn a corner and it's still lit, just barely.

"I wish I would have met Mom and Dad," Polly says. "That's all I wanted. I don't want to die without even meeting them."

"Who says we're going to die?" Tick asks.

"What do you mean? Once the light goes out the creepers are going to get us."

"Not necessarily," Tick says. "Remember what Darcy said? They hunt by sound. If we keep really quiet they might not notice us."

"But listen to how loud we are," Polly says. "We're panting too heavily, our shoes make echoes with each step, and I can't guarantee I won't scream out in pain at any given moment."

"We can do it," Tick says. "Just move one inch at a time. Take shallow breaths. Only focus on keeping quiet."

"But do you really think we'll get anywhere in the dark?" she asks.

"We'll have to feel along the walls," Tick says. "I have one idea of where we can go."

The suit makes a clicking-pop noise, like a light bulb as it dies. Then the power goes out and they are swallowed by darkness. They freeze in their tracks. Their sense of sight is completely wiped black.

They try not to even breathe.

In the dark, raspy breaths hit the backs of their necks. They are in the middle of a crowd of the creatures. The pungent smell of wet animal fills their nostrils. Shaggy hair brushes against jagged horns. Wiry tongues lap drool onto pointed teeth.

Polly tightens her grip on Tick's hand. They see absolutely nothing. There's no light in any direction. But they can sense the beasts all around them as they grunt and snort in their ears.

For several minutes, they don't even move. They just stand there in the dark wondering if the creatures will notice them. Although they are surrounded by beasts, nothing attacks them. Not yet. The crowd moves around them, traveling as a pack.

One bumps Polly in the back, slamming into her with a loud grunt. Polly's rib pops out of place for a moment and she bites her tongue, trying not to shriek at the pain. Tears pour from her eye.

When they don't hear any of the beasts in front of them, they take small steps forward. Polly trembles in Tick's grasp. Moving this slowly is even more painful for her than moving quickly. The creatures continuously bump into them or brush against their arms, sending shooting pains through Polly's bones even at the slightest touch.

Tick can only think of one option to find light. There is supposed to be a row of elevators up ahead. If the elevators work, maybe they can take it up to the third floor, where the power was on when they were up there earlier.

It takes them what seems like hours to get to where the elevators are supposed to be, but they can't find anything in the dark. Tick feels along the walls with his free hand, searching for doors or buttons, but there's nothing there. Just a flat wall.

He feels along until he touches the chest of a creeper leaning against a wall, scraping its antlers as if to sharpen them. It turns around and shrieks in his face. Tick doesn't move. He just closes his eyes and tries not to breathe as the thing yells at him, bouncing rancid hot breath against his forehead. The sounds it makes are a combination of grunts, snorts, and screams, as if it's some kind of language, scolding Tick for not watching where he's going. Tick stands there, trying not to breathe or move a muscle until it gets bored of shouting and wanders off. Then they continue to move, one step at a time. The elevators are nowhere to be found.

Tick wonders how long they will be able to survive in the dark with the creepers. Will they have to attempt to sleep around them? Find food and water in the dark around them? How long can they keep it up?

Polly can barely move now. Tick feels her weight becoming heavier against him. Her head dangles forward on her neck like she's passing out drunk. She's about to drop to the floor at any minute.

Just when Polly is about to give up and fall to her knees, something grabs their attention. It's the sound of footsteps. A dim light appears in the distance. It becomes brighter. The footsteps become louder. Polly taps excitedly on Tick's arm, signaling him to look forward. But he doesn't need her to signal him. There's no way he could miss it.

Up ahead, a maid comes around a corner and enters the hallway. It is an exact replica of the maid they saw before, only this one is still functioning.

As it moves, a section of the ceiling brightens above it, shining down over the robot. The light moves along the ceiling with it, only one panel of light shining at a time, as if to preserve power. Tick doesn't understand how the robot is able to turn the lights on above it. There are no switches. It's like the robot can remotely control the power of the lighting using its internal circuits.

Polly and Tick smile when they see the maid. But then their smiles fade when the robot moves in the opposite direction down the hall, away from them. They try to speed their pace to catch up, but even at the maid's casual walking pace she's just too fast for them.

"Hey," Polly yells to the robot. "Over here. Help us!"

Tick squeezes Polly's wrists. He whispers, "What are you doing? You're going to get us killed."

"Come back," Polly says. "We need your help!"

The maid doesn't notice them. She continues moving through the hallway, going about her standard routine. The creepers, on the other hand, turn toward her voice. Their eyes glare at her, gnashing their teeth, aiming their antlers forward.

"Run," Tick yells.

Polly hesitates only for a minute. Then she pushes herself off of Tick and runs on her own. The pain is intolerable at first, but soon the shock and adrenaline kick in and cause her to go numb.

"Get behind me," she says.

She lowers her antlers and rams the oncoming creepers out of the way like a deer in mating season. Once they break free from the crowd, they just have to run.

"Wait for us," Tick screams.

The creepers scream and snarl at their heels. The horde is so dense their antlers clack and scrape against each other. Polly slows down and Tick has to push her forward. When they reach the light above the maid, they fall to the ground. The creepers dissipate around them. Polly rolls over to catch her breath.

The maid continues moving, taking the light with her. Just before Polly is resubmerged into the shadows, Tick yells, "Stop."

The maid stops.

The two children drop their heads to the floor and let their muscles relax, catching their breath under the safety of one small panel of light.

The maid doesn't say anything. She just stands in place, obeying the stop order.

"Do you speak?" Tick asks her.

The robot does not respond, just staring forward.

"Can you help us?"

Tick goes to the front of the robot. She has a calm look on her face. She's not like Nanny. She doesn't speak or have the same spark of life. Nanny must have been a much more sophisticated machine.

"Where did you come from? Are there people in your section of the house?"

She looks a little older than Polly, but with short purple hair and no antlers. Her big purple eyes look wet as if she's about to cry, but that's impossible. They must be self-lubricating or have a gloss coat.

"We need you to guide us."

Tick helps Polly to her feet. As he holds her up, getting ready to continue their journey, he says, "Move forward."

The maid moves forward. Tick and Polly walk behind her, but she goes too quickly. They almost fall behind, into the shadows.

"Slow down," Tick says.

The maid slows down.

"Help me carry Polly," Tick says.

Tick is surprised to see the maid turn around, step slowly to Polly and pick her up. She carries her like a stack of pillows in her mechanical arms.

"Okay, now let's keep going," Tick says.

They travel through the hallways for a couple of hours, one

panel of light at a time, exploring the ground floor. Other than the maid, there are no signs of life. Nothing seems to work. Tick wonders if the maid can help more than just carrying Polly or lighting the way for them.

"Do you know where our parents are?" Tick asks the robot.

The robot doesn't respond.

"What are you doing?" Polly asks him. "She doesn't know anything."

"But what if she does? Just because she can't speak doesn't mean she doesn't know things."

"Take us to our parents," Tick says.

The robot continues walking forward.

"Take us to the owners of the house," he says.

The robot stops.

Polly and Tick look at each other.

It pauses there for a moment. Then the maid turns around. She takes a different route, turning a corner, heading into a more ornate hallway with flowery red carpeting and ancient Chinese vases on display.

"It's working," Tick says. "We're going there."

They still spend hours traversing through the massive building, but now they have hope. The shadows don't seem as dark. The house doesn't seem as dead. Their smiles don't leave their faces.

"We're going to make it, Polly," Tick says. "We're going to be okay."

He looks up at Polly to see she's shaking. Sweat pours down her face.

"No, we're not," Polly says.

"Why?"

"I can feel another fit coming on."

"You have to fight it," Tick says, but Polly is already grinding her teeth and growling.

Tick turns to the maid.

"We have to move faster," he tells the maid. "Run."

The maid picks up her pace until she is at a running speed, as Polly twitches in her arms. Tick runs alongside them, trying to keep up.

"Hang on, Polly," Tick says. "Just relax."

But the fit hits her as violently as always. She whips her arms around and kicks her legs at the maid.

"Restrain her," Tick says. "Don't let her get away."

The maid tightens her grip around Polly, holding her in the air as the young woman thrashes and bites. She just allows herself to be attacked as Polly swings her antlers and rams them into her chest.

"Keep moving," Tick says.

Polly screams and struggles. She can no longer feel pain and is likely splitting her wound open again. The maid charges forward, racing down the hall. The creepers scratch and shriek around them.

When Tick sees it, he can't believe his eyes. Up ahead, at the end of the hallway, there are double doors with light shining through the cracks. The power works beyond those doors. Tick wonders if this is really it, the place they've been looking for. He wonders if this really is where his parents have been all this time.

"We're almost there, Polly," Tick says. "Hold on."

Tick doesn't see it happen. He just hears a loud crack and a shower of sparks and then the maid's head flying into the shadows. The robot falls to the ground and Polly pulls herself out of its dead arms. Tick falls back when he sees his raving mad sister impale the maid repeatedly with her antlers, cutting open the maid uniform with her stumpy claws.

The light above them is still on. Destroying the robot did not switch it off. But it is only one panel of light. Tick needs to keep her in that small area until she calms down. He doesn't speak. He just sits there, keeping his guard, watching the girl tear apart the corpse of the dead robot.

But the maid doesn't hold her interest for long. The creepers surround them in the shadows, growling and clacking their antlers together. Polly looks up from the robot and growls at the creatures in the dark. She kneels down and arches her back as if preparing to lunge forward and attack.

Tick jumps at her and wraps his arms around her legs just before she leaves the light, holding her in place. Polly looks down at him with her ravenous red eye. Then she turns her attack on him.

"Polly, stop," Tick yells, as his sister slams her antlers against his back. "Snap out of it."

She punches and claws at him, but Tick won't let her go. He allows her to tear open his shirt and slice up his flesh.

"Stop…"

This goes on for quite some time, so long that Tick goes numb, but it doesn't go on long enough to return Polly back to normal. With all the creepers in the shadows around them, she eventually loses interest in Tick. She gets off of him, then screams and claws at the darkness. Tick tries to hold her in place with all of his strength.

"Don't," Tick cries. "Don't attack them. Attack me."

But she slides out of his grasp and connects antlers with a creeper in the shadows. Tick gets to his feet and grabs her around the waist, pulling her back into the light.

"Come on," Tick yells.

He slaps her on the back and she turns to him, snarling.

"Attack me," he cries.

She arches her back in an attack stance, growling at him and glaring hungrily into his eyes.

Then Tick runs into the darkness. Polly follows.

"Come on," he cries. "Attack me!"

Tick runs down the corridor toward the lighted doors. Polly chases after him.

"Attack me!"

She's not as fast with her wounds, so she can't catch up to him, clawing at the air behind his back. He continues hollering at her to keep her attention on him, so she doesn't notice all the creepers they pass in the darkness.

"Tick? What's going on?"

Polly has regained her senses, waking to find herself in the dark.

"Keep running," he says. "We're almost there."

When the pain returns to Polly, it shoots through her chest and she nearly collapses to the ground.

"Tick..." she says.

He goes back and blindly grabs her in the dark, then helps carry her toward the end of the corridor. With their speed lowered dramatically, the creepers close in on them.

"Faster," Tick yells.

The screams and rancid smells of the creepers hit them on the backs of their necks. When they burst through the double doors and fall to the ground, the creatures pop out of existence as the light floods the hallway.

When they get to their feet and look around, they see a crowd of adults staring back at them.

CHAPTER NINETEEN

"Where in the world did they come from?"

"Are they children?"

"What are children doing in the house?"

Tick and Polly stagger forward into the elegant ballroom with crystal chandeliers and glistening ice sculptures—their clothes torn to shreds, dirt and wounds covering their skin, blood dripping onto the spotless tile floor.

"People…" Tick says.

There are so many of them, dozens of adults in black tuxedos and long elegant white evening gowns. The men have gold jewelry and military metals decorating their coats. The women have antlers that reach all the way to the ceiling, wrapped in ribbons and bows, with gems dangling from the tips like holiday trees.

"Ewww, they're so gross," one woman says, giggling.

"They're like sick stray dogs," says a large man with a great yellow beard, chuckling so loudly he almost spills his flute of champagne.

"Look at how small her claws and antlers are," a woman says, pointing at Polly. "She's practically a guy!"

Tick and Polly can't find the right words to speak. The adults gather around them. They all seem so powerful and frightening to the children. Each one of them so pristine and majestic.

"We're looking for our parents," Tick says.

They all laugh and applaud their words, as if they are the most amusing things they've seen in a long time.

One of the women looks similar to the mother Tick used to draw back in the nursery. She has long green curled hair like Polly. She's the prettiest woman in the room.

Tick steps toward her and asks, "Are you my mom?"

She nearly falls over with laughter as Tick comes near.

"No, no, no!" she giggles. "Get it away!"

Tick turns from her and steps to the middle of the group.

"Who owns the house?" he asks. "Our parents are supposed to own this house."

A drunken couple steps forward. They wear the most elegant attire of anyone in the room. Like a king and queen with glittering crystal clothing.

"We own the house," says the man, taking a last swig of his drink. "But I don't remember having any kids." He turns to his wife. "Do you remember having any kids, my darling?"

She shrugs and then giggles. "No, I'm pretty certain I'd remember if we made any children."

They touch their finger tips together and wiggle them around in some kind of flirtatious finger-kiss. Then they turn to the children.

"Were you born in this house?" asks the man, leaning down to Tick.

"Yes," Tick says, inching away from his piercing gaze. "We came from Nursery #507."

The man straightens up and looks back at his wife.

"So that explains it," he says. "They're the previous owner's kids."

"Previous owners?"

"About a decade ago, they went bankrupt and lost this house. They must have left the birthing machine going."

"What's a birthing machine?"

"That's the place where little babies come from," says the woman, leaning down and making a cutesy condescending baby voice. "Mommies and daddies insert their DNA inside the big birther, then it grows eggs and sends them to all the nurseries in the house where they grow up to be big boys and girls."

"So our parents don't even know we were born?"

"Don't know and don't care," says the man. "They aban-doned this place a long time ago. They're probably dead in a gutter somewhere."

Tick can do nothing but cry. They've come all this way, been through so much, just to learn this. The crowd laughs and cheers when they see his tears fall.

"Nanny died," he says, crying. "Our nursery caught on fire. We had to survive in the dark with the creepers. How could Mom and Dad leave us to that?"

The owners look at each other with confused expressions.

"What's a creeper?" asks the woman.

The yellow bearded adult says, "I think they mean the natives."

The male owner looks down at Tick. "Is that what you mean? The Terramytes? I guess there would be tons of them lurking inside an old house like this…"

"Terra…what?" Tick asks.

"Terramytes," he says. "They were the native people of this planet before we colonized it. They were a savage race. Brutal."

"Like animals," says the woman.

"Yes," continues the man. "They were too territorial and wouldn't give up their land. So, naturally, we had to wipe them out. What else could we do? It's not like we could go back to Earth. That place is nothing but a garbage dump now."

"Nobody of any significance lives there anymore," says the woman.

"Yes," continues the man. "So we killed off every Terramyte on the planet."

The yellow bearded man chuckles. "Only the bastards didn't die!"

"Yes," says the man. "Their ghosts, you see, are different than the ghosts of humans. When they die, their spirits remain alive in the shadow realm. They are ghosts just like the ghosts of humans when in the light, but in the dark they become solid living beings."

"And the buggers are impossible to kill," says the yellow bearded man. "We finally wiped them all out only to make them indestructible."

"They usually aren't that dangerous," says the female owner. "The shadow gates normally keep them out."

"Yes," says the male. "We have blockades set up in the shadow realm. In the light, humans can pass through them, but nothing can get through in the dark. The shadow gates around this house must have crumbled a long time ago. They'll need to be repaired eventually."

The other adults seem bored with the children. They move away and socialize in their own circles. It is some kind of cocktail party. When Tick looks over at Polly he sees she's not doing very well. The excitement of meeting the adults is fading. The damage caused by walking on her wounds is taking over.

"My sister needs help," Tick says. "She's seriously hurt."

"Eww," says the woman, examining Polly carefully. "You're right. She needs a doctor... or a vet."

Tick is bleeding from the antler cuts on his back, but he doesn't care about himself right now. He needs to save his sister.

"You're a doctor, aren't you, Mortimer?" the male says to the yellow bearded man.

"Yes, yes," says Mortimer. He holds up his glass. "But I've had too much to drink to practice medicine tonight." Then he looks at Polly and chuckles. "Plus the young lady could never afford my fees!"

Everyone chuckles and applauds the doctor. Then they change the subject, ignoring the children and their cries for help.

Tick helps Polly to a couch and lies her down.

As the female owner of the house sees them dirtying her nice furniture with their blood and filth, she calmly marches away from her guests and whispers in Tick's ear.

"Not there," she says.

She snaps her fingers and an old servant comes forward. He lifts Polly to her feet.

"This way," the woman says. "Let's get them out of sight."

They take the children out of the ballroom into the back kitchen where servants quickly prepare hors d'oeuvres and cocktails for the guests. There is a couch in a lounge beyond the kitchen.

When Polly is dropped off, the lady of the house says, "Take care of them until the party's over. Then drop them off at one of the education centers."

"Yes, my lady," says the servant.

As the woman leaves, she says. "And get somebody to stop the birthing machine. We don't need any more of these things popping up all over the place like cockroaches."

When she's gone, the servant hands the children a plate of sausages and mushroom pockets. They guzzle it all down within minutes. He is an older gentleman with a small grey mustache and a bald scalp.

"Why do they use birthing machines?" Tick asks the servant. "I thought mothers gave birth to their babies. Is it so they don't have to go through the pregnancy themselves?"

The servant gives Polly some strong painkillers. Then he cleans her wounds. He answers Tick's questions as he works.

"They have to use them," says the servant. "It's the only way humans can reproduce these days." He replaces Polly's bandages with sterile cloth. "A long time ago, when humans colonized this planet, they learned that the atmosphere was unsuitable for human life. It caused women to become barren. Humans could no longer reproduce. To save themselves from extinction, humans had to alter their DNA. They crossbred with the local natives." He pointed at Polly's antlers. "This resulted in many changes in human anatomy."

"Humans now reproduce using a birthing mother," says the servant. "The natives didn't have only two genders. They had three. All three are needed in order to reproduce. There is a mother, a father, and a birthing mother."

"So the birthing machine isn't a machine?" Tick asks. "It's a person?"

"They are living beings, but they are not viewed as real people in this society. They have to be biologically engineered. Because they are created and not born they are seen as machines. Only the wealthiest citizens can afford them."

"The kind that are rich enough to afford a house this big?" Tick asks.

The servant nods and gets them a second helping of food.

"This house is what they call a Super Mansion," says the servant. "There are dozens of them on this planet. Each one is like a nation in itself. There is one birthing mother per household, kept in the basement level of the mansion, which populates the house with children. These children are like the citizens of the nation. The owners of the house are like the rulers."

"They sound like insects," Tick says.

"Humans have become very much like insects," says the servant. "Each Super Mansion is like a hive, populating a workforce to serve the parents."

"It sounds horrible."

The servant shakes his head. "It's not as cold as it sounds. The people are happy. Some are even allowed to be artists, entertainers, scientists or philosophers. It's a comfortable lifestyle. The people in the nation usually intermarry, but are not allowed to have children. Only the parents of the household are able to reproduce until they name successors to take their place."

"So people only live in these mansions? Nobody lives outside?"

"Actually, there are many cities outside the mansions," says the servant. "Not all children stay in the home after they are born. Many move out into the cities. It's not as comfortable of a lifestyle but some people prefer the freedom from their parents' rule."

Polly groans on the couch. She looks pale. Although the pain killers have cured her discomfort, she is still in serious condition.

"She's not looking well," the servant says, touching her forehead.

"What can we do?" Tick asks.

"There's a medical station on this floor, a couple of miles

away," says the servant.

"Does it work?"

"The operating machines should be functional," he says. "If not I can get them going again."

"Then we should go," Tick says, trying to help Polly up.

The servant pushes her back down.

"No, no," he says. "I can arrange transportation. She should be taken by hall car."

Then he leaves the kitchen in a rush.

While waiting for the servant, Tick holds Polly's hand. He's upset about their parents, but is happy they have made it someplace safe, away from the creepers.

"I don't buy it…" Polly says.

"What?"

"All of this," she says. "It doesn't seem real."

"How do you mean?"

"This party. These people. How can they be in the middle of this dark dead house, acting so casual? It's creepy."

"The house is old. They haven't fixed it up yet."

"They're ghosts," Polly says. "Just like the creepers in the hallways. They're just ghosts that live in the light instead of the dark."

"But we spoke to them. They have to be real."

"Do you remember when we saw the outside of the house?" she asks. "There were no signs of life anywhere. It wasn't just this house that was dead, it was all the houses. It was the whole planet. Civilization fell a long time ago."

"But they're right here," Tick says. He points at the servants preparing food in the kitchen. "Right in front of us."

"These people can't be real," she says. "They don't belong here."

The children wait for an hour, but the servant doesn't return. Tick leaves the couch and peeks out of the kitchen door to find the servant in the ballroom, serving drinks and food to the guests.

"Has he forgotten about us?" Tick asks.

He enters the ballroom and signals the servant.

"Aren't we taking my sister to the medical station like you said?"

The servant looks at him as if he has no idea what he's talking about. He doesn't even recognize Tick. None of the people in the room recognize Tick.

When the party guests see him, they say the same things they said when he first arrived.

"Where in the world did he come from?"

"Is that a child?"

"What is a child doing in the house?"

It is the same people who said those things before.

Polly staggers into the room behind Tick and gives him a look.

"I told you," she says.

Tick tries to get Polly to sit back down and get off her feet, but she refuses. The pain killers are strong enough to keep her going for now.

"Look at how small her claws and antlers are," a woman says, pointing at Polly. "She's practically a guy!"

Then the children notice the weird people. Many party guests are in the center of the room, frozen in place, vibrating and staring forward. Some of them are trapped halfway inside the walls, wiggling back and forth. One of the servants is on top of the ceiling, walking around with a bottle of champagne, as if trying to serve a group of invisible guests.

"It's like our school," Polly says. "It's all a simulation. None of it is real."

"But when we went to the school, only our minds were

192

teleported inside," Tick says. "Not our whole bodies."

"This is probably a different kind of virtual reality program," Polly says. "A holographic room. Different technology, but basically the same kind of thing."

They explore the room, ignoring the annoying party guests that swarm them with questions. There is a door leading out of the hall into a large bedroom. The room has dim lighting, lit by a cage of light exactly like the one Tick and Polly used in order to get around the mansion.

In the bed, there lie the remains of an adult human being who must have died in his sleep. The corpse has probably been there for years, maybe decades.

"He's probably the one who was running the simulation," Polly says. "The last living adult in this house, spending his final days living inside a fictional world."

"He had food, water, light, and companionship," Tick says. "I guess that's all he needed."

They search the room and come across a dusty book by the side of his bed. When they blow on the cover, it creates a cloud of dust in the brown air.

"It's his journal," Polly says.

She scans through the pages, picking out useful bits of information. Tick waits patiently as she reads through section after section, trying to learn all she can about the life of this dead adult lying before them.

"It says the planet was abandoned ten years ago," Polly says.

"Ten years before he wrote that, you mean," Tick says. "Who knows how long ago it really was. It could have been fifty years since he died."

Polly ignores her brother's comment. She continues, "The people here created a device that would change the orbits of the other planets in the solar system, bringing them closer to the sun so they could be terraformed."

"What does that mean?"

Polly shakes her head. "But something went wrong. Now all

the planets in the system are slowly coming together. They're on a collision course with each other. It won't happen for another two hundred years, but eventually the worlds will collide and this system will come to an end."

"That's why we could see all those planets in the sky?" Tick says. "I wonder how long we have left…"

Polly continues, "Once the people of this planet found another inhabitable world, they abandoned this one. This man here says he chose to stay behind, because he wanted to die in the place where he was born."

"So why did they leave the power on?" Tick asks. "Why did they allow children to still be born after they left?"

"Maybe this guy is responsible," Polly says. "He turned the power on for his own sake, not realizing everything else that was going on in the house."

Tick lets out a long sigh when Polly finally closes the journal and puts it aside. At least he knows what really happened to his parents now; they left the planet with everyone else. It is kind of a relief to know for sure, but it makes him feel alone and small. Irrelevant.

He goes to the cage of light in the corner of the room. When he touches it, the room brightens. Tick wonders if the cage of light is a common style of lighting in this house. Like a lantern that never needs more fuel. With it, they will be safe from the creepers.

"Come on," Tick says, heading toward the exit.

"Where to now?" Polly says.

"Let's get you to the medical station," he says. "We still need to fix you up."

CHAPTER TWENTY

Staggering down the corridors with the cage of light, Tick and Polly come across something they weren't expecting to find. A girl is standing in the dark, frozen in place, trying not to breathe so that the creepers don't attack her.

"Is that Darcy?" Polly asks.

When they get closer, Tick realizes that it is her, staring at them, a wild look in her eyes.

"What is she doing in the dark?"

Darcy jumps into their light once they get close enough and falls to her knees, trying to catch her breath.

"You have to help me," Darcy says.

"What happened?" Tick asks.

When Tick gets to her, he sees Leech strapped to her back, sleeping peacefully. The bug probably doesn't even realize she was just in the dark with a pack of creepers.

"Drool," Darcy says. "He took my light and left."

Tick pulls Leech off of her back and straps her to his. When her big eyes open to see him, she squirts and squeaks excitedly, probably because she thinks she's going to get fed.

"*Your* light?" Polly cries. "You stole that light from us and left us to die. Looks like you got a taste of your own medicine."

"You have to help me find him," Darcy cries. "He's practically a baby. He'll die out there on his own."

"Not our problem," Polly says. "You abandoned us, so why shouldn't we abandon you."

"I didn't abandon you," Darcy says. "I was just upset and ran away. Once I realized what I was doing, I came back and you were gone."

"Sure you did."

"I went looking for you," Darcy cries. She looks at Tick. "Honestly, I did."

Tick looks back at her. He can't tell if she's telling the truth or not.

She goes to him and holds him by the hand, trying to communicate with him through the warmth in her palm.

"Please," she says, her eyes sopping wet. "He's all I have."

"Fine," Polly says. "But not for you. We'll do it for the bug kid."

Darcy drops Tick's hand and goes to Polly. "Thank you!"

"But there's one condition," Polly says.

"What?"

"Give me your knife," she says. "I don't trust you around sharp objects."

"But I need it to protect myself," Darcy says.

"Against what?" Polly says. "You can't hurt the creepers with it. Your mother is imaginary. The only people you can hurt with it are us and yourself. You don't need it."

Darcy looks down. Before she can get it out herself, Polly grabs it out of her belt and tosses it over her shoulder. Darcy watches as it lands in the darkness, far out of reach.

"Lead the way." Polly turns the girl around and pushes her forward. "And if you try to take our light one more time, I'll ram my antlers into your eyeballs."

Darcy says that Drool left her because a vision of his mother told him to find her in the basement levels. When Darcy refused to take him there, he threw a tantrum, stole the light when she wasn't paying attention, and ran away from her.

"Are you thinking what I'm thinking?" Tick asks Polly, as they travel through the halls, searching for the bug boy.

Polly looks over at him.

"The servant said that the birthing mother lived in the

basement levels," Tick says.

"But he wasn't real," Polly says. "That was all an illusion."

"Just because the people were fake doesn't mean the information wasn't real. What if the birthing mother still lives down there? What if she's the one who has been coming to us in our dreams?"

"You think she's still alive down there?" Polly asks.

"I'm sure of it," Tick says. "How do you think Leech was born? Or either of us? She must still be down there, giving birth to new children all the time."

"What are you two talking about?" Darcy asks.

Tick explains much of the information that they just learned about the house and their species. She just listens, but does not react.

"We don't have just two parents," Tick says. "We have three of them. A mother, a father, and a third parent called a birthing mother."

"She's the one who actually gave birth to us," Polly says.

"She's our *real* mom," Tick says.

"I don't care," Darcy says. "Let's just find Drool."

But Tick and Polly are excited by the idea of meeting one of their parents. Their birthing mother has called to them in their dreams for so long. She probably needs their help. She's been locked down in the basement for so long. Somebody has to set her free.

"What is this?" Polly asks.

They come to a staircase in the center of the corridor. It is not the typical stairwell they have traveled through in the past. This is a small spiral staircase made of black metal, twisting into the ground like a drill.

"This is it," Tick says. "It's our way into the basement."

"Are you sure the kid went down there?" Polly asks.

Darcy goes to the steps and looks down into the black hole.

"He must have," she says.

Then she goes down.

"Mommy!"

As they descend the algae-covered metal staircase, they can hear Drool's voice echoing through the basement.

"Drool?" Darcy shouts out.

He's too far away to see.

The basement is a deep cavernous pit. Yellow stalactites hang from the ceiling like demon fangs. A green mist rises in the air. It doesn't feel like they are inside the house anymore. It's like they are descending into a swampy canyon.

The basement doesn't have any rooms. It is just one large pit a hundred miles wide. And it's so deep it would take up five floors of the house if it were above ground.

"Mommy, where are you?" Drool cries through the mist.

He's somewhere down there, but he could be anywhere. Tick and Darcy scan the canyon as they descend the rickety staircase. They don't look for Drool, they search for the light he was carrying. But there are many lights scattered across the basement. They look like hundreds of tiny birthday candles across a giant cake.

"Drool, where are you?" Darcy calls out. "Come to us."

The closer to the ground they get, the slimier and more rusted the steps become. Polly nearly slips off twice, catching herself on the wobbly railing.

"Mommy! Mommy!" the boy's voice continues.

"How can she be down here?" Polly asks. "This is a dungeon."

"She wasn't treated like a human," Tick says. "They thought of her as a machine. She's probably locked in a cell somewhere down here."

"Or she doesn't really exist."

When they get to the ground, their feet sink in the mud. It instantly sucks them down to their ankles like quicksand.

"Drool went through this?" Darcy cries.

They see holes in the mud that trail off into the distance. He must have sunk all the way down past his knees. It's amazing that he was able to keep moving through it at his size.

"Mommy…" Drool's voice echoes faintly.

"It sounds like he's getting further away," Tick says.

"Let's hurry," Darcy says.

They travel slowly through the mire, following the sound of the boy's voice. They come to one of the lights scattered across the basement ground. It is another cage of planets, lying on its side.

"Is it Drool's?" Darcy asks.

Tick examines it. The cage is covered in algae and a little rusted.

"No," Tick says, he hands it to Darcy to carry. "This one looks as if it's been here a while."

They continue on and find another cage of light. Then another. All the lights in the basement seem to be from the planetary cages. They seem to form a trail, creating a safe path through the swamp. It is safer following the lights. It doesn't feel so much like they are walking in quicksand. Based on the footprints in the mud, this is the direction Drool has gone.

"Mommy! Mommy!" Drool is screaming. He's no longer calling out to his mother, he's screaming for her.

Darcy picks up the pace, rushing through the green mist, leaping over rocks and massive clusters of mushrooms.

"Help me!" Drool cries. "Mommy, help me!"

When they see him, he is cowering beneath a creature as tall as the basement is deep. It's a giant blubbery mass, half-submerged in the quicksand. Black antlers the size of trees grow from its pale white skull, twisting into the mist above.

"Drool!" Darcy cries, rushing toward him.

The giant beast lowers its head and sucks Drool into its mouth, slurping him up with its black rubbery lips. The creature moans as it sucks on him, as if savoring his flavor.

"Mommy! Help me!"

Drool struggles and fights the creature, but he's smaller than even its tongue. Darcy doesn't care about the size of the thing. She runs through the quicksand toward it and grabs Drool by the arms.

"Mommy! Mommy!"

The boy isn't calling out for his real mother. He's calling out for Darcy—the girl who raised him ever since he was born.

"Save me, Mommy," Drool says. "Don't let it eat me."

"I'm right here, baby," Darcy says, tugging on his arms while punching the creature's goopy lips.

The creature's globe-like eyes peer down at Darcy as it consumes the child. She screams out, kicking and pulling on him, fighting against the suction.

Tick hands Leech off to Polly who tosses the bug on the ground, then rushes to help Darcy. He comes up behind her and grabs Drool by the waist. Using his feet to brace himself against the beast's mouth, he pulls with all his strength. With a smacking pop noise, Drool breaks free. They pick him up and run.

"Let's get out of here," Tick cries.

They flee through the mud, running away from the massive beast as quickly as they can. But their legs just don't go fast enough. They feel like they're sinking in quicksand.

"Where are you going, my darlings?"

The children freeze. Tick recognizes that voice. He's heard it almost every night since he was Drool's age. It's the voice of his paper mom.

He turns around.

"Aren't you happy to see me?" says their mother.

The voice is coming from the massive creature. Its black lips curl into a smile. Now that he looks more carefully, Tick can see that she resembles a human. Her eyes are big alien blue globes, but her nose and mouth resemble the shape of a woman's.

"It can't be…" Tick says.

"Is that her?" Polly asks, trembling under the size of the enormous woman. "The birthing mother?"

"Mommy's so happy to see you," says the beast, her voice booming across the cavernous dungeon. "I've been waiting so long for more of my lovely children to come to me."

The woman pulls herself out of the quicksand, exposing her insectoid lower abdomen. Her form is somewhere between human, animal, and insect. Mud-caked breasts dangle from her chest like useless blobs of pudding. Her belly swells out, rumbling and sloshing. A crusted hole of a belly button hangs in the center. Tubes run out of her lower abdomen, connecting to the ceiling in a dozen directions.

"Are you the birthing mother?" Tick asks her.

The creature smiles.

"I am the Human Queen," she says. "I am mother of all children in this hive. Each year, over a hundred of my eggs are sent above to the nests where you grow big and strong."

The blubbery giant rolls forward like a worm, shaking the ground around them.

"My mates have left me alone," says the queen. "Left me to fend for myself. I was regularly fed through tubes to keep me satiated. But one day, the food stopped coming."

The creature rolls closer, but the children do not flee. They are hypnotized by their mother's gaze.

"So I implanted a message into the embryo of every egg I laid," she says. "*Come find me.* Those words echo through the mind of every one of my children as they grow up. And once they are old enough to leave the nursery, that's what they always do. They come find me."

Tick looks around at all of the cages of light littering the ground of the basement. All of them were brought by children who had come down to the basement, looking for their mother.

"It's so sad," the mother says. "But I must have food. I must survive, even if it means that I must eat my little darlings." She peers down on them, licking her lips with a fat white tongue. "Now, come to Mommy. Save her from this frightful hunger."

The creature opens her mouth toward the group of children. None of them move. They are too captivated to escape.

But just before her lips touch them, Tick holds out his hands and yells, "Stop!"

The mother opens her eyes and peers down.

"There's got to be another way," Tick says.

"Oh, there's no other way, my sweet boy," she says. "It is the new cycle of life. I lay eggs, they are hatched in nurseries, the children grow up, they come to me, I eat them, and then I am able to continue living to produce more eggs. If I don't eat, then the human species on this planet will die."

"But then what's the point in growing up if we're only to become food?"

"You had a happy childhood, didn't you?" she asks. "You were cared for and nurtured. You had a life better than most living beings. Your sacrifice will make it possible for future children to live as you did. You must see how necessary it is. Without your sacrifice, it all ends."

"It all ends anyway," Tick says. "The nurseries are dying. One by one, their power is going out. Your eggs have been going to dead nests. Our sacrifice will not be for the future of our species. It will be for nothing."

"You have seen these dead nests?" the queen asks.

"Yes," Tick says. "They must be fixed. If somebody doesn't do something to make these machines run again no children will be born."

"My children have visited me so rarely these past few years," she says. "I feared something like this might have happened. Are you capable of fixing these machines?"

"No, but I might be able to learn," Tick says.

"Very well," she says. "I will spare you so you can learn to fix the machines."

The mother opens her mouth over her other children.

"Hey," Tick cries. "I thought you said you would spare us?"

"I said I would spare *you*," she tells Tick. "Not the others."

"I can't fix the machines alone," Tick says. "I need them."

"But I must eat some of you," she says. "I haven't been fed in a very long time."

"You don't have to eat anyone," Tick says. "We can bring you something to eat from the food machines upstairs. It won't take us long."

"No," says the mother. "If anything happens to you along the way I will starve. At least one of you must be devoured."

The creature eyeballs the children one at a time.

"You there," she says to Polly. "Step forward."

Polly steps forward. Tick gets in front of her, trying to push her back.

"My darling, you can't possibly survive with that wound of yours," the creature says, smiling down on Polly. "Let Mommy eat you."

Polly tries to get past her brother, trying to step toward the queen's mouth.

"Let me end your suffering," the creature says.

"Polly, get away from her," Tick says.

"No," Polly says, looking at her brother. "She's right. We both know I'm not going to make it."

"You *will* make it," Tick says. "We just have to get you to the medical station."

"There is no medical station and you know it," she says. "Everything upstairs died a long time ago."

"We don't know for sure," Tick says. "We can at least try and see."

"Tick, stop." She looks him in the eyes. "Stop always trying to save me." She puts her hands on his shoulders. "I should have died a long time ago but you keep saving me and pushing me forward. Do you know how much pain I've had to endure because you wouldn't let me give up?"

She wraps her arms around him.

"I'm tired now," she says. "I want you to let me go."

Tick hugs her back, but he doesn't think he'll be able to let her go.

"That's my darling," says the creature. "That's a good girl. Good girls know how to make Mommy happy."

Polly leaves her brother and goes toward the birthing mother. The creature lowers her mouth to the girl.

"Come inside, my baby," whispers the creature. "Let me taste your love."

When Tick sees his sister entering the creature's mouth, an explosion of anger swells inside of him. He can't believe his sister would just let herself die like that after all they've been through. The birthing mother is not more important than Polly. The planet is going to die some day. There's no need to continue the human species. The birthing mother is not important at all anymore.

"Polly!" Tick cries, charging forward.

He grabs his sister by the antlers, pulling her back. The creature closes its lips around her lower body.

"I'm not letting you go," he says.

"What did I tell you?" Polly cries. "I said stop trying to save me."

"Do I ever listen to you?"

He takes her arms and pulls, pushing against his mother's lips.

"You're so useless," Polly cries.

Darcy joins him. She pulls a knife out of her boot and stabs the creature in the mouth. Although it doesn't cause major damage to the creature, it feels like a bee sting. The beast spits

Polly out and recoils.

Tick lifts Polly to her feet, holding her upright. His sister looks down at the crazy young girl pointing a knife at the creature.

"I thought I threw that away," Polly says, looking at the knife.

"You think I only had one knife?" Darcy says, smiling up at her.

The creature roars and shakes the earth beneath their feet.

"How dare you treat your mother this way," says the creature. "No good child would refuse to feed their poor hungry mother. You are all very bad children. Now you must all be eaten."

She opens her mouth to attack, moving too quickly for the children to run. But then something stops the queen. She freezes in place. Then she groans weakly.

"What is happening?" asks the mother. "Why am I dizzy? I'm so tired…"

The creature sways back and forth, as if unable to keep itself upright. When Tick sees what is causing her to go weak, he can hardly believe it. A pink balloon the size of a small hippopotamus is attached to the creature's back. The balloon swells larger and larger with each passing moment.

"Is that Leech?" Polly asks.

The baby has been drinking blood from the birthing mother this whole time, guzzling down an enormous feast. Tick realizes that it was all true. A human baby really does have a bottomless stomach.

"Stop eating your mommy," the creature says to Leech. "You're hurting your mommy."

The birthing mother tries to brush Leech away, but she doesn't have the strength. She loses consciousness and collapses into the mud, rumbling the ground beneath their feet.

The children look at each other, and then look back at the massive pink balloon Leech has become.

"Should we make her stop?" Darcy asks. "Or should we have her suck the rest of the monster's blood out?"

Tick shakes his head. "Let's stop her. If she drinks anymore she's going to burst."

Then they climb up on top of the blubbery creature, wondering how the heck they're going to roll the baby out of there.

"She's not what I was expecting," Polly says to her brother, staring down at the giant fleshy monster before them.

"Who?" Tick asks.

He watches over the giant squeaking ball of Leech as she rolls across the mud, making sure she doesn't pop on a sharp rock.

"Our mother," Polly says. "I thought she would be prettier."

Tick laughs. "I thought she would be shorter."

Polly smiles for a moment, but then it fades.

"So that's it," she says. "It's all over. At least I can die satisfied that I met my mother."

"You're not going to die," Tick says.

"Of course I am," Polly says.

"Look at you," Tick says. "You haven't died yet. You're still walking."

"It's just the painkillers."

"It doesn't matter what it is. The old type of human would have probably died by now. But you're not human. You're a hybrid of human and Terramyte. You're stronger than a normal human. Even if we never find a working medical station, I think you'll still survive."

Polly shrugs.

"It doesn't really matter if I survive now, does it?" she says. "There's nothing to live for. We have no future. Everybody is dead or gone. The house is in ruins. This is the end."

"It's not the end," Tick says. "It's only the beginning. We can rebuild this place."

"With what?"

"We have all of these lights." He points at all of the cages of planets spread across the basement. "We can be safe from the creepers. We can explore the house room by room and find all the other kids who live here. There are also surely some working robots and nannies who can help us fix things."

"But there are things that the robots and nannies might not know anything about, like how to fix robots."

"There are probably books on these things somewhere in the house. We also have a whole ballroom full of adults we can get information from."

"But those adults aren't real."

"Yeah, but neither were our school teachers and they taught us everything we know."

Darcy passes by, pulling lamps out of the mud with Drool. She whispers in Polly's ear, "Listen to him. He knows what he's talking about." Then she looks over at Tick and smiles before continuing on.

Polly shakes her head and gazes out across the flickering swamp.

"You think we can really do it?" Polly says.

Tick gives her a shoulder to lean on.

"Of course we can."

EPILOGUE

The bell rings outside Nursery #637.

Children jump out of the toy room with excitement, wondering if their dream is finally coming true. One is age five, the other is ten. Both of them have smiles that won't leave their faces.

"Nanny, what's that noise?" says the little girl.

"Well, I don't know, Sally," the nanny says. "Maybe it's your mommy and daddy coming to visit."

Both of the children look at each other with wide open mouths. They follow the nanny into the entry room and peek around the corner.

"Do you think it's really them?" Sally asks the boy.

"I don't know…" says the boy.

The nanny unlocks and unlatches the door, then opens it. There is a man and a woman standing in the doorway. When the children see them, their eyes sparkle. The man with his short dark hair and nicely pressed brown suit looks so smart and the girl with her tall majestic antlers and long blue hair looks so beautiful and nice.

"Come in," the nanny tells them. Then she turns to the little ones hiding in the hallway. "Children, you have visitors."

The kids step cautiously into the entryway, the smiles still on their faces. The little girl looks up at the woman with the long blue hair and giant antlers.

"Are you my mommy?" the girl asks.

The woman bends down and smiles at the child. "Yes, I am."

When she picks the girl up into her arms, the feeling of warmth overwhelms them both. The girl curls up against her mother's chest, digging her face into her clothes to absorb her scent.

The older brother steps toward the man.

"Is it true?" the boy asks. "Are you really our parents?"

"That's right," the man says, resting his hand on the boy's shoulder.

"Are you here for me?" the boy asks. "Is it time for you to take me away?"

The man nods. "You won't be taken too far. Just to another part of the house. There's a lot of work to be done. We could use your help."

"But what about Sally?" the boy asks. "She'll be left all alone."

"Don't worry about Sally," the father says. "She has a baby brother coming soon. She won't be alone. Plus, she has Nanny to look after her."

"But I'll miss her," he says.

The father is surprised to see he cares so much for a younger sibling. His own older sister would have left him in a second if she were in this boy's shoes.

"You'll see her again when she's your age," the father says. "It won't be so long."

"Can't I come visit her here?"

"Unfortunately, that would be too dangerous," says the father. "This area of the house is still unprotected."

"You mean, from the stalkers?"

"Yes," says the father. "The lower levels of the house have been made safe. There are shadow gates set up that make it impossible for the stalkers to enter. But up here, the hallways are dangerous. Once you leave, you must not return."

The boy nods his head.

"Now go pack your things," says the father. "We have a long journey ahead of us."

The boy nods again and runs to his room to get ready.

The father looks over at the little girl with her arms wrapped around his wife's neck. They giggle and rub each other's noses. They're instantly in love with one another. His wife has that effect on all of the children they've visited in the nurseries.

"Mommy, come look at my toys," the girl says.

The woman sets the girl down. "Okay, let's go play."

The little girl leads her by the hand down the hallway toward the toy room, laughing and yelling the whole way.

The man is left in the entry room with the nanny. She looks him up and down. Then she shakes her head.

"You're not really the masters of the house, are you?" the nanny asks.

The man smiles at her, surprised she's so quickly come to that conclusion.

"How'd you know?" he asks.

"You care too much for the children," she says. "Their real parents would have demanded their love without giving any in return."

The man snickers. "Well, their real parents abandoned this house a long time ago."

"What do you mean? How?"

"They found a better place to live and left the children behind. All the adults did."

"But you're an adult, aren't you?"

"I wasn't at the time," he says. "My wife, my sister, and I were merely children when we started bringing this house back together. We went from nursery to nursery, recruiting help from other kids. The first ten floors of this house have complete power now. Seventy-six people live there."

"Let's go into my room, just in case the children hear," says the nanny, her eyes peeking around the corner. "They aren't ready for this kind of information."

The man agrees. He follows the nanny into her quarters and sits down with her at a small table by the end of her bed.

"The younger kids started calling us Mother and Father," the man continues, "so we've kind of took on the role. We're not the oldest adults down there, but we seem to be the only ones willing to bear the weight of responsibility."

The man tells the nanny everything about his experiences in the house and what has become of human life. The only piece of information he leaves out is the fact that the planet they live on will eventually be destroyed. He decided a long time ago that it would be best if nobody knew about this, at least not for a few decades. They still have a hundred and fifty years until the end. That is not a bad lifespan for a civilization. Perhaps, some day, they will figure out a way to leave the planet as their parents did and find a new world.

"So things have changed a lot out there, haven't they?" says the nanny.

"Probably for the better," the man says. "I've read much of the history of my parents' society on this planet. I don't think I like it much."

"No, I don't think anybody really did," the nanny says. "That's why these nurseries closer resemble life in ancient times, when human society was more pleasant. More... *human.*"

The man nods.

"You do a good job," the man says. "You nannies have always done a good job of raising kids."

He smiles at the nanny when she isn't paying attention, then looks away before she notices.

"I have a favor to ask you," he says.

The nanny raises her eyebrows. "What's that?"

"It'll only be for a short while, but you can refuse if you want. I'm not sure if it will work anyway..."

He places something onto the table. It is in a box, wrapped in a shirt.

"What is it?" the nanny asks.

He pushes it across the table to her.

As she unwraps it, he says, "I recently visited my own nursery for the first time in about ten years. The place was on fire when we left it. Everything burned down. I assumed nothing would be left of my nanny's body when I found it."

The nanny opens the box to find a large computer chip.

"But I discovered that her memory card was still intact," the man says. "I was able to save it."

The nanny looks at the chip.

"Do you think it can be fixed?" he asks.

The nanny nods. "Yeah, it just needs to be cleaned up a bit. There's a bit of corrosion, but I can get it functioning again soon."

She tries to stand to get her computer cleaning supplies, but the man stops her.

"That's not the favor I was asking," the man says. "I was wondering if you would be willing to let me swap it with yours. Just for a while. Then I'll swap it right back. I promise." He looks down at the chip. "I never got a chance to say goodbye to her."

The nanny puts her hand on his shoulder.

"Of course you can," the nanny says. "Just wait here and I'll be back in a moment."

The man sits in the garden next to the robot, putting the new chip inside and turning it back on. When the nanny comes to life, she takes a deep breath and then exhales with a smile, staring at the blooming marigolds in front of her.

"Hi, Nanny," the man says to the robot.

She turns her head, looks up at the man seated next to her. At first she doesn't recognize him, but then she squints her eyes at his face.

"Ricky?" she says. "Is that you?"

"Yes, Nanny Warburough," he says. "It's me."

She blinks her mechanical eyes at him.

"You're all grown up," she says, her lips wrinkling into a smile.

"Well, you've been away for a long time," he says.

"Have I?" says Nanny Warburough. She turns to the flowers and nods. "Yes, I guess I have…"

The man moves closer to the nanny and takes her hand. He

doesn't care what they talk about. He just wants to be with her.

"So what's become of you?" she asks. "What kind of man has the troublesome little Ricky grown into?"

He decides not to tell her anything about the world outside the nursery. He doesn't want her to know about what happened to him or what he's gone through.

"Well, I'm happy," he says. "I'm a hard worker. I have lots of responsibility. I try to help people whenever I can."

The nanny smiles and pats his knee.

"That's the Ricky I imagined," she says. "Did you ever get married?"

The man says, "Do you remember that girl Darcy I always had a crush on at school?"

"I knew it," the nanny says.

"What do you mean you knew it?"

"I knew that you would find her outside of the nursery and one day marry that girl. You were destined to be together."

"How could you know?" He didn't even know the nanny knew Darcy's name. "The girl I liked at school wasn't even real."

"That's just how schooling works," the nanny says. "It's designed to introduce you to a fictional version of the girl you're destined to spend the rest of your life with."

"I'm really lucky I found her," the man says.

"And what about Polly?" the nanny says. "What is she up to?"

"She's a doctor now," he says. "A really important person in the household. She got married to a slightly older man. He's considered the most handsome and popular guy in the house, but if you ask her about him she'll say he's completely useless."

The nanny laughs.

"And what about Kajhug?" she asks. "How's she?"

"Who?"

"Your baby sister."

He thinks about it for a moment, and then remembers.

"Oh, you mean Leech. I completely forgot you used to call her Kajhug. Nobody's actually ever called her that besides you."

The nanny seems a little disappointed that she ended up going with her nickname.

"She turned into a hellion," the man says. "She does whatever she wants whenever she wants, never listens to anybody, and always gets herself into trouble all the time."

"She sounds like she takes after her older brother," the nanny says.

"I'm terrified of what she'll be like once her antlers grow in." The nanny laughs again.

The two of them sit there in the garden room for what seems like hours, just gazing at the plants and flowers, reminiscing about old times in the nursery. He wishes the moment would last forever, but he knows it's already time for this nursery to get its real nanny back.

"Nanny," he says. "I just want to say…" He turns away from the flowers to face her. "Thank you. Thank you for everything."

She shakes her head. "You don't have to thank me for anything, Ricky."

"No, I do, Nanny," the man says. "I spent my whole life searching for my mother, because I wanted so badly to have somebody who would love me and comfort me, read me stories when I was bored, stay up late with me when I was scared. Every night, I dreamed about my mother. I spent all my time drawing pictures of what I thought she might look like."

"Of course, every child is like that," the nanny says.

"But I recently found one of those pictures," he says. "I found it hidden in the crawlspace of the nursery, where it survived the fire."

He pulls the folded up piece of paper out of his pocket.

"I remembered it being my most treasured drawing of my mother I ever created," he says. "The one I felt best captured her true likeness. But for the life of me I couldn't remember what the drawing looked like or why I always kept it hidden." He unfolds the drawing. "Until I saw it."

He hands the drawing to the nanny.

She looks down at the image, and says, "But this is a picture of me?"

The man nods his head.

"After spending my whole life wishing and praying that I could be with my mother," the man says, "I had no idea that I was with her all along." He takes the drawing from her hands and puts it aside. "If only it weren't against the rules to hug you and love you, I would never have needed another mother in my life."

The nanny nods at him and puts her hand on his shoulder.

"Well, you're an adult now," she says. "You don't have to follow the rules anymore."

"No, I don't," the man says.

He hugs the pudgy old woman with all of his strength, squeezing her so tightly that he can feel the warm machinery behind her synthetic flesh. And when she hugs him back, it feels as if he's finally found what he's always been searching for. He's finally hugging his mother for the first time in his life. And because he knows this hug is also the last, he makes sure it's one that will last a whole lifetime.

As they embrace, the nanny looks down and smiles at the drawing on the floor. It is a drawing of the boy and the nanny holding hands, smiles brightening their crayon-drawn faces. Above the boy, the word *Tick* is written in sloppy handwriting. Above the nanny, there is the word *Nanny* that has been crossed out and replaced with another word: *Mommy*.

After the chip is removed, tears fall onto the man's lap. But he's not sure if they fell from him or from his mommy's warm mechanical eyes.

THE END

BONUS SECTION

This is the part of the book where we would have published an afterword by the author but he insisted on drawing a comic strip instead for reasons we don't quite understand.

I hope you enjoyed my new book *Quicksand House*

It's me CM3!

Like most of my books, I wrote Quicksand House during a writing marathon.

A writing marathon is where I start and finish a book in a single session. I lock myself away from the world for days or even weeks with no distractions or contact with the outside world.

That's my room!

RED LION

RED LION

When I wrote Quicksand House, I checked into the Red Lion Hotel by the Portland Airport for almost three weeks.

I conned them into thinking I'm important enough to stay at a 70% discount!

This is the room I stayed in. The first night is always the hardest. Sometimes I spend the whole night working on just the first page. It takes me hours to get into "writing mode."

Usually, I'm in "breakdance mode."

Once I'm in writing mode, I'll work for twenty hours straight. I usually write at the pace of ?00 words per hour but when I'm flying I can do 2000.

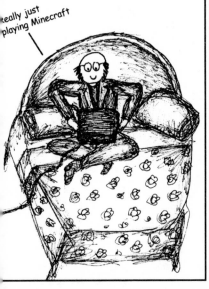

Really just playing Minecraft

When I can't write anymore, I'll collapse for eight to ten hours. I usually fall asleep thinking about my book, dream about my book, and then wake up thinking about my book.

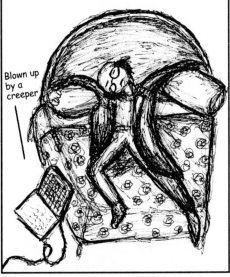

Blown up by a creeper

When I need to brainstorm ideas, I'll usually go outside for a cigarette break and have awkward conversations with the other hotel guests.

And if I'm in need of inspiration, I'll stop by the room next door to see what my neighbors are up to.

Somtimes I'll get so into a scene I'm writing that I'll forget who I am or where I am and become completely immersed in the story.

writing a scene about tacos

And if I do a good job, gooboo fairies will come and reward me with little cakes.

It's rainbow-flavored!

One thing I don't like about marathon writing is how my brain feels like it's on fire whenever I consume too many energy drinks.

I also hate getting all of those annoying phone calls from management every time I decide to throw ninja stars out of my hotel room window.

Even though it requires a lot of endurance, writing a book marathon-style is always the fastest way to write a quality story.

Which is really important to me because I am often plagued by the constant irrational fear that the world is going to spontaneously explode before I can finish the book I'm working on.

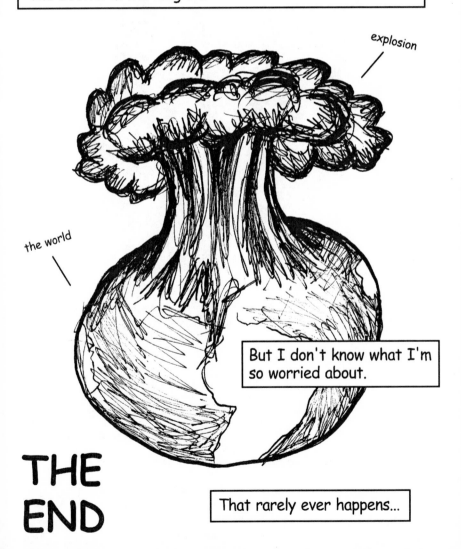

explosion

the world

But I don't know what I'm so worried about.

THE END

That rarely ever happens...

ABOUT THE AUTHOR

Carlton Mellick III is one of the leading authors of the bizarro fiction subgenre. Since 2001, his books have drawn an international cult following, despite the fact that they have been shunned by most libraries and chain bookstores.

He won the Wonderland Book Award for his novel, *Warrior Wolf Women of the Wasteland*, in 2009. His short fiction has appeared in *Vice Magazine, The Year's Best Fantasy and Horror #16, The Magazine of Bizarro Fiction,* and *Zombies: Encounters with the Hungry Dead*, among others. He is also a graduate of Clarion West, where he studied under the likes of Chuck Palahniuk, Connie Willis, and Cory Doctorow.

He lives in Portland, OR, the bizarro fiction mecca.

Visit him online at **www.carltonmellick.com**

BIZARRO BOOKS

CATALOG   SPRING 2013

ERASERHEAD PRESS

Your major resource for the bizarro fiction genre:

WWW.BIZARROCENTRAL.COM

Introduce yourselves to the bizarro fiction genre and all of its authors with the Bizarro Starter Kit series. Each volume features short novels and short stories by ten of the leading bizarro authors, designed to give you a perfect sampling of the genre for only $10.

BB-0X1
"The Bizarro Starter Kit" (Orange)
Featuring D. Harlan Wilson, Carlton Mellick III, Jeremy Robert Johnson, Kevin L Donihe, Gina Ranalli, Andre Duza, Vincent W. Sakowski, Steve Beard, John Edward Lawson, and Bruce Taylor. **236 pages $10**

BB-0X2
"The Bizarro Starter Kit" (Blue)
Featuring Ray Fracalossy, Jeremy C. Shipp, Jordan Krall, Mykle Hansen, Andersen Prunty, Eckhard Gerdes, Bradley Sands, Steve Aylett, Christian TeBordo, and Tony Rauch. **244 pages $10**

BB-0X2
"The Bizarro Starter Kit" (Purple)
Featuring Russell Edson, Athena Villaverde, David Agranoff, Matthew Revert, Andrew Goldfarb, Jeff Burk, Garrett Cook, Kris Saknussemm, Cody Goodfellow, and Cameron Pierce **264 pages $10**

BB-001 "The Kafka Effekt" D. Harlan Wilson — A collection of forty-four irreal short stories loosely written in the vein of Franz Kafka, with more than a pinch of William S. Burroughs sprinkled on top. **211 pages $14**

BB-002 "Satan Burger" Carlton Mellick III — The cult novel that put Carlton Mellick III on the map ... Six punks get jobs at a fast food restaurant owned by the devil in a city violently overpopulated by surreal alien cultures. **236 pages $14**

BB-003 "Some Things Are Better Left Unplugged" Vincent Sakwoski — Join The Man and his Nemesis, the obese tabby, for a nightmare roller coaster ride into this postmodern fantasy. **152 pages $10**

BB-005 "Razor Wire Pubic Hair" Carlton Mellick III — A genderless humandildo is purchased by a razor dominatrix and brought into her nightmarish world of bizarre sex and mutilation. **176 pages $11**

BB-007 "The Baby Jesus Butt Plug" Carlton Mellick III — Using clones of the Baby Jesus for anal sex will be the hip sex fetish of the future. **92 pages $10**

BB-010 "The Menstruating Mall" Carlton Mellick III — "The Breakfast Club meets Chopping Mall as directed by David Lynch." - Brian Keene **212 pages $12**

BB-011 "Angel Dust Apocalypse" Jeremy Robert Johnson — Meth-heads, man-made monsters, and murderous Neo-Nazis. "Seriously amazing short stories..." - Chuck Palahniuk, author of Fight Club **184 pages $11**

BB-015 "Foop!" Chris Genoa — Strange happenings are going on at Dactyl, Inc, the world's first and only time travel tourism company.
"A surreal pie in the face!" - Christopher Moore **300 pages $14**

BB-032 **"Extinction Journals" Jeremy Robert Johnson** — An uncanny voyage across a newly nuclear America where one man must confront the problems associated with loneliness, insane dieties, radiation, love, and an ever-evolving cockroach suit with a mind of its own. **104 pages $10**

BB-037 **"The Haunted Vagina" Carlton Mellick III** — It's difficult to love a woman whose vagina is a gateway to the world of the dead. **132 pages $10**

BB-043 **"War Slut" Carlton Mellick III** — Part "1984," part "Waiting for Godot," and part action horror video game adaptation of John Carpenter's "The Thing." **116 pages $10**

BB-047 **"Sausagey Santa" Carlton Mellick III** — A bizarro Christmas tale featuring Santa as a piratey mutant with a body made of sausages. 124 pages $10

BB-048 **"Misadventures in a Thumbnail Universe" Vincent Sakowski** — Dive deep into the surreal and satirical realms of neo-classical Blender Fiction, filled with television shoes and flesh-filled skies. **120 pages $10**

BB-053 **"Ballad of a Slow Poisoner" Andrew Goldfarb** — Millford Mutterwurst sat down on a Tuesday to take his afternoon tea, and made the unpleasant discovery that his elbows were becoming flatter. **128 pages $10**

BB-055 **"Help! A Bear is Eating Me" Mykle Hansen** — The bizarro, heartwarming, magical tale of poor planning, hubris and severe blood loss... **150 pages $11**

BB-056 **"Piecemeal June" Jordan Krall** — A man falls in love with a living sex doll, but with love comes danger when her creator comes after her with crab-squid assassins. **90 pages $9**

BB-058 "The Overwhelming Urge" Andersen Prunty — A collection of bizarro tales by Andersen Prunty. **150 pages $11**

BB-059 "Adolf in Wonderland" Carlton Mellick III — A dreamlike adventure that takes a young descendant of Adolf Hitler's design and sends him down the rabbit hole into a world of imperfection and disorder. **180 pages $11**

BB-061 "Ultra Fuckers" Carlton Mellick III — Absurdist suburban horror about a couple who enter an upper middle class gated community but can't find their way out. **108 pages $9**

BB-062 "House of Houses" Kevin L. Donihe — An odd man wants to marry his house. Unfortunately, all of the houses in the world collapse at the same time in the Great House Holocaust. Now he must travel to House Heaven to find his departed fiancee. **172 pages $11**

BB-064 "Squid Pulp Blues" Jordan Krall — In these three bizarro-noir novellas, the reader is thrown into a world of murderers, drugs made from squid parts, deformed gun-toting veterans, and a mischievous apocalyptic donkey. **204 pages $12**

BB-065 "Jack and Mr. Grin" Andersen Prunty — "When Mr. Grin calls you can hear a smile in his voice. Not a warm and friendly smile, but the kind that seizes your spine in fear. You don't need to pay your phone bill to hear it. That smile is in every line of Prunty's prose." - Tom Bradley. **208 pages $12**

BB-066 "Cybernetrix" Carlton Mellick III — What would you do if your normal everyday world was slowly mutating into the video game world from Tron? **212 pages $12**

BB-072 "Zerostrata" Andersen Prunty — Hansel Nothing lives in a tree house, suffers from memory loss, has a very eccentric family, and falls in love with a woman who runs naked through the woods every night. **144 pages $11**

BB-073 **"The Egg Man" Carlton Mellick III** — It is a world where humans reproduce like insects. Children are the property of corporations, and having an enormous ten-foot brain implanted into your skull is a grotesque sexual fetish. Mellick's industrial urban dystopia is one of his darkest and grittiest to date. **184 pages $11**

BB-074 **"Shark Hunting in Paradise Garden" Cameron Pierce** — A group of strange humanoid religious fanatics travel back in time to the Garden of Eden to discover it is invested with hundreds of giant flying maneating sharks. **150 pages $10**

BB-075 **"Apeshit" Carlton Mellick III** - Friday the 13th meets Visitor Q. Six hipster teens go to a cabin in the woods inhabited by a deformed killer. An incredibly fucked-up parody of B-horror movies with a bizarro slant. **192 pages $12**

BB-076 **"Fuckers of Everything on the Crazy Shitting Planet of the Vomit At smosphere" Mykle Hansen** - Three bizarro satires. Monster Cocks, Journey to the Center of Agnes Cuddlebottom, and Crazy Shitting Planet. **228 pages $12**

BB-077 **"The Kissing Bug" Daniel Scott Buck** — In the tradition of Roald Dahl, Tim Burton, and Edward Gorey, comes this bizarro anti-war children's story about a bohemian conenose kissing bug who falls in love with a human woman. **116 pages $10**

BB-078 **"MachoPoni" Lotus Rose** — It's My Little Pony... *Bizarro* style! A long time ago Poniworld was split in two. On one side of the Jagged Line is the Pastel Kingdom, a magical land of music, parties, and positivity. On the other side of the Jagged Line is Dark Kingdom inhabited by an army of undead ponies. **148 pages $11**

BB-079 **"The Faggiest Vampire" Carlton Mellick III** — A Roald Dahl-esque children's story about two faggy vampires who partake in a mustache competition to find out which one is truly the faggiest. **104 pages $10**

BB-080 **"Sky Tongues" Gina Ranalli** — The autobiography of Sky Tongues, the biracial hermaphrodite actress with tongues for fingers. Follow her strange life story as she rises from freak to fame. **204 pages $12**

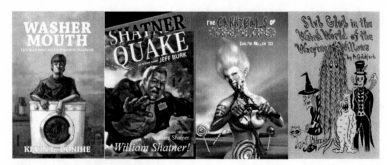

BB-081 **"Washer Mouth" Kevin L. Donihe** - A washing machine becomes human and pursues his dream of meeting his favorite soap opera star. **244 pages $11**

BB-082 **"Shatnerquake" Jeff Burk** - All of the characters ever played by William Shatner are suddenly sucked into our world. Their mission: hunt down and destroy the real William Shatner. **100 pages $10**

BB-083 **"The Cannibals of Candyland" Carlton Mellick III** - There exists a race of cannibals that are made of candy. They live in an underground world made out of candy. One man has dedicated his life to killing them all. **170 pages $11**

BB-084 **"Slub Glub in the Weird World of the Weeping Willows"**
Andrew Goldfarb - The charming tale of a blue glob named Slub Glub who helps the weeping willows whose tears are flooding the earth. There are also hyenas, ghosts, and a voodoo priest **100 pages $10**

BB-085 **"Super Fetus" Adam Pepper** - Try to abort this fetus and he'll kick your ass! **104 pages $10**

BB-086 **"Fistful of Feet" Jordan Krall** - A bizarro tribute to spaghetti westerns, featuring Cthulhu-worshipping Indians, a woman with four feet, a crazed gunman who is obsessed with sucking on candy, Syphilis-ridden mutants, sexually transmitted tattoos, and a house devoted to the freakiest fetishes. **228 pages $12**

BB-087 **"Ass Goblins of Auschwitz" Cameron Pierce** - It's Monty Python meets Nazi exploitation in a surreal nightmare as can only be imagined by Bizarro author Cameron Pierce. **104 pages $10**

BB-088 **"Silent Weapons for Quiet Wars" Cody Goodfellow** - "This is high-end psychological surrealist horror meets bottom-feeding low-life crime in a techno-thrilling science fiction world full of Lovecraft and magic..." -John Skipp **212 pages $12**

BB-089 "Warrior Wolf Women of the Wasteland" Carlton Mellick III
— Road Warrior Werewolves versus McDonaldland Mutants...post-apocalyptic fiction has never been quite like this. **316 pages $13**

BB-091 "Super Giant Monster Time" Jeff Burk — A tribute to choose your
own adventures and Godzilla movies. Will you escape the giant monsters that are rampaging the fuck out of your city and shit? Or will you join the mob of alien-controlled punk rockers causing chaos in the streets? What happens next depends on you. **188 pages $12**

BB-092 "Perfect Union" Cody Goodfellow — "Cronenberg's THE FLY on a
grand scale: human/insect gene-spliced body horror, where the human hive politics are as shocking as the gore." -John Skipp. **272 pages $13**

BB-093 "Sunset with a Beard" Carlton Mellick III — 14 stories of surreal
science fiction. **200 pages $12**

BB-094 "My Fake War" Andersen Prunty — The absurd tale of an unlikely soldier
forced to fight a war that, quite possibly, does not exist. It's Rambo meets Waiting for Godot in this subversive satire of American values and the scope of the human imagination. **128 pages $11**

BB-095 "Lost in Cat Brain Land" Cameron Pierce — Sad stories from a sur-
real world. A fascist mustache, the ghost of Franz Kafka, a desert inside a dead cat. Primordial entities mourn the death of their child. The desperate serve tea to mysterious creatures. A hopeless romantic falls in love with a pterodactyl. And much more. **152 pages $11**

BB-096 "The Kobold Wizard's Dildo of Enlightenment +2" Carlton
Mellick III — A Dungeons and Dragons parody about a group of people who learn they are only made up characters in an AD&D campaign and must find a way to resist their nerdy teenaged players and retarded dungeon master in order to survive. 232 **pages $12**

BB-098 "A Hundred Horrible Sorrows of Ogner Stump" Andrew
Goldfarb — Goldfarb's acclaimed comic series. A magical and weird journey into the horrors of everyday life. **164 pages $11**

BB-099 "Pickled Apocalypse of Pancake Island" Cameron Pierce—A demented fairy tale about a pickle, a pancake, and the apocalypse. **102 pages $8**

BB-100 "Slag Attack" Andersen Prunty— Slag Attack features four visceral, noir stories about the living, crawling apocalypse. A slag is what survivors are calling the slug-like maggots raining from the sky, burrowing inside people, and hollowing out their flesh and their sanity. **148 pages $11**

BB-101 "Slaughterhouse High" Robert Devereaux—A place where schools are built with secret passageways, rebellious teens get zippers installed in their mouths and genitals, and once a year, on that special night, one couple is slaughtered and the bits of their bodies are kept as souvenirs. **304 pages $13**

BB-102 "The Emerald Burrito of Oz" John Skipp & Marc Levinthal —OZ IS REAL! Magic is real! The gate is really in Kansas! And America is finally allowing Earth tourists to visit this weird-ass, mysterious land. But when Gene of Los Angeles heads off for summer vacation in the Emerald City, little does he know that a war is brewing...a war that could destroy both worlds. **280 pages $13**

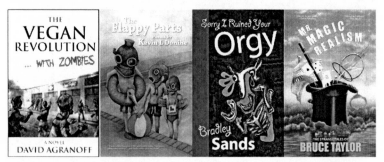

BB-103 "The Vegan Revolution... with Zombies" David Agranoff — When there's no more meat in hell, the vegans will walk the earth. **160 pages $11**

BB-104 "The Flappy Parts" Kevin L Donihe—Poems about bunnies, LSD, and police abuse. You know, things that matter. **132 pages $11**

BB-105 "Sorry I Ruined Your Orgy" Bradley Sands—Bizarro humorist Bradley Sands returns with one of the strangest, most hilarious collections of the year. **130 pages $11**

BB-106 "Mr. Magic Realism" Bruce Taylor—Like Golden Age science fiction comics written by Freud, *Mr. Magic Realism* is a strange, insightful adventure that spans the furthest reaches of the galaxy, exploring the hidden caverns in the hearts and minds of men, women, aliens, and biomechanical cats. **152 pages $11**

BB-107 "Zombies and Shit" Carlton Mellick III—"Battle Royale" meets "Return of the Living Dead." Mellick's bizarro tribute to the zombie genre. **308 pages $13**

BB-108 "The Cannibal's Guide to Ethical Living" Mykle Hansen— Over a five star French meal of fine wine, organic vegetables and human flesh, a lunatic delivers a witty, chilling, disturbingly sane argument in favor of eating the rich.. **184 pages $11**

BB-109 "Starfish Girl" Athena Villaverde—In a post-apocalyptic underwater dome society, a girl with a starfish growing from her head and an assassin with sea anenome hair are on the run from a gang of mutant fish men. **160 pages $11**

BB-110 "Lick Your Neighbor" Chris Genoa—Mutant ninjas, a talking whale, kung fu masters, maniacal pilgrims, and an alcoholic clown populate Chris Genoa's surreal, darkly comical and unnerving reimagining of the first Thanksgiving. **303 pages $13**

BB-111 "Night of the Assholes" Kevin L. Donihe—A plague of assholes is infecting the countryside. Normal everyday people are transforming into jerks, snobs, dicks, and douchebags. And they all have only one purpose: to make your life a living hell.. **192 pages $11**

BB-112 "Jimmy Plush, Teddy Bear Detective" Garrett Cook—Hardboiled cases of a private detective trapped within a teddy bear body. **180 pages $11**

BB-113 "The Deadheart Shelters" Forrest Armstrong—The hip hop lovechild of William Burroughs and Dali... **144 pages $11**

BB-114 "Eyeballs Growing All Over Me... Again" Tony Raugh— Absurd, surreal, playful, dream-like, whimsical, and a lot of fun to read. **144 pages $11**

BB-115 **"Whargoul" Dave Brockie** — From the killing grounds of Stalingrad to the death camps of the holocaust. From torture chambers in Iraq to race riots in the United States, the Whargoul was there, killing and raping. **244 pages $12**

BB-116 **"By the Time We Leave Here, We'll Be Friends" J. David Osborne** — A David Lynchian nightmare set in a Russian gulag, where its prisoners, guards, traitors, soldiers, lovers, and demons fight for survival and their own rapidly deteriorating humanity. **168 pages $11**

BB-117 **"Christmas on Crack" edited by Carlton Mellick III** — Perverted Christmas Tales for the whole family! . . . as long as every member of your family is over the age of 18. **168 pages $11**

BB-118 **"Crab Town" Carlton Mellick III** — Radiation fetishists, balloon people, mutant crabs, sail-bike road warriors, and a love affair between a woman and an H-Bomb. This is one mean asshole of a city. Welcome to Crab Town. **100 pages $8**

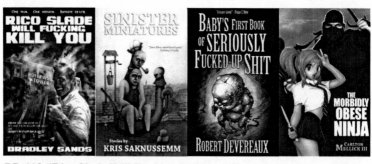

BB-119 **"Rico Slade Will Fucking Kill You" Bradley Sands** — Rico Slade is an action hero. Rico Slade can rip out a throat with his bare hands. Rico Slade's favorite food is the honey-roasted peanut. Rico Slade will fucking kill everyone. A novel. **122 pages $8**

BB-120 **"Sinister Miniatures" Kris Saknussemm** — The definitive collection of short fiction by Kris Saknussemm, confirming that he is one of the best, most daring writers of the weird to emerge in the twenty-first century. **180 pages $11**

BB-121 **"Baby's First Book of Seriously Fucked up Shit" Robert Devereaux** — Ten stories of the strange, the gross, and the just plain fucked up from one of the most original voices in horror. **176 pages $11**

BB-122 **"The Morbidly Obese Ninja" Carlton Mellick III** — These days, if you want to run a successful company . . . you're going to need a lot of ninjas. **92 pages $8**

BB-123 **"Abortion Arcade" Cameron Pierce** — An intoxicating blend of body horror and midnight movie madness, reminiscent of early David Lynch and the splatterpunks at their most sublime. **172 pages $11**

BB-124 **"Black Hole Blues" Patrick Wensink** — A hilarious double helix of country music and physics. **196 pages $11**

BB-125 **"Barbarian Beast Bitches of the Badlands" Carlton Mellick III** — Three prequels and sequels to *Warrior Wolf Women of the Wasteland*. **284 pages $13**

BB-126 **"The Traveling Dildo Salesman" Kevin L. Donihe** — A nightmare comedy about destiny, faith, and sex toys. Also featuring Donihe's most lurid and infamous short stories: *Milky Agitation, Two-Way Santa, The Helen Mower, Living Room Zombies,* and *Revenge of the Living Masturbation Rag.* **108 pages $8**

BB-127 **"Metamorphosis Blues" Bruce Taylor** — Enter a land of love beasts, intergalactic cowboys, and rock 'n roll. A land where Sears Catalogs are doorways to insanity and men keep mysterious black boxes. Welcome to the monstrous mind of Mr. Magic Realism. **136 pages $11**

BB-128 **"The Driver's Guide to Hitting Pedestrians" Andersen Prunty** — A pocket guide to the twenty-three most painful things in life, written by the most well-adjusted man in the universe. **108 pages $8**

BB-129 **"Island of the Super People" Kevin Shamel** — Four students and their anthropology professor journey to a remote island to study its indigenous population. But this is no ordinary native culture. They're super heroes and villains with flesh costumes and outlandish abilities like self-detonation, musical eyelashes, and microwave hands. **194 pages $11**

BB-130 **"Fantastic Orgy" Carlton Mellick III** — Shark Sex, mutant cats, and strange sexually transmitted diseases. Featuring the stories: *Candy-coated, Ear Cat, Fantastic Orgy, City Hobgoblins,* and *Porno in August.* **136 pages $9**

BB-131 **"Cripple Wolf" Jeff Burk** — Part man. Part wolf. 100% crippled. Also including *Punk Rock Nursing Home, Adrift with Space Badgers, Cook for Your Life, Just Another Day in the Park, Frosty and the Full Monty*, and *House of Cats*. **152 pages $10**

BB-132 **"I Knocked Up Satan's Daughter" Carlton Mellick III** — An adorable, violent, fantastical love story. A romantic comedy for the bizarro fiction reader. **152 pages $10**

BB-133 **"A Town Called Suckhole" David W. Barbee** — Far into the future, in the nuclear bowels of post-apocalyptic Dixie, there is a town. A town of derelict mobile homes, ancient junk, and mutant wildlife. A town of slack jawed rednecks who bask in the splendors of moonshine and mud boggin'. A town dedicated to the bloody and demented legacy of the Old South. A town called Suckhole. **144 pages $10**

BB-134 **"Cthulhu Comes to the Vampire Kingdom" Cameron Pierce** — What you'd get if H. P. Lovecraft wrote a Tim Burton animated film. **148 pages $11**

BB-135 **"I am Genghis Cum" Violet LeVoit** — From the savage Arctic tundra to post-partum mutations to your missing daughter's unmarked grave, join visionary madwoman Violet LeVoit in this non-stop eight-story onslaught of full-tilt Bizarro punk lit thrills. **124 pages $9**

BB-136 **"Haunt" Laura Lee Bahr** — A tripping-balls Los Angeles noir, where a mysterious dame drags you through a time-warping Bizarro hall of mirrors. **316 pages $13**

BB-137 **"Amazing Stories of the Flying Spaghetti Monster" edited by Cameron Pierce** — Like an all-spaghetti evening of Adult Swim, the Flying Spaghetti Monster will show you the many realms of His Noodly Appendage. Learn of those who worship him and the lives he touches in distant, mysterious ways. **228 pages $12**

BB-138 **"Wave of Mutilation" Douglas Lain** — A dream-pop exploration of modern architecture and the American identity, *Wave of Mutilation* is a Zen finger trap for the 21st century. **100 pages $8**

BB-139 "Hooray for Death!" Mykle Hansen — Famous Author Mykle Hansen draws unconventional humor from deaths tiny and large, and invites you to laugh while you can. **128 pages $10**

BB-140 "Hypno-hog's Moonshine Monster Jamboree" Andrew Goldfarb — Hicks, Hogs, Horror! Goldfarb is back with another strange illustrated tale of backwoods weirdness. **120 pages $9**

BB-141 "Broken Piano For President" Patrick Wensink — A comic masterpiece about the fast food industry, booze, and the necessity to choose happiness over work and security. **372 pages $15**

BB-142 "Please Do Not Shoot Me in the Face" Bradley Sands — A novel in three parts, *Please Do Not Shoot Me in the Face: A Novel*, is the story of one boy detective, the worst ninja in the world, and the great American fast food wars. It is a novel of loss, destruction, and--incredibly--genuine hope. **224 pages $12**

BB-143 "Santa Steps Out" Robert Devereaux — Sex, Death, and Santa Claus ... The ultimate erotic Christmas story is back. **294 pages $13**

BB-144 "Santa Conquers the Homophobes" Robert Devereaux — "I wish I could hope to ever attain one-thousandth the perversity of Robert Devereaux's toenail clippings." - Poppy Z. Brite **316 pages $13**

BB-145 "We Live Inside You" Jeremy Robert Johnson — "Jeremy Robert Johnson is dancing to a way different drummer. He loves language, he loves the edge, and he loves us people. These stories have range and style and wit. This is entertainment... and literature."- Jack Ketchum **188 pages $11**

BB-146 "Clockwork Girl" Athena Villaverde — Urban fairy tales for the weird girl in all of us. Like a combination of Francesca Lia Block, Charles de Lint, Kathe Koja, Tim Burton, and Hayao Miyazaki, her stories are cute, kinky, edgy, magical, provocative, and strange, full of poetic imagery and vicious sexuality. **160 pages $10**

BB-147 **"Armadillo Fists" Carlton Mellick III** — A weird-as-hell gangster story set in a world where people drive giant mechanical dinosaurs instead of cars. **168 pages $11**

BB-148 **"Gargoyle Girls of Spider Island" Cameron Pierce** — Four college seniors venture out into open waters for the tropical party weekend of a lifetime. Instead of a teenage sex fantasy, they find themselves in a nightmare of pirates, sharks, and sex-crazed monsters. **100 pages $8**

BB-149 **"The Handsome Squirm" by Carlton Mellick III** — Like Franz Kafka's *The Trial* meets an erotic body horror version of *The Blob*. **158 pages $11**

BB-150 **"Tentacle Death Trip" Jordan Krall** — It's *Death Race 2000* meets H. P. Lovecraft in bizarro author Jordan Krall's best and most suspenseful work to date. **224 pages $12**

BB-151 **"The Obese" Nick Antosca** — Like Alfred Hitchcock's *The Birds*... but with obese people. **108 pages $10**

BB-152 **"All-Monster Action!" Cody Goodfellow** — The world gave him a blank check and a demand: Create giant monsters to fight our wars. But Dr. Otaku was not satisfied with mere chaos and mass destruction.... **216 pages $12**

BB-153 **"Ugly Heaven" Carlton Mellick III** — Heaven is no longer a paradise. It was once a blissful utopia full of wonders far beyond human comprehension. But the afterlife is now in ruins. It has become an ugly, lonely wasteland populated by strange monstrous beasts, masturbating angels, and sad man-like beings wallowing in the remains of the once-great Kingdom of God. **106 pages $8**

BB-154 **"Space Walrus" Kevin L. Donihe** — Walter is supposed to go where no walrus has ever gone before, but all this astronaut walrus really wants is to take it easy on the intense training, escape the chimpanzee bullies, and win the love of his human trainer Dr. Stephanie. **160 pages $11**

BB-155 **"Unicorn Battle Squad" Kirsten Alene** — Mutant unicorns. A palace with a thousand human legs. The most powerful army on the planet. **192 pages $11**

BB-156 **"Kill Ball" Carlton Mellick III** — In a city where all humans live inside of plastic bubbles, exotic dancers are being murdered in the rubbery streets by a mysterious stalker known only as Kill Ball. **134 pages $10**

BB-157 **"Die You Doughnut Bastards" Cameron Pierce** — The bacon storm is rolling in. We hear the grease and sugar beat against the roof and windows. The doughnut people are attacking. We press close together, forgetting for a moment that we hate each other. **196 pages $11**

BB-158 **"Tumor Fruit" Carlton Mellick III** — Eight desperate castaways find themselves stranded on a mysterious deserted island. They are surrounded by poisonous blue plants and an ocean made of acid. Ravenous creatures lurk in the toxic jungle. The ghostly sound of crying babies can be heard on the wind. **310 pages $13**

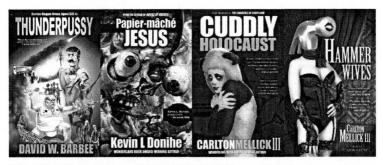

BB-159 **"Thunderpussy" David W. Barbee** — When it comes to high-tech global espionage, only one man has the balls to save humanity from the world's most powerful bastards. He's Declan Magpie Bruce, Agent 00X. **136 pages $11**

BB-160 **"Papier Mâché Jesus" Kevin L. Donihe** — Donihe's surreal wit and beautiful mind-bending imagination is on full display with stories such as All Children Go to Hell, Happiness is a Warm Gun, and Swimming in Endless Night. **154 pages $11**

BB-161 **"Cuddly Holocaust" Carlton Mellick III** — The war between humans and toys has come to an end. The toys won. **172 pages $11**

BB-162 **"Hammer Wives" Carlton Mellick III** — Fish-eyed mutants, oceans of insects, and flesh-eating women with hammers for heads. Hammer Wives collects six of his most popular novelettes and short stories. **152 pages $10**

CPSIA information can be obtained at www.ICGtesting.com
Printed in the USA
BVOW05s0118170915

418217BV00001B/77/P